I've travelled the world twice over,
Met the famous: saints and sinners,
Poets and artists, kings and queens,
Old stars and hopeful beginners,
I've been where no-one's been before,
Learned secrets from writers and cooks
All with one library ticket
To the wonderful world of books.

© JANICE JAMES.

QUOTH THE RAVEN

Sam Tree was an honest and pleasant man, but he had married into trouble. He was husband number three of a charming woman who was adept in the art of protracted evasion. Sam wondered how Violet had come by the hundred-dollar bills she scattered about, why she had to pay off her worthless second husband, and whether she was connected with the shady dealings of her first husband. When Sam's grocery store was invaded by a gunman and his house was broken into, he felt obliged to take drastic action.

Books by Bruno Fischer
in the Ulverscroft Large Print Series:

MORE DEATHS THAN ONE
THE EVIL DAYS

BRUNO FISCHER

QUOTH THE RAVEN

Complete and Unabridged

ULVERSCROFT
Leicester

First published in the
United States of America

First Large Print Edition
published October 1993

Copyright © 1944 by Bruno Fischer
All rights reserved

British Library CIP Data

Fischer, Bruno
    Quoth the raven.—Large print ed.—
Ulverscroft large print series: mystery
I. Title
813.54 [F]

ISBN 0–7089–2952–4

Published by
F. A. Thorpe (Publishing) Ltd.
Anstey, Leicestershire
Set by Words & Graphics Ltd.
Anstey, Leicestershire
Printed and bound in Great Britain by
T. J. Press (Padstow) Ltd., Padstow, Cornwall

1

The Third Husband

THAT Tuesday evening Sam Tree had three visitors in his grocery store. The first was his wife's former husband. The second was a rich man who believed in the persuasive power of money. The third carried a gun.

The first arrived a few minutes before closing time. Sam Tree was slicing American cheese for Mrs. Anchor when he noticed a tall, stooped man standing unobtrusively near the bag of walnuts. The door had a way of slamming like a pistol shot, but this time it hadn't made a sound. "Front!" Sam called, and Ted Hanley appeared from the back room and sidled his lazy fat bulk along the grocery counter.

"Yes?" Ted said to the customer.

The tall man made a weary motion with his limp hand and remained where he was. Without interest his eyes roamed the grocery shelves.

"What can I do for you?" Ted persisted.

The hand waved again, this time toward the dairy counter behind which Sam stood. He turned his face with the gesture, and Sam saw that he was Felix Skinner.

"Finish up Mrs. Anchor," Sam told Ted. He went around the counter and down the length of the store and extended his hand to Felix Skinner. "How are you?"

Skinner's hand had the character and texture of a floor mop. "I'm always the same. How's Violet?"

"She just returned from a visit to Cape Cod."

"To her mother, eh?" Skinner muttered, moodily examining the cereal packages on the top shelves. His gaunt face held utter weariness; he seemed to have trouble keeping his long body together.

Sam waited, finding it hard to make conversation with the man who had been his wife's husband. "Were you in the neighborhood?" he asked for the sake of saying something.

2

"I made a special trip to New York." Skinner said it as if Queens were at the other end of the world. His eyes did not leave the grocery shelves. "I'd like a loan."

"For gambling?"

"Listen," Skinner said, his eyes everywhere but on Sam. "This is a good thing. I can make a couple of thousand if I can get my hands on a few hundred bucks tonight."

Sam felt a little sick with contempt. This was the man Violet had lived with for five years. He said: "If you need money for food or clothing or rent, you're welcome to it. But not for gambling".

Skinner looked at him then, and his mouth was crooked. "I heard about you from Naomi. A plaster saint."

"My stepdaughter doesn't talk about me that way," Sam said stiffly.

"Not in those words, maybe, but that's what she means." His tired gaze was again on the shelves. "So you're not lending me the money?"

"No."

"Damn you!" Skinner said. "You took Violet away from me. Now you won't even lend me a few lousy bucks."

"Violet wasn't living with you when I met her."

"She would have come back to me. She — "

"Quiet!" Sam whispered.

Mrs. Anchor was staring at them over her shoulder. Behind the grocery counter Ted wore a fascinated smirk.

Skinner's long body drew into itself. "Sorry I bothered you," he said with a flash of pride and turned to the door.

A wave of pity swept over Sam as the door slammed. It wasn't nice to see a man in the final stages of disintegration. Sam went after him.

In the street Skinner turned at the sound of Sam's voice. He was humble again and eager. "So you changed your mind?"

The store window caught the images of the two men. Sam was almost as tall as Skinner, but his shoulders were broader, and he had the wiry build of a man who keeps himself fit even in his forties. Skinner was about the same age; he could have passed for fifteen years older.

"You've got a lot of good years ahead of you," Sam said. "I might be able to help you find a job."

Skinner threw harsh laughter into Sam's face. "Now the plaster saint is trying to be a good Samaritan. To hell with you!" He shuffled up the street.

Mrs. Anchor was coming out of the store with her bundles. Sam, turning, almost ran her down, veered at the last moment, said good night to her. Inside the store Ted Hanley leaned on the counter and grinned at his boss.

"I remember him now," Ted said. "I met him coming out of the Paramount with Naomi. She introduced us. He's Naomi's father."

"Her stepfather," Sam muttered.

"I thought you're her stepfather. Then who's — "

"It's nearly eight," Sam snapped irritably. "Start cleaning up."

The second visitor appeared a few minutes later. Sam Tree was counting out the change in the cash register when he heard the door open and slam. Ted, who was straightening up the disorganized counter display, whispered: "Pipe that, Sam."

Sam raised his eyes to the man who came up to the grocery counter. He looked as if he had stepped out of the kind of movie in which everybody was rich. A black camel-hair coat was kind to his dumpy figure. He wore a white silk scarf and a derby, and his rigid formality was punctuated by a silver-headed cane.

"Mr. Tree?" he asked, looking from Ted to Sam and back to Ted.

"That's right," Sam said.

"I'm Douglas Faulcon, Senior."

Sam dropped the change he was counting into the till and stretched a hand across the counter. Suddenly he was acutely aware that his white coat was dirty. "Doug's father, eh? I'm glad to know you."

"Yes," Faulcon said noncommittally. "I thought it time we two got together. May I drive you home?"

"It's only four blocks. I'll be with you in a couple of minutes."

Faulcon retreated from the counter and leaned patiently on his cane. He looked around curiously, as if he had never before been in a grocery store. Probably he never had been.

Again Sam lifted the dimes from the till and started the count from the beginning. He found that he was slightly nervous, and it made him angry with himself. He was as good as Douglas Faulcon, Senior, or any other man on earth.

Ted kept glancing at Faulcon in awe. He stooped near the register to pick up a bag from the floor and whispered up to Sam: "I read about the Faulcons in the gossip columns. Snazzy society. So Naomi is marrying into that family!"

Sam didn't answer. The cash again wasn't right. There was a shortage of eleven dollars and change; last night it had been thirteen dollars, the night before that eight. He started to count the money over, then changed his mind and put the bills into a paper bag and stuck the bag into his hip pocket.

"I'll wait outside in my car," Faulcon said. He wasn't the sort of man who would care to hang around a store.

"I'll be out in five minutes," Sam said.

Ted was already in his overcoat. He

opened the door for Faulcon and then put out the window lights. "I'd like to make the movies, Sam."

"Go ahead," Sam said.

Sam went to the washroom and washed his hands. As he was drying them, he heard the store door open and close. Ted leaving, he thought, and combed his hair by running his fingers through its thickness. He was ready then. He wore a coat only on coldest midwinter days and never a hat.

As he moved between the piled cases in the back room, something clicked in his mind. On his way to the washroom he had heard Ted leave. A minute later the door had opened again. If that had been Ted returning to get something, why hadn't he heard him in the store? Why wasn't he hearing now whoever had come in?

There was nobody in the store. Sam stood in the doorway between the back room and the store and tried to recall if he had really heard the door close twice. It was so quiet that he could hear his own breathing — and another sound, like stealthy movement, behind him.

His was one of the few grocery stores in the neighborhood which had never been held up, but he knew that holdup men usually chose this hour, just at closing time. His eyes dropped to an egg crate standing against the wall. On it lay a hatchet used to open wooden boxes. He swooped down, closed his fingers over the handle.

"Take it easy and you won't be hurt," a quiet voice said.

Sam straightened up with the hatchet in his hand and looked over his shoulder. A man had stepped from behind a pile of cases. In the dimness of the room a pair of gray eyes regarded Sam. That was all Sam could see of the man's face. A gray slouch hat was pulled low over his brow. His coat collar was pulled up around his chin and a gray muffler covered his mouth and nose. He was small, slight, and not young or even middle-aged. A slim nickeled revolver rested easily in his gloved hand.

"A holdup," Sam said.

He wasn't greatly afraid. Most of the store money was in checks, and the cash was certainly not worth risking a bullet.

He reached around to his hip pocket.

"Keep your hands in sight," the gray man ordered.

"The money is in my pocket."

"How much?"

"The cash comes to about sixty dollars."

The gray man laughed without mirth. "I want a lot more than that, and I want it in one-hundred-dollar bills."

"What?"

"Don't act dumb. You've still got that money in its original denominations. Chances are you keep it here or in your house."

"You've got me confused with somebody else," Sam said.

"Your name is Sam Tree, isn't it?"

"Yes."

"Then you've got it," the gray man asserted as if with certain knowledge. "Is it here?"

The hatchet lay against Sam's thigh. He wondered why the gunman let him hold it, and then he realized that his body blocked off view of the hatchet from the other.

The gun muzzle tilted toward Sam's

heart. "I'm not in the mood for horsing around."

"If you'll tell me what you want — "

"Cut it out!" Those gray eyes were ugly now. The flesh around them was wrinkled. They were very old eyes — tired eyes and cruel eyes.

"Cut out what?" Sam said. "If you'll stop talking in riddles, I might get an idea what you want."

"One-hundred-dollar bills. A lot of them." The gray eyes narrowed. The gun moved out.

Fear swept over Sam in icy waves. This was not just a holdup where you could give over what money you had and be done with it. The man was stark, raving mad, and he was going to shoot.

"Maybe you don't keep the dough here in the store," the gray man was saying. "But you're going to tell me where it is and how much is left. I'll give you ten seconds."

"All right," Sam told him thickly. "It's there in the desk."

It hadn't occurred to Sam to try trickery. Desperately he was sparring for time. But when the man impulsively turned his head toward the desk against the back of the refrigerator, Sam saw his chance. Almost without thinking he threw the hatchet.

The gray eyes shifted back in time to see the hatchet coming. The man threw up his gun arm to ward it off. The sharp edge of the hatchet grazed his arm; the head struck his cheekbone a glancing blow. He reeled.

Sam didn't wait to see how much damage he had done. He plunged into the store and ran along the grocery counter. The gray man's feet sounded in pursuit. Sam ducked behind the end of the counter.

Crouching there, Sam felt salt sweat on his lips. He should have headed toward the door, chancing a bullet in his back. There was nothing to save him now. Perhaps if he yelled, the gunman would be scared off. Faulcon was in his car outside, and people were always passing on this main street, and the two broad windows made all of the store visible from outside.

Sam was opening his mouth to scream

when he heard the door open and then close.

Cautiously Sam raised his head above the counter. The slight form of the gray man was outside the door, his back to the store. He pulled down his coat collar and muffler, and Sam saw that both his gloved hands were now empty. His back remained to Sam as he walked past the farther window and disappeared.

Sam's legs were watery as he stood erect. He knew that he was still alive only because the gray man hadn't wanted him dead. One could not learn anything from a dead man. His gun had been a bluff to intimidate him.

Somehow the gray man had made a grotesque mistake. Had he mistaken him for somebody else named Sam Tree? Whatever it was, the gray man obviously had the wrong person in mind.

Sam put out all the lights except the night light and locked the store.

A swanky, low-slung sedan was parked at the curb. Douglas Faulcon, Senior, reached sideways from behind the wheel to open the door. Sam settled beside him in the remarkably comfortable seat.

13

"Would you like to go somewhere for a drink?" Faulcon suggested.

"I don't drink, thanks. Why not come to my house?"

Faulcon took off his derby and looked into it as if he expected to find something there. He was bald except for a fringe of graying hair. With the automatic satisfaction of a man no longer very young, Sam ran his fingers through his own thick, unruly mop of hair.

"I'd rather not," Faulcon said slowly. "I'd like to talk to you alone. Sort of man to man." He put his hat on again, and Sam enjoyed the nervousness of the millionaire.

Sam settled deeper in the seat. "In other words, you don't approve of Douglas Faulcon, Junior, marrying a grocer's daughter."

"Oh no, that's not it, quite."

"Quite?" Sam said. "Does that mean that it is it?"

Faulcon gave a strained laugh. "If it comes to that, Naomi isn't your daughter."

"All right, stepdaughter."

"Stepdaughter twice removed." Faulcon

fumbled inside his pocket. "You'll like these cigars. They're my private stock."

"I don't smoke, thanks," Sam said.

Faulcon looked mildly surprised. He returned one cigar to his pocket and slipped the band off the other. As he lifted a flame to the tip of his cigar, Sam noticed that his face was peculiarly hawklike. That was odd, because Faulcon was inclined to fleshiness. It was probably his eyes that did it, Sam decided.

"Doug came home this morning," Faulcon said. "He believes it will be his last leave before he goes overseas. I would not want him to do anything foolish."

"Marrying Naomi seems like good sense to me."

"Doug will be a poor man if he marries her," Faulcon pointed out acidly.

"That's Doug's problem. Meanwhile, he draws a second lieutenant's pay."

"That's what has made him so headstrong. I can't do a thing with him. He's my only child, Tree; I've so many things planned for him. Now he plunges into this marriage, and she might have a baby, and he might — well, let's be frank, he

15

mightn't come back."

"I don't get it," Sam said. "If Doug is your only child, wouldn't you want him to leave an offspring if he doesn't come back?"

"That offspring!" Faulcon spat out.

Without a word Sam turned to the door and pushed down the door handle. Faulcon grabbed his arm.

"Wait, Tree. You appear to be a reasonable man. I'm not sure I'd object to the marriage if you were Naomi's father. I'm a — well, we're living in a democracy, aren't we? I mean, you appear to be decent and honest and — "

"Oh hell!" Sam cut in. "Get down to cases. Did you hire private detectives?"

Faulcon's eyebrows arched. "What makes you think that?"

"You're the kind who would."

"You know, I'm beginning to like you, Tree. I'm a blunt man myself." The dashboard showed Faulcon's face sober abruptly. "I considered it my duty to have Naomi's past investigated. I learned that her father was a criminal named Ira Pram. He was killed while trying to escape from the police."

16

"That happened when Naomi was a child of five."

"Which doesn't change the fact that Pram's blood flows in her veins. Her mother married again a year or two later — a man named Felix Skinner. When Naomi was twelve her mother — your wife — separated from Skinner, but Naomi has constantly remained under his influence. To this day she continues to see him. You know what Skinner is — a drunkard and an incorrigible gambler."

"So what?" Sam said. "That hasn't affected Naomi."

"It's in the blood. Her father was a desperate criminal. Her stepfather, who brought her up during her formative years, is an utterly dissolute individual."

"Is that all you have against Naomi?"

Faulcon squirmed. "Well, my wife and I — " He decided to return to his original approach. "Blood is important, you know."

Sam studied the fleshy profile with the fierce, sunken eyes. "Maybe you believe that nonsense. Maybe you believe that the Faulcon blood is better because it's

17

the blood of parasites who got rich on New York real estate which was made valuable by the work and sweat of millions of poor, common people. What's the real reason, Faulcon? Is there a society girl Doug was thinking of marrying before he met Naomi?"

Faulcon chuckled. "I like you, Tree."

"You said that before."

"Did I?" Faulcon blew cigar smoke at the windshield. "What I can't understand is why a man of your spirit and intelligence is content to be the owner of a small grocery store. You could expand considerably if an investor were to invest, say, ten thousand dollars cash in your business."

"With no return on the investment, of course," Sam said dryly.

"Of course. The investor would appreciate it if you would talk reason to Naomi. She is not your daughter, but I have no doubt that she has faith in your advice. All that would be necessary is that she does not marry Doug before he goes overseas."

"Hoping," Sam said, "that by the time he returns, if he does return, he will

18

marry a girl of his class and blood who is fit to carry on the Faulcon line."

Faulcon nodded once. "I trust the future to take care of itself. Quite likely the investor in your business will not want his money back for a long time to come, if at all."

"I don't like rich people," Sam said quietly. "They try to buy too much with their money." He opened the car door and got out and turned back to Faulcon. "Don't try bribing my wife. She's a placid woman, but she hasn't got my philosophic calm."

The dash light caught the savage glitter in Faulcon's hawklike eyes. He wasn't used to the open contempt of any man, certainly not to that of a mere grocer. "Your wife, Tree, is a fortune hunter. She's after every cent of the Faulcon money."

"Don't tell me you've tried to work on her also?"

"My wife visited her," Faulcon said with his mouth tight. "She wasted her time, the way I wasted mine."

Sam enjoyed the mental picture of Violet receiving the great lady that

Mrs. Douglas Faulcon, Senior, doubtless was, and being flightily effusive over her without ever giving her a chance to come to the point. But why, he wondered, hadn't Violet mentioned the visit to him?

The motor sprang into life. Sam stepped back from the car a moment before it started rolling. Faulcon hadn't repeated his offer to drive Sam home; he hadn't even said good night. He was now a very angry man.

Sam walked four blocks to a row of two-story gray brick houses, each separated from its neighbor by a narrow driveway. Automatically Sam counted the fourth house from the corner; it was the quickest way to tell his from the others. Coming from the opposite direction, a red brick chimney running up the side of the house distinguished it, for Sam had violated suburban sameness by tearing down the living-room wall and erecting a fireplace. The neighbors considered that a bohemian gesture.

Dim light lay against the drawn living-room shades. No other window was lit, which probably meant that Violet was curled up with a book. He walked up the five steps to the tiny open porch and turned to take in the Manhattan skyline across the river. The mast of the Empire State Building was an obelisk in the moonlight dominating the hunched masses of mid-town Manhattan. Violet and Naomi would have preferred to move from Queens to the other side of the river, but Sam insisted on living close to the store. In this one matter, at least, they humored him.

The house door opened. Sam glanced over his shoulder, and a little shock went through him when he saw Felix Skinner come out. Skinner had never before been in this house; Violet had absolutely forbidden her former husband to come here to visit Naomi, and she herself would have nothing to do with him.

Sam opened his mouth and closed it without a sound when he realized that Skinner did not notice him standing in the shadows. Sam could do very well without another talk with him.

At the foot of the porch steps Skinner stopped and pulled his right hand out of his coat pocket. A loose wad of money came out with it. By the slanting light of a street lamp Skinner slowly counted the money, then carelessly stuffed the wad back into his pocket. One of the bills fluttered to the cemented walk.

Sam downed the impulse to call out to him. He watched Skinner, his tall body still drooping wearily in spite of his newly gained wealth, shuffle up the street. When he was out of sight, Sam went down the porch steps and picked up the money. It was a one-hundred-dollar bill.

2

One-Hundred-Dollar Bill

VIOLET TREE rose quickly from the fireplace when she heard Sam enter. The poker was in her hand. In the fireplace a small flame flared, then subsided.

"I burned some papers." She put down the poker, adding, "Old bills I cleaned out of the desk."

She looked at that moment like somebody Sam hardly knew. Violet was a round woman who escaped being buxom only through diligent dieting — the soft, cozy, pretty kind of woman older men especially found attractive. It was probably the light, or the lack of it, that caused the change in her now, Sam told himself. Only a single floor lamp was lit some distance from where she stood, and the fringe of it made planes and shadows of her face, giving her features a strangely pinched effect.

23

"Felix Skinner was in the store tonight," he said casually. "He asked me for money."

"Did you give it to him?"

"You know I didn't. That's why he came to you for it."

Her fingers toyed nervously with the zipper of her flowered housecoat. "Felix said he would be evicted from his apartment tomorrow if he didn't pay back rent. I — I let him have a few dollars."

"How much?"

"Oh, I don't know," she said with that typically vague toss of her head. "Whatever was in my bag."

Violet was like that, careless about money, never knowing even approximately how much she had on her or how much she had spent. Or else she pretended to be. In five years of marriage to her Sam hadn't been able to decide which it was.

"I thought you hated him," he said.

"I wouldn't call it hate."

"Whatever it is, you've never let him come here, and you're always scolding Naomi because she sees him."

"I was sorry for Felix tonight. He

24

looked so — so completely crushed. After all, I was married to him for five years. I couldn't simply stand by while he was put out on the street."

"Don't you know what he'll use that money for?"

"You mean for gambling? Well, he promised me he'd pay his rent with it."

"How much rent?"

Her shoulders stirred with impatience. "I won't be questioned like this. He was behind two or three months. I don't know; I didn't ask him."

Sam Tree took the hundred-dollar bill out of his pocket and walked across the room with it. "Felix Skinner dropped this in front of the house. He had a handful. I don't know if the others were one-hundred-dollar bills, but there must have been enough to pay the rent on his dive for a year or two."

She looked down at the money without touching it. Her bosom stirred against the tight bodice of her housecoat. "Sam, I didn't think you capable of tricking me." She said it accusingly, making it sound as if he were the one who was completely in the wrong.

"I'm your husband," he reminded her. "I'm entitled to know what's going on."

"I didn't want to bother you with my personal problems, and an ex-husband is a very personal problem. It was a few hundred dollars. Three hundred, to be exact, and it was my money."

"Evidently you don't dislike Felix Skinner as much as you pretend."

"Don't tell me you're jealous of poor Felix?" She was very good at turning the tables; the burden of denial had been shifted to him.

He said nothing for a while, looking at her. From where he stood he had an illusion that the raven was perched on top of her head.

It was on the mantelpiece behind her, of course, squatting on top of the helmeted head of the Greek goddess Pallas Athene. The whole business, white head and black raven, was a single plaster cast and was supposed to illustrate Poe's poem. Sam had always considered the figure particularly shoddy as art, but Violet and Naomi liked it, and they ran the household.

"Do you keep hundred-dollar bills

loose in the house?" Sam persisted.

"I drew money from the bank before I visited East Wiston. I wanted to give Mother a present, and I had some money left when I came home yesterday."

"Three hundred in cash? You must have taken quite a sum with you."

She flared up then, getting that cold glow in her pale blue eyes which he had seen only a few times before. Violet was essentially placid, but not always.

"I won't be questioned like a criminal," she said now. "It's my money."

"Yes, it's your money." Sam stepped sideways to get the raven off Violet's head and back on the bust of Pallas where it belonged. "How much did you pay for the fur coat you bought Naomi last month?"

"I told you at the time — a few hundred dollars."

"How much is a few hundred in your language?"

"Four hundred dollars, and it was a bargain."

"I'm sure it was," he said dryly. "Naomi came into the store the other day wearing that coat. Bosher, the tailor next door, came in later and said jokingly that business must be great for me to be able to afford expensive mink coats like that. When I told him it cost only a few hundred dollars, he laughed and said he'd give me thirteen hundred for it in cash even though it had been worn."

Violet left the fireplace and put an arm about Sam's waist and snuggled up to him. She was nearer the light now, and she looked the way she always had, soft and restful and years younger than her age.

"Sam, darling, I see I was wrong. When Father was alive, Mother never used to tell him how much things cost. She said it only upset him."

"You know I'm not that way about money."

"It's silly of me." She snuggled her face into his shoulder. "I simply had to buy Naomi that mink coat. You can't expect her to be dressed shabbily in the circles she moves in now."

"When are Naomi and Doug Faulcon getting married?"

"Very soon. Doug came home on leave this afternoon. He has five days; he thinks he will be sent abroad when he gets back to camp. I've been trying to persuade her to marry him right away — a quiet wedding with only a few people right here at home."

"And without his parents," Sam said.

"That's what's making Naomi hesitate. Doug wants to go through with it anyway. I can't believe that Doug's parents would really cut him off without a cent. After all, he's their only child."

His hand stroked her hip. She was good to hold close. He said: "Faulcon, Senior, was around to see me this evening."

She stiffened against him. "What did he want?"

"To use my influence to break it up."

"What did you tell him?"

"What do you think?"

She relaxed, and her mouth was on the side of his neck. "You're a sweet man, darling."

"This marriage means a lot to you, doesn't it?"

"Naturally I want Naomi to be happy. I want her to marry into a good family with a good background, and not make the mistake I did." Her laughter fluttered against his neck. "I mean, of course, my first two marriages. You're a perfect husband."

Her words brought him back to where he had started. As usual, he had received affection, but no answers. He slid out of her embrace.

"I'm perfect, all right," he said. "Away at the store all day while you two women run everything. Where do you get all that money, Violet?"

"What money?"

"Hell!" He understood now how a man could strangle a woman he loved. "You know damn well I mean all the money you've been spending these last couple of years."

Distractedly she brushed a loose wisp of hair from her face. "Please, Sam, don't nag me tonight. I have a frightful headache. You know very well that Ira left me a five-thousand-dollar life insurance policy."

"That was fifteen years ago. You needed money plenty of times since then, especially after your father died penniless and you had your mother on your hands in addition to Naomi. From all I've heard, Felix Skinner never earned much, even when he worked, which wasn't often, and after he left you he didn't contribute anything to your support."

"He did so. For a while Felix sent me fifteen dollars a week, almost."

"Huh!" Sam sniffed. "Fifteen dollars a week, for a while and almost, wouldn't have kept you and Naomi in clothes."

"Naomi has a job."

"Only since last year, and she never has any extra money. It doesn't wash, Violet. You must have dug deep into that five thousand before you met me. And after that deeper. You spent well over two thousand for furniture when I bought this house and hadn't anything over. You've been sending your mother a fat allowance every month which doesn't come out of my pocket. On top of that you buy Naomi a mink coat for at least fifteen hundred dollars, maybe a lot more, and you still seem to have plenty left."

Her back was to him now; she was fingering the lace doily on the table. "You're right, the insurance money is almost gone, Sam. From now on you'll have to provide all the money."

"I make enough for ordinary decent living."

"Of course you do, darling." Violet returned to him and placed a hand on his cheek. "I promise to stop being so dreadfully extravagant."

He looked down at her, not sure how she did it. Every time he launched an attack, he found himself neatly switched to the defensive. Now suddenly she was the understanding wife willing to make sacrifices in order to get along on her husband's inadequate income, and everything he had said up to now was brushed aside and lost. Well, this time he wouldn't let her get away with it.

"It doesn't figure out, Violet. Five thousand dollars which you received fifteen years ago — "

"Please, darling! My headache is killing me. I'm going to bed."

"Are you afraid to talk to me?"

"Silly!" She gave him her slow, comfortable smile. "I always talk to you, don't I? Are you coming to bed soon?"

"No," he said.

He heard her go up the stairs. Pacing the room, he did sums in his head, but every way he figured the result was a lot more than five thousand dollars. Naomi's job didn't count. She was an office worker in a war plant in Long Island City. She made thirty-two dollars a week. After tax and war-bond deductions and the small sum she insisted on contributing to the household, there was barely enough left for working expenses and clothes.

Sam realized that the one-hundred-dollar bill was still in his hand. He stared at the money. The gray man had asked for one-hundred-dollar bills. There was probably no connection. Bills of that denomination were not too uncommon.

Yet the gray man had been very sure that Sam Tree was the man he wanted. Could he have meant Violet Tree? Then why hadn't he come here to Violet?

Sam placed the bill on the table doily and went to the fireplace.

The fireplace had been swept clean that afternoon. Sam had given up trying to persuade Violet that a layer of ashes made the best base for a fire. Between the andirons lay a fluffy heap of still smoldering ashes. Sam poked the ashes; some of the bottom papers were not completely consumed. With the poker he pulled toward him the lower couple of inches of a letter written on expensive rag paper. Gingerly he picked up one corner. What remained of the letter read: ' . . . millions of kisses until I see you Monday.' And it was signed: 'Ira.'

Over and over Sam read those few scrawled words. Once Violet had mentioned that her marriage to Felix Skinner had been held up for several weeks until Ira Pram was declared legally dead, yet that had been almost two years after Pram was killed. The details were sketchy in his mind; Violet never wanted to speak about them.

Did that mean that there had been doubt about Pram's death? How long ago had this letter been written? Monday could be any time. It could be yesterday.

He peered into the fireplace and pulled out an envelope which was practically intact. It was addressed: 'Miss Violet Wilson, East Wiston, Mass.' There was no return address, but beyond doubt the handwriting on the envelope was the same as in the letter. Wilson was Violet's maiden name and East Wiston her home town.

Breathing easier now, Sam stood up. The letter had been sent from Boston, but the date on the postmark was somewhat blurred. He took the letter under the light and deciphered the date: 1923. That was the year Ira Pram and Violet were married. The letter had probably been written a few months before their marriage, when he had been courting her.

So that was all it was, Violet burning old love letters in the fireplace. And like a fool he —

Suddenly he was very still, looking at the charred scrap of letter in one hand and the envelope in the other without seeing them. Violet had burned the letters tonight as soon as Felix Skinner left the house. She might have been about to burn them when Skinner arrived and had put it off until he left.

Then why had she lied about it? She had told him she was burning old bills, and she had been very nervous saying it. And she had given Skinner a lot of money tonight.

Sam dropped into a chair. He was always tired after a day at the store, and now the tiredness was in his head too. Did Violet give Skinner the money in return for the letters? But that didn't make sense either. There couldn't be anything incriminating in the letters of a man she had married — a man dead fifteen years. And the gray man . . .

His thoughts dulled. He sat there, trying to think and not able to, and all at once he was asleep.

When he awoke it was almost eleven o'clock. The charred fragments of letter and envelope lay at his feet. He picked them up and got a match from the kitchen and burned them in the fireplace. When he rose, the raven leered down at him from the helmet of Pallas. He locked the front and back doors and went upstairs.

As he undressed by the light of the dresser lamp, he looked at himself in the mirror. He had practically no stomach, and his wiry body retained its straight lines. His face wasn't much, but Violet

36

said it was sweet. Being married to her was very pleasant, but tonight something had come between them.

Standing there, he had an oppressive feeling that part of each of her former husbands — the crook and the pan-handling bum — somehow shared this house with Violet and Naomi and himself and that Violet had never ceased being their wife when she had become his. Not their wife in a physical way, of course — one was dead — but in a way that went deeper and was terrifying.

He shook himself, as if to throw the weight of her former husbands off his shoulders, and turned to the bed. Violet was watching him with her pale eyes wide.

"How's your headache?" he asked.

"What? Oh, it's much better."

She used every woman's weapon to fight him, he thought as he got into his pajamas. Even a phony headache. But fight him why and for what?

He said: "Do you know a small, elderly man with gray eyes?"

"What's his name?"

"I don't know." He hestitated. He did

not want to frighten her by telling her that he had almost been killed today. He added: "It was busy in the store, and I didn't catch his name. He said he knew you."

She seemed to be sincerely puzzled. "A small gray-haired man. What did he want?"

"I'm not sure about his hair. I said his eyes were gray. It's not important." He tied the cord of his pajamas. "Was there ever any doubt about Ira Pram being dead?"

"Doubt?" She pulled the blanket up to her chin. "Ira was killed by the police."

"You never told me the details."

"Please darling." Even in bed she could manage that fluttering, distracted gesture. "I told you that talking about it only brings back the past. I want to forget."

He stood looking down at her. Then he turned to the dresser and put out the light.

3

The Prowler

THE first two or three times Sam Tree heard the sound he paid little attention to it. Every house at night had its own peculiar meaningless noises. Then, after a pause, it came again, half-muted and small and directly below the bedroom, and it was not like any sound that creaking furniture or a settling house makes.

It might be Naomi downstairs. But he would have heard her come home from her date with Doug Faulcon. For well over an hour he had lain awake in bed, the penalty for having dozed off downstairs; and now he lay still and wide-eyed beside Violet, waiting for the sound to return.

It did, at the regular intervals of three or four heartbeats. It was, he decided, a long-drawn squeak, like the agony of some inanimate thing. Ordinarily he would have dismissed it, but not tonight after his experience with the gray man.

He slipped out of bed and in darkness groped for his bathrobe. Barefooted he went out to the hall and listened. There was silence, and there had been since he had left the bed. *It's nothing,* he thought. *I'm upset and worried, so my imagination is playing tricks.*

He was turning back to the bedroom when there was a thump downstairs. It was as small as the other sounds had been and would have been inaudible except for the silence.

Sam went down the stairs on his bare feet. In the hall he stopped, hearing himself breathe and hearing nothing else. He was cold suddenly; a breeze hit his bed-warmed body. For long seconds he wondered about that before he understood.

His bedroom was directly above the living room, and he had heard somebody raise a window. Damp weather had caused the windows to stick; opening and closing them was a strain and produced those spaced squeaks. Whoever had stood at the side of the house raising the window had done so gradually, in spurts, to deaden the squeaks and because the window would not move easily. And now the window was wide open and cold air was sweeping into the hall from the living room. Which meant that somebody was in there.

The gray man?

Abruptly light glowed in the living-room doorway. Not the brilliant ceiling light, certainly, nor any of the table or floor lamps, because the light was low and peculiarly concentrated. Then it moved, dimming in the doorway and then returning and dimming again as the flashlight swept the living room.

Straining to hear, Sam caught the whisper of feet over the carpet. The gray man, if it was he, was searching the living room. Or perhaps it was Felix Skinner, prowling in the house for some reason connected with his earlier visit here tonight.

The light moved by the door, almost touching Sam, and in panic he retreated toward the stairs. Fear made him angry, and when the light was elsewhere in the other room he crossed the hall. The umbrella stand stood near the street door. He jerked out the umbrella and stepped into the living room.

The flashlight beam hit Sam squarely in the face, blotting out everything but the glare of it. A moment later it went out and he was momentarily blind.

In the street a truck chugged by, louder than anything that could be heard in the room. Sam raised the umbrella; the weight of it was ridiculously frail. It was hardly a weapon. When the noise of the truck died, Sam could hear strained breathing that was not his own.

A little of the fear lifted from his chest. If it was the gray man, he had a gun, and he could have used it when his light had hit Sam. Yet he wasn't here to kill, unless he found it necessary. He could have killed him in the store, and he hadn't.

Sam's eyes became accustomed to the darkness. The prowler had pulled up the shade of the window through which he had entered, and the fringe of the street lamp sent an opaque glow into the room. Sam's gaze found the whitest thing, the plaster bust of Pallas barely discernible.

The raven on the head was merged with the darkness. His eyes focused nearer and distinguished the darker mass of what was doubtless a man standing not ten feet from him. No sound or motion came from that form.

He's as afraid as I am, Sam thought. *I've trapped him, and if he has a gun, he'll have to use it whether he wants to or not.*

"Who are you?" Sam said hoarsely.

His voice died into taut silence. Sam decided that his only chance was to attack. He was bigger and stronger and younger than the gray man.

Raising his umbrella, Sam rushed toward the shape. He had to cross the window, and the prowler saw him coming and side-stepped. Sam twisted, trying to follow him, but he never completed the turn. The flashlight struck him on the skull, just below his temple.

Sam felt the blow drive sickness down to the pit of his stomach. His legs buckled; his knees hit the carpet. He got his left hand on the floor and propped himself up with it.

As if from a distance Sam heard a

chair crash. Groggily he raised his head. The prowler was at the window, pausing there as if in indecision; then he started to slip through into the driveway. The street light vaguely outlined very wide hips and heavy thighs.

Fury gave Sam strength. He pushed himself erect. His legs wobbled, but they bore him to the window. When he reached it the prowler had vanished. He stuck his head out into the brisk air. The street lamp sent a shaft of light down the driveway; the prowler was running away from the street, away from the range of light. Sam glimpsed his labored, waddling gait before he vanished out of sight into the back yard of the house next door.

Slowly Sam withdrew his head. He leaned against the wall, feeling his stomach churn. The gray man was scarcely half the size of the prowler. Felix Skinner was as tall, but never as wide. It had been a burglar, then — a very big man, a fat man — who had come to steal the store receipts.

Sam crossed to the door and snapped on the ceiling light. Nothing in the room was disturbed except the chair the burglar had knocked over. Sam picked it up, and pain jabbed his skull with the downward motion of his head. As he replaced the chair against the table, his eyes fell on the one-hundred-dollar bill which he had left on the doily earlier that evening.

It was still there; it hadn't been touched.

Leaning heavily against the chair, Sam tried to remember how long he had stood outside the hall while the flashlight searched the room. Long enough for the light to have picked out the money. The light had crossed the room several times, and on that white doily the bill was as conspicuous as anything in the room. A burglar's first instinct would have been to snatch it up. He couldn't have hoped for more than that in cash from the store receipts, yet he had been quite a distance from the table when Sam had entered the room.

In short, the prowler was not the gray man and he was not Felix Skinner and he was not a burglar.

But nobody entering a house by stealth would resist stealing one hundred dollars for the mere effort of picking it off the table. Nobody but somebody who was after something so urgent and important that that money was insignificant by comparison and he had put off taking the time to cross to the table. Somebody who was not a burglar, but who had come into the house like a burglar.

Sam shook his head, and the pain caught him again. He was lifting his hand to feel the wound when he heard gay voices outside and then feet coming up the porch steps. He went out to the hall and put on the light. A key turned in the lock.

He knew who it must be, but he was again afraid. Not until Naomi came in through the open door did he breathe normally.

"Hello, Sam," Naomi said in surprise. She was particularly attractive tonight in her new mink coat and her black wool fascinator over her dark brown hair. She was dark-eyed and tall and big-boned. She did not look anything at all like her fair and soft and round mother. Violet said that she was like her father, Ira Pram, who had been a big, dark man.

Naomi snapped her handbag shut and then looked at him again with puzzled eyes. Sam realized that the umbrella was still in his hand and that his feet were bare.

There was no point frightening her by telling her the truth. "I came down for a drink of water and found that this umbrella had fallen out of the stand," he said.

"You do look rather ridiculous holding that umbrella like a club," Naomi said with a laugh. She came all the way into the hall. "For a moment I had a notion that you intended to brain me with it."

Now that she was no longer in front of the door, Sam could see that two other people were out on the porch — a soldier and a woman. Sam dropped the umbrella into the stand and turned back as Doug Faulcon, Junior, entered.

"How are you, sir?" Doug said with his inevitable politeness.

He put down the valise he carried and shook Sam's hand. He was hardly taller than Naomi, and he had a pug-nosed, freckled face which was not handsome. It was a frank, open face, the kind Sam

47

liked in a young man. He found himself wishing suddenly that he had a son like that or a daughter like Naomi.

"It gives me a shock to hear an officer call me sir," Sam said. "In my experience in the Army it was always the other way around."

"Naomi's been telling me you were in the last war. In the artillery also."

"I thought you were in the Rangers," Sam said.

"I was, but they transferred me. Guess I wasn't rugged enough. Did you see much action in the last war, sir?"

Sam grinned wryly. "I never got overseas. I'm the kind of man who's always a buck private and to whom nothing ever happens, even when it happens to millions of others."

Naomi called out: "Come in, Blythe."

The woman entered diffidently from the porch, as if she were intruding and knew it. She was considerably older than Naomi, close to thirty, if not over. Sam thought he knew all of Naomi's friends, but he had never seen her before.

"Blythe Brice — my stepfather, Sam Tree," Naomi introduced them. "Blythe

48

is spending the night with me."

The woman nodded solemnly and tried to make herself obscure against the hall wall. Evidently the valise Doug had brought in was hers. Her high cheekbones gave her face a gaunt, sallow appearance, and she wore little or no make-up. Her eyes were deep-set, lusterless. She couldn't be Naomi's friend; she was too old, too timid.

"Sam!" Naomi exclaimed. "You're bleeding!"

Gingerly he touched his temple and felt the stickiness of blood. They were all staring at him. Doug's eyes dropped to Sam's bare feet and then up again to his head.

"It's nothing," Sam said with a feeble little laugh. His stomach refused to settle. "I was coming down the stairs in the darkness and tripped and struck my head against the banister."

"And you say nothing ever happens to you!" Naomi said.

"It wasn't funny," Sam muttered. She couldn't guess how unfunny it was. Things were happening to him now, all right, but he wished he knew what.

Doug shifted his feet like an embarrassed schoolboy. "Well, sir, if Naomi doesn't break the news, I guess I'll have to. We're getting married."

"That's fine," Sam said. "When?"

"The minute the law lets us," Naomi said. "We got our license and blood tests this afternoon."

Sam kissed Naomi. As he moved to shake Doug's hand again, he had a mental picture of Douglas Faulcon, Senior's, anger at the news, and he enjoyed it. Then Naomi tucked a hand through Doug's arm and dragged him out to the porch to say good night in private. The door closed, and instantly Sam was aware that he was alone in the hall with Blythe Brice and that his feet were bare and that there was blood on his temple.

"They make a sweet couple," Blythe Brice said. Her shoulders were tight against the wall.

"Yes." Sam groped for words. He was never any good at casual conversation. "Are you married?"

Pointedly she twisted a gold band on her finger. "My husband's in the Navy."

"Oh," Sam said.

Conversation died. Evidently she wasn't any better at conversation than he was. The silence seemed to oppress her. She said without interest: "This is a very nice house."

Sam was about to reply that it was a pretty good house when Naomi relieved the situation by returning. He muttered good night and went into the kitchen for a drink of water. When he moved his head it hardly hurt at all, though his stomach remained squeazy.

Before he went upstairs he locked every downstairs window and tried the front and back doors. Idly he wondered if he should try to get a permit for a gun. Twenty-six years ago in the Army he had been a pretty good shot. He had been not quite twenty then and was anxious for excitement. He had never found any.

Walking along the upstairs hall, he heard the girls talking in Naomi's room. He went into the bathroom and washed his wound with hot water. It was hardly more than a skin break; his thick hair would hide it. He was lucky that the prowler hadn't had anything more vicious than a flashlight in his hand. A burglar would have had a gun.

His breath came out sharply. There was one other possible reason why the prowler hadn't taken that one-hundred-dollar bill. He was an honest man; he would not steal. But murder was different. It would be hard for any man, especially a fat man, to climb up to a second-floor window from outside. The entrance was through the ground floor, and he had been on his way upstairs.

Not to murder me, Sam said into the towel against his face. *If he had a weapon in his pocket, a gun or a knife, I was in his power after he struck me. Violet, then. He came up to murder Violet in her sleep, both of us if necessary, but not just me alone.*

He finished wiping his face. His hands shook; his stomach bounced. Then he laughed wildly, thinking: *I'm all wrong. I've got to be. In college I learned that logic can deduce any answer you want it to. My mind is getting melodramatic on me.*

In the hall he met Naomi coming out

of her room. She wore pajamas and had a fresh towel over her arm.

"Sam, I want to explain about Blythe," she said. "I never saw her before tonight."

He wondered why he tensed. "Who is she?"

"Her husband is in the Navy. His ship sailed tonight from Brooklyn Navy Yard, and she came all the way from Indiana to spend a single night with him." She looked away from him. "I can understand how she feels. I'll have only a day or two with Doug after we're married."

"Is that why you brought her home with you?"

"Well, I guess that's what decided me. Doug and I were in a night club tonight, and I happened to sit next to her at the bar. We got to talking. She told me that she was trying to get over her loneliness. She said she had no place to sleep. You know how the hotel situation is these days, and she hadn't made a reservation in advance."

"What about the place where she spent last night with her husband?"

"It was in the apartment of a friend of

his. She hardly knows him; in fact, she says she knows nobody in New York."

He remembered that he had left the one-hundred-dollar bill on the living-room table. "Are you putting her up on the day bed?"

"My bed is big enough for two, and the poor girl feels so sad and lonely."

"You're a fine girl, Naomi," Sam said.

She placed a hand against his cheek — a gesture she had learned from Violet. "You're a fine man, Sam. I didn't approve of Mother marrying a third time, but I'm not sorry now."

"You were hoping that Violet would go back to Felix Skinner."

She didn't deny it. Her dark eyes went grave. "Sam, I wish you'd do something about Felix."

He was annoyed at the jealousy that went through him. Naomi was fond of him, but not the way she was of her first stepfather.

"What's the matter now?" he asked.

"The same thing, only more so. I was up to see him yesterday. His place was like a pigsty, and he's always been neat.

He looks — well, as if he's falling apart. Sam, he can be saved. If you were to find a decent job for him — "

"I offered to find him one this evening," Sam said. "He told me to go to hell."

"Felix came to see you? What did he want?"

"Money for gambling. I didn't give it to him, but your mother did."

She looked at him in disbelief. "Mother gave him money? Are you sure?"

"Yes."

"I don't understand it," she said. "This morning I spoke to her about doing something about Felix and she was very angry because I'd seen him."

So Naomi didn't know anything either. Violet was in this alone, whatever it was.

"Well, I've a store to open tomorrow morning," he said. "Good night."

Naomi muttered good night as if she didn't know that she was speaking. At the door Sam looked back. She hadn't moved. She stood there in the hall, a tall, charming statue in pajamas, and her eyes were like a statue's.

Sam went into his room and shed his bathrobe and looked down at Violet, a sleeping shadow in what light entered the windows. He closed the open window and locked it and the other two and then got into bed.

4

Felix Skinner

AT noon Violet Tree phoned the store. "I have wonderful news, darling. Naomi and Doug took out their marriage license yesterday."

Sam had left the house while Violet still slept, so he had not spoken to her since early the night before. He said: "When did you find that out?"

"Naomi told me as soon as I got up. I've been on the phone since then, telling everybody. I'm afraid I ran up a frightful bill talking long-distance to Mother."

"And when there was nobody left to tell," Sam said, "you decided that you might as well let me know too. I'm grateful. It's the first time in a long time you've let me in on anything."

"Don't be sarcastic, darling," Violet said blithely. "It doesn't become you. Aren't you delighted at the news?"

"Why not? Did you find that hundred-dollar bill I left on the living-room table?"

For long seconds Violet did not say anything, and when she spoke her voice was small and thin and tired. "Naomi gave it to me this morning. Will you be home for supper tonight?"

"Violet, let me help you."

"Help me how? What do you mean?"

"Violet, do you know a big, fat middle-aged man?"

"A fat man!" she echoed shrilly. "O God!"

"Then you do know him? Who — "

"I know several fat men," she broke in, her voice almost normal. "Ted Hanley is fat. So is Grover Langford."

"Cut it out, Violet. I'm your husband. I've a right to know what's going on."

"Sam, you didn't answer me. Are you coming home for supper?"

"Yes. Violet, are you in any danger? You've got to tell me if — "

"There goes the doorbell," she said. "Good-by, Sam."

He heard the click of the line going dead.

The store telephone was in the back room, behind the refrigerator. Ted Hanley was opening a case of peas just outside the back door leading into the store, so that Sam didn't see him until he stepped away from the telephone.

"What's the idea listening in to my private conversation?" Sam said.

"I was just opening a can of peas."

"There are plenty of peas on the shelf."

Ted straightened up. "Gee, you're touchy today, Sam."

He knew that he was and couldn't help it. In the afternoon he was snappish with a cranky customer and felt a little better when she stalked out in a huff. He found himself writing on a paper bag numbers which had nothing to do with store business. No matter how he cut the figures down, the answer was always well over five thousand dollars.

He tore up the bag and telephoned Grover Langford's law office in downtown Manhattan.

"Congratulations," Grover said.

"On what?"

"Naomi's coming marriage. It was in

all the morning papers. That's the beauty of marrying into money. Don't you read the papers, Sam?"

"Not the society pages," Sam said. "I want you to do something for me. You know about Violet's first husband?"

"Sure. A lad named Ira Pram."

"When he died, he left a life-insurance policy. Now possibly there were some policies Violet didn't know about. I want you to check up on it. Pram lived in East Wiston, Massachusetts. Probably he got his insurance from Boston brokers."

Grover Langford's voice sounded puzzled. "Didn't Violet collect?"

"On that one policy. He might have carried more and Violet didn't know about it and took no steps to collect it."

"Assuming that the companies had no knowledge that Ira Pram was dead," Grover said, using his legal tone, "they would have continued to attempt to collect premiums. Violet would have received his mail."

"You know the kind of person he was. Suppose he had another address in Boston."

"Then the mail would have been returned and the insurance companies would have investigated. They're very efficient that way."

In the store Sam heard Ted say, "He's in back," and he heard a woman answer, "I'll go right in." He glanced around and saw Martha Underhill enter the back room.

"A friend of yours is here," Sam told Grover. "Martha."

"Give her my love," Grover said, "but not the way I'd like to myself."

"Will you attend to this little matter for me?"

"You're footing the bill, kid," Grover said cheerfully.

Sam hung up. Martha Underhill was setting fire to a cigarette with mannish nonchalance. There was very much of the man about her. She went in for severely tailored suits and low-heeled shoes and cropped hair. She was the kind of woman you would call handsome. Violet was her closest friend; had been since they were girls together on Cape Cod.

"That was Grover," Sam said. "He

sends his love. Why don't you marry him?"

Martha exhaled smoke through her nostrils. "He's too jolly and he has a potbelly. Why don't all men keep their figure like you, Sam?"

"I suppose it's a matter of glands." He looked around the back room, cramped by full and empty cases, and decided that he ought at least to get a chair for visitors to sit on. "Did you stop at the house?"

Martha crushed out her cigarette under her toes after having taken only a few puffs. It was only then that Sam realized she was agitated. "Sam, you've got to do something about Felix Skinner."

"You, too? Naomi asked me the same thing last night. She said he was going completely to pieces."

"That's not what I mean. I visited Violet a couple of hours ago. As I came from the subway, I met Felix. It was unlikely that he had come anywhere but from your house."

"Again!" Sam blurted.

She looked at him. "So it's not the first time. I don't understand it. Violet despises that man. What can he want?"

Sam knew, but he didn't say it.

"He acted strange," Martha went on. "I mean, he nodded to me in an abstract sort of way and went past without stopping to talk. I knew Felix almost as well as Violet did, and we'd always been friendly." She fumbled in her bag for another cigarette. "When I rang the bell of your house, nobody answered. I tried the door and it was open, so I went in. And there in the hall Violet was stretched out on the floor."

"What!"

"Don't get frightened. She'd only fainted and was coming out of it. I went to the kitchen for water. When I returned, a girl was coming down the stairs. She said her name was Mrs. Price."

"Brice. Is she still there?"

"Isn't she supposed to be?"

"It's all right. Naomi brought her home last night. Her husband's in the Navy and — Never mind. Go on."

"I thought Felix must have hurt Violet," she said, "but she denied it. I believe it, because Felix is not the kind, though I suppose you never can tell. I could see that he had upset her very much. She said that after Felix left she was on the way to her room when everything turned black. It's a lucky thing she didn't faint on the stairs."

"What did Violet say happened between her and Skinner?"

Martha shrugged. "You know Violet. She talks and talks, and when she's finished you realize that she hasn't told you anything."

"I know," Sam said grimly

"Sam, I don't know what you can do, but Felix is very bad for Violet. He's always been. She'll have a nervous breakdown if he sees her again. Maybe you ought to have a talk with him."

Sam felt his jaw muscles ridge. "What's his address?"

"It's on West Eleventh Street. Here, I'll write it down."

When she handed him the address on a scrap of paper, she saw something in his face that frightened her. "Sam, don't do anything rash!"

Slowly he expelled breath. "Don't worry. I won't beat him up, if that's what you mean."

"What else could I mean?" She kept looking at him. "Sam, be careful. Maybe I shouldn't have told you."

"I'm glad somebody tells me something," he said.

When Martha Underhill was gone, Sam took off his white coat and told Ted that he would be back in a couple of hours. He walked home.

The front door was locked. When he let himself into the hall, the silence of the house hit him. He called Violet's name, and his voice came back to him unanswered. A giant fist squeezed his heart. Violet was always going places, but she had fainted a few hours ago and would not be feeling well.

He went through the house room by room, thinking: *It's my fault if anything happened to her. After the gray man and the prowler, I had no business leaving her alone.*

She was not in any room. He went up to the attic and then down to the cellar before he could convince himself that she was not at home. He laughed then and his knees were weak. He had told her that he was coming home for supper; she had gone to the butcher or somewhere. It was almost five; she would be back shortly. He waited.

At six o'clock he was standing on the porch, looking up and down the street for her. She knew that he had to eat early so that he could relieve Ted for supper. At ten minutes to seven he left the house. When he reached the store, he phoned home every ten minutes.

Shortly before closing time at eight o'clock Violet answered the phone. His nerves untied at the sound of her voice.

"Where have you been? I told you I was coming home for supper."

"That's right, you did," Violet said vaguely. "I forgot. I went to the movies."

"In the late afternoon? And after Martha found you fainted on the floor?"

"So Martha spoke to you? I was upset, and a movie always makes me relax."

"How much did you give Skinner this time?" Sam said.

"Now, Sam, I refuse to be nagged about poor Felix. I'm trying to — to get him back on his feet. Do you object to that?"

It was possible. Violet was bitter about

her former husband, but after all she had lived with him for five years. Though it wasn't as simple as that. There was the prowler last night, and Violet's fright at the mention of a fat man. She wouldn't tell him anything, he knew. Maybe he could get it out of Skinner.

"I won't be home till late tonight," he said.

"Where are you going?"

"Business," he said.

* * *

The dim-out had been lifted in New York, but West Eleventh Street was dark and wind-swept. Hatless and coatless, Sam shivered a little and dug into a pocket for the address. It would be a renovated tenement house cut up into tiny apartments for single people and business couples. Sam had inhabited a number of them in Greenwich Village during his long bachelor years.

Sam pushed the bell under Felix Skinner's name. There was no answering buzz. Probably Skinner wasn't home, but there was a chance that the buzzer didn't work. The vestibule door wasn't locked. He went up three flights of sickly lit stairs to apartment 3C and knocked on the door. "Come in," Skinner called.

There was a foyer which hardly had room for a right turn into the apartment. That one room was all there was to it except for a bathroom. A tiny kitchenette recessed in one wall was supposed to be covered by a curtain, but the curtain was gone. The sink and the ancient squat icebox were piled with dirty dishes and scraps of food. The covers of the unmade bed were flung about; layers of the harsh black dust which plagues householders in downtown New York lay over everything; there was not a chair free of magazines or newspapers or clothes. Skinner was not in the room.

"Skinner?" Sam said.

The half-open bathroom door was kicked all the way back on its hinges. Skinner appeared, wiping lather off his face with a towel, the stub of a lit cigarette in the corner of his thin mouth. His shirt was off and his ribs punched against his very white skin. At the sight of Sam his eyebrows arched.

"Well, well! What are you doing here — Slumming?"

Sam said: "I want you to let Violet alone."

"Ah, the gallant husband." Skinner tossed the towel on a chair. "You've got a nerve coming here, Tree. Violet is old enough to know what she's doing."

"Why did she give you money?"

In the room the bell buzzed. Skinner glanced vacantly at the button near the door and did not go near it. He opened the bottom drawer of an unpainted pine dresser and rummaged through a pile of dirty shirts until he found a clean one. Sam stood watching him, waiting for him to speak first.

"Because she still loves me," Skinner said with a feeble grin.

"Damn you!" Sam's fists clenched. He found himself taking an angry step toward Skinner. Skinner made a hoarse sound in his throat and cowered back like a child about to be struck. That stopped Sam. You couldn't hit a man like that.

"Go ask Violet." Skinner's voice was edged with hysteria.

"Let her alone," Sam said again.

Skinner wet his lips and then fumbled the pins out of his shirt with unsteady hands. "Sure. I don't want any trouble with you or anybody. I told Violet this afternoon she'd never see me again."

"Is that why she fainted after you left?"

"Did she faint? I'm sorry." He put an arm into a shirt sleeve. "Violet's all right. I guess I made her pretty unhappy." His face screwed up, like that of a blubbering drunk, though he didn't appear to be drunk. "I'm no good. We started off swell. We loved each other, and Naomi was like my own child. Then — I don't know. Maybe if I'd been a better man — " His voice faded. His fingers shook on the shirt buttons.

The man could go through a lot of moods within a few minutes, and all of them were contemptible. To Sam his self-pity was the worst. He said: "That doesn't settle anything. Why did Violet give you money?"

There was a knock on the door.

Skinner said, "Come in," and Naomi and Doug Faulcon entered the tiny foyer and made the turn into the apartment.

"So you came, Sam," Naomi said delightedly. "I'm glad."

He couldn't tell her then that he wasn't there to rehabilitate her stepfather. He nodded to Doug and watched Naomi cross the room to Skinner and throw her arms about his neck and kiss him hard on the mouth. A pang of jealousy jabbed Sam. She had never kissed him like that, not even last night when he had congratulated her on her coming marriage. And abruptly Felix Skinner looked years younger.

"You're going out?" Naomi said. "I'm glad we caught you. I'm getting married tomorrow, Felix. I brought Doug here to meet you."

"So this is the lucky man?" Skinner's thin, younger-looking face beamed. They shook hands heartily. Skinner touched the bar on Doug's shoulder. "A captain, I see."

"Only a second lieutenant, sir." All three laughed as if Skinner's mistake were very funny.

Sam felt in the way, out of it. He cleared his throat. "Guess I'll be going."

"This occasion deserves a little party."

71

Skinner was enthusiastic. "At least one drink all around. Oh yes, you don't drink, Tree." He said it without malice. Naomi's presence had put still another mood on him. He was the friendly host now; his gaunt face was almost pleasant. "Anyway, join me in toasting the happy couple. I think there's some ginger ale."

"All right," Sam said.

Carelessly Naomi tossed her mink coat on the bed. Doug was trying to hide his distaste at the mess in the apartment. He unbuttoned his olive-drab coat but did not take it off.

Felix Skinner was fishing whisky glasses out of the sink. He located three and rinsed them and brushed papers off the table to make room for the glasses. "I've been saving some fine scotch," he said, returning to the kitchenette. Over Doug's shoulder Sam saw Skinner open the door of the cupboard above the icebox.

The world exploded in a chaos of sound and blinding light. Something went wrong with Sam's eyes. He put his hands up to them. "Doug!" Naomi screamed, and her voice told Sam that he could hear again. He took his fingers

72

from his eyes, and he could see in a blur.

Between himself and the kitchenette Doug Faulcon sat on the floor, doubled over, his right hand clutching his left arm. He was strangely motionless and silent.

Naomi screamed again. "O God, Felix!"

She swayed toward Doug and then stopped, burying her face in her hands.

Sam looked again at Doug; his vision straightened out, and he could see beyond the hunched back of the sitting soldier. Felix Skinner lay against the side wall like a rag doll carelessly tossed there. His white shirt was no longer white. It did not seem possible that there could be so much blood in one man.

Quickly Sam looked away, and his eyes stopped in the line with the cupboard over the icebox. Two vast gun muzzles gaped at him.

5

Captain Gavigan

A CARICATURIST could have drawn Detective Captain Gavigan in a sequence of three inverted triangles. From a wide forehead and protruding cheekbones his face sloped sharply to a pointed chin. His immense shoulders tapered down to a comparatively slender waist. His hips, spreading womanishly, formed the base of the third triangle, with the apex at the ankles.

He was a restless man. Running his fingers through his graying hair, he prowled between Skinner's apartment and the hall. Sam watched him with a kind of dazed fascination. There was no other room in the apartment in which Sam and Naomi could wait, so they huddled in the narrow hall against the banister, while members of the homicide squad bustled in and out and uniformed policemen kept the other tenants on that

74

floor from spilling out into the hall.

Whenever Captain Gavigan appeared, he barked impatient questions at Sam and Naomi. Nearly always Sam answered for both, because Naomi was too numb to talk.

Then the ambulance intern led Doug Faulcon out. The ambulance driver had come up with a stretcher, but there was no need for it. Leaning heavily on the intern, Doug was able to walk. Naomi stirred then, quickly crossing the hall diagonally to meet him.

"I'll survive," Doug told her with a forced smile on his bloodless lips. "What a hell of a note, being wounded without even seeing action!"

"He's got only a few buckshots in his chest and arm," the intern told Naomi. "He'll be all right in a couple of days."

She started to move along with Doug. Gavigan swooped out of the apartment and grabbed her arm. "Hey, are you forgetting this is a murder?"

"Forgetting?" Naomi looked at him and shivered. That was the first word she had uttered in a long time, and the last.

The captain made his voice low and gentle. "I mean you're an important witness. I can't let you go just like that." A couple of more plain-clothes men came up the stairs and squeezed by. "This is a hell of a place. You come with me to headquarters. Meers, tell Lieutenant Goldblatt to take over here."

A police sedan was waiting for them at the curb.

★ ★ ★

In his office Gavigan continued to prowl while Sam sat on the captain's desk and tried to persuade Grover Langford's Filipino valet on the other end of the telephone wire that his business was important.

"I don't care if Mr. Langford is asleep," Sam said. "Wake him up."

Reluctantly the valet gave in. Sam sat patiently on the desk and waited.

Naomi was perched stiffly on the edge of the chair, her coat thrown back over her broad shoulders, her fingers tense on her handbag. She hardly seemed to breathe.

At the opposite end of the desk from Sam a police stenographer was cleaning his pipe with a feather pipe cleaner. A detective sergeant, named Jones, was planted at the door, as if to bar an attempt to escape. He did not look like a man who could lose himself in a crowd of two people.

Grover Langford's voice came sleepily over the wire. Sam told him what had happened.

"What, poor Felix knocked off!" Grover exclaimed. "You say you were there when it happened? I'll be right over. You know you don't have to tell the police a thing before you've seen your lawyer."

"What do you mean?" Sam said. "You don't imagine that I — "

"Never mind that now. Don't tell them anything."

Captain Gavigan dropped behind his desk when Sam cradled the phone. "Why are you so anxious to have a mouthpiece?"

"It seems like the right thing to do after you drag us here."

"Your conscience bother you?"

"Don't talk like a movie cop," Sam said.

Gavigan's restless eyes studied Sam. "Where did you leave your hat and coat? I didn't see them in Skinner's apartment."

"I didn't wear a hat or coat."

"In weather like this?"

"You get used to it," Sam said. "What has that to do with the murder?"

"Could be you left it where you shouldn't have been. We'll see." Gavigan picked up a pencil and put it down. "Now, Miss Tree — "

"Miss Skinner," Naomi said listlessly.

"That's right, Tree told me he's your stepfather. Skinner's your father."

She recited dully: "He was also my stepfather. He married Mother when I was a child. She changed my last name to Skinner at that time. When Mother married Sam Tree, I was already grown up and saw no reason to change it again."

"I see," Gavigan said. "Did your mother divorce your father?"

She looked at her knees. "He died when I was five."

Gavigan had sat too long. He got up and prowled again. "Jones, go see Mrs. Tree. Mr. Tree will give you the address. You know the questions."

Sam felt his insides tighten. At least Violet wouldn't be dragged here. He jotted down the address for Jones, and the sergeant departed.

"Did Skinner have any enemies?" Gavigan asked lazily.

"I hardly knew him."

Gavigan pounced. "Then what were you doing in his apartment?"

"He owed me some money."

"You said you hardly knew him."

"Not well. But he came around to my store last night to borrow fifty dollars. He said he would return it this afternoon. When he didn't, I went to his place to try to collect."

"Why the terrific hurry?"

Sam tried not to squirm. He'd said the wrong thing. It would have simplified matters if he had said that he had visited Skinner to try to induce him to take a job. Now he had to go through with it.

"Fifty dollars is a lot of money," Sam said.

"And when you came there, you met your stepdaughter and Lieutenant Faulcon visiting him?"

"They arrived a few minutes later to tell Skinner of their coming marriage."

Gavigan swung to face Naomi. "How did your mother feel about Skinner?"

"Well, she'd divorced him," Naomi muttered.

"Was she still fond of Skinner? I mean — put it this way: was she seeing a lot of him?"

Naomi was still too dazed to think. "No. She even objected to me seeing — " She caught herself and bit her lower lip.

"In other words, she disliked him?"

"I didn't say that," Naomi protested.

Gavigan smiled, and suddenly Sam was very much afraid of him.

"How did you feel about him, Miss Skinner?"

Naomi was silent so long that the captain repeated the question.

Her voice quavered when she spoke. "He was always very sweet to me."

"You saw a lot of him?"

"About every week or two."

"Did your mother object?"

Naomi pulled her fur coat back over her shoulders. She was on guard now. "I'm a mature person, and Mother treats me like one."

"That's not an answer."

"I think it is."

Gavigan prowled for a long minute. The police stenographer knocked out the ashes of his pipe and yawned. Gavigan came back to the desk on which Sam still sat.

"How's your duck shooting?" he inquired affably.

"Huh?" Sam said blankly.

"You hunt ducks in season, don't you?"

"I never shot a duck in my life."

"Then what do you hunt with your shotgun?"

"I haven't any gun." Sam stood up to stretch his legs. "The trap you're trying to spring is too obvious. Anyway, I thought guns are easy to trace."

"Not shotguns," Gavigan said. "There are no laws regulating them the way there are with pistols and revolvers."

Sam said: "Wasn't that a very complicated way to murder somebody? I mean

81

you ought to be looking for somebody who knows a lot about guns."

Gavigan scratched his pointed chin. "Whom are you trying to divert the hunt from, Tree?"

"I merely made a suggestion."

"So you did. Well, it didn't need much knowledge. It was the simplest form of gun trap. The killer prepared it at home, sawing off both barrels of the shotgun — which, by the way, made it an illegal weapon — and mounted the stock on a wooden block. Then he — or maybe she — slipped into Skinner's apartment when he was out. Any skeleton key could open that lock. Skinner drank a lot, didn't he?"

"Yes."

"That's plain enough," Gavigan said. "There was more liquor than food in that cupboard. The killer knew that it wouldn't be long after Skinner got home tonight that he would go for a drink. The bottom shelf was on a level with his chest. Strings were drawn about both triggers of the sawed-off shotgun and attached to the inside of the cupboard door. Because that kitchenette is so cramped, whoever opened the cupboard would have to stand directly in front of it. The killer was out to do a thorough job. A pistol would have been easier to rig up, but a pistol bullet would as likely wound as kill. I can't think of anything deadlier than two barrels of buckshot at close range. It blasted Skinner halfway across the room and tossed him against the side wall, and the edge of the charge caught Lieutenant Faulcon. That killer was playing for keeps."

Naomi moaned.

"Sorry, Miss Skinner," Gavigan muttered. "You'll read about it in the papers anyway." He turned back to Sam. "So Skinner went all the way out to Queens last night to borrow fifty bucks from you?"

"You Manhattanites think Queens is in another country. By subway Greenwich Village is closer to Queens than to uptown Manhattan."

"Then how come he had a thousand dollars in his wallet tonight? Ten one-hundred-dollar bills."

Sam stood very straight. Sooner or later the police were bound to come to it. And last night Violet had lied to him even about the amount she had given Skinner. Three hundred dollars, she had said; actually it had been one thousand. Eleven hundred, counting the hundred-dollar bill Skinner had dropped.

And the gray man had said that he was after a lot of money in one-hundred-dollar bills.

"I don't know anything about Skinner's finances," Sam said carefully. "Most likely that was the money he expected when he promised to pay back the next day."

"Expected from where?"

"I haven't any idea."

Sam's gaze shifted past the captain's ear and rested on Naomi. She was bent forward from her hips, her fingers clutching the opening of her coat, and her eyes were alert now and frightened. Sam thought: *She's wondering why I'm lying. Last night I told her I hadn't given Skinner a cent, and I told her that Violet had.*

Gavigan's voice pounded at him. "You said at the house that Skinner had no job. What did he do for a living?"

"As far as I know, he gambled. I'm not sure."

"This can be checked, you know."

Sam made an impatient turn away from Gavigan. "Check and be damned. If you want Skinner's life history, you're asking the wrong person."

"I want to know about that dough. Is it your notion that overnight he boosted your fifty up to a thousand by gambling?"

"It's possible. I know nothing about gambling."

Gavigan sighed and returned to his desk. "We'll tie up the loose ends, all right. You two will see a lot more of me before I'm through."

"Does that mean we can go?" Sam asked.

Captain Gavigan waved toward the door. "Go ahead, but don't suddenly decide that you want to take a trip out of town."

"Don't be foolish," Sam said. He took Naomi's elbow, and she rose without looking at him.

Reporters and cameramen were waiting for them in the lobby. Naomi bowed her head when bulbs flashed and ignored the reporters, who clamored for a statement about herself and Lieutenant Douglas Faulcon, Junior. They appeared to be more interested in romance than in murder. Sam muttered, "We have nothing to say," and pushed through with Naomi to the street door.

The door swung outward as they reached it, and they were face to face with Douglas Faulcon, Senior. Evidently he had been hurrying, because he was breathing hard and his fleshy face was flushed. He stopped dead, holding the door open with one hand and agitatedly swinging his cane with the other as if undecided whether to make a club of it. His derby was askew on his bald head. His dignity was gone.

"I knew something like this would happen!" he screeched at Naomi. "That's what comes of Doug getting mixed up with such trash. If my boy dies it'll be your fault. I'll — "

"Shut up!" Sam said.

Faulcon's hawkish eyes blazed with incipient madness. He raised his cane. Sam closed in and wrenched it out of his hand, and then the reporters were on them. The cameramen had a field day. Faulcon stared blankly at them and brushed by Naomi as if he were no longer aware of her. She cowered against Sam.

Sam tugged her through the door. He still held Faulcon's cane. He pushed the door open again and dropped the cane on the lobby floor. Faulcon was hidden by the newspapermen who surrounded him, but Sam could hear his voice murmuring: "My boy . . . they said . . . shot . . . where is he?"

Sam turned back to Naomi. She had moved all the way out to the sidewalk, where she was speaking to Grover Langford.

"He wanted to strike me with the cane," she sobbed. "And he's going to be my father-in-law."

"He lost his head," Sam said. "I guess they only told him Doug was shot, without any details, and he just about went crazy."

"Stuffed shirt," Grover dismissed Faulcon airily. He unbuttoned his overcoat from the great curve of his belly. "Well, Sam, it seems you didn't have to drag me out of bed after all."

"I didn't know what Gavigan might be up to."

"Good thing you called me at that," Grover said. "A lawyer is like a doctor. Never take a chance when you think you need one. So poor old Felix Skinner was shot! I knew him when he was a better man. Let's have the dope, Sam."

"Please!" Naomi said. "I can't stand any more."

"I know how you feel, kid, but I'm here to protect your interests."

"I don't need any protection. I haven't done anything." She added with a vehemence that startled Sam: "And neither has Sam."

"Sure, sure," Grover said placatingly. "But I've got to know — "

"We're going home," Sam told him wearily.

The lawyer shrugged. "That's up to you. I'm going inside for the dope. Who's in charge? Captain Gavigan? Good man. Very good. Don't worry, Sam, I'll be watching out for developments. So long, Naomi."

A cruising taxi was coming down the street. Sam stepped to the curb to hail it.

6

Too Much Money

NAOMI was a dim huddle of fur in the corner of the taxi seat, her face turned toward the window. Once she fumbled in her handbag for her handkerchief. Sam wanted to put an arm about her, to comfort her, but he felt a wall barring him from her.

She spoke for the first time when the taxi was crossing the Queensboro Bridge, and she sounded as if she were taking up a conversation. "Mother said the one-hundred-dollar bill I found this morning in the living room was hers."

"I left it there for her."

"No, Sam," she said firmly. "Where could Mother have changed it? You have a store; you always have smaller bills. And the captain said that Felix had ten one-hundred-dollar bills in his pocket."

Sam shifted along the seat until he

was close against her. "The driver!" he warned.

She looked at the dark back behind the wheel and then around at Sam. Their faces were inches apart, but in the darkness Sam couldn't see her clearly. He was glad that he didn't have to meet her eyes.

"Mother paid for this coat with hundred-dollar bills," Naomi murmured. "There were eighteen of them, and she had more. I remember asking her why she carried that much cash with her instead of a check. I was so excited over the coat at the time that I didn't realize till now that she didn't answer me directly."

"What are you getting at?"

"I wish I knew. Sam, why did you lie to the captain about having lent Felix money?"

"Well, I did let him have fifty. I forgot to mention it to you last night."

Her fur-covered shoulder shifted against his side. "You never forget anything, Sam. And Felix had a thousand dollars in hundred-dollar bills, and Mother always seems to have one-hundred-dollar bills. You told me that Mother had given

90

Felix money, but you never told it to the captain."

"They'd just annoy Violet with questions."

"Sam!" she cried, and then looked at the driver's back and lowered her voice. "Sam, what are you trying to shield Mother from?"

"Police annoyance."

"Tell me the truth."

"I've told you what I know," he said quietly, and in a way that was the truth.

She leaned away from him, staring out of the window again, and they sat like that until the taxi pulled up in front of the house.

Every light in the house seemed to be on. *Sergeant Jones is still there*, Sam thought, and his stomach muscles knotted at the prospect of facing the police again. But only Violet and Blythe Brice were in the living room.

Violet rose from the easy chair. "Mother!" Naomi sobbed and rushed into her arms. She was almost a head taller than Violet.

"You poor dear!" Violet said. "The policeman told me that Felix was killed right in front of your eyes." She looked sideways at Sam. "I thought he would never leave. He kept asking questions and questions."

"What did he want to know?"

"I hardly remember," Violet replied vaguely.

She was under perfect control, and that was like her. People who did not know her well thought her flighty and even shallow; she had a way of dismissing whatever was annoying or unpleasant by one of her helpless gestures or by talking around and then away from the subject. But Sam had learned that for all her external softness there was a hard core to her and a coldly calculating intelligence. Now it frightened him.

Blythe Brice moved forward from the bust of Pallas. "You'd better get to bed, Naomi," she said gently. "Come, I'll take you up."

Naomi nodded and slipped out of her mother's arms.

At the door Blythe paused. "Don't you think it would be better for her if I slept with her tonight, Mrs. Tree?"

"You're sweet," Violet said.

Sam waited until the two girls were upstairs. Then he said: "Is Mrs. Brice going to be a permanent boarder?"

"Don't be like that, darling. She went to look for a room this afternoon and found one. When she came back for her valise, the detective was here, and she didn't want to leave me alone until you and Naomi came home. That shows what a fine person she is."

"Why did she wait until midnight to come back for her valise?"

"It was only a little after eleven. I'm surprised at you, darling. That poor girl is all alone in New York, with her husband fighting for his country, and you — "

"All right, all right," he said testily. He sat down on the couch and punched the cushion at his side. "Come here."

She snuggled up beside him, and she was the coziest woman he had ever known. She patted his cheek. "Poor darling! It must have been horrible seeing a man killed."

"Not just a man," Sam said. "Felix Skinner, your former husband."

"Yes, I know. But I can't feel anything,

Sam. He'd become like a stranger to me."

"A stranger to whom you'd given a thousand dollars."

She took his knowledge without surprise. "I suppose the police told you. The detective who was here said a thousand dollars was found in his pocket."

"What did he ask you?"

"Oh, you know, just like in books. Where was I every minute of today."

"Did you tell him you were in the movies?"

"Why, of course. That's where I was."

"Did he ask you where Skinner had gotten the money?"

She spoke against his chest. "I thought it would be too complicated if I told him."

"What do you mean, complicated?"

"They might get the wrong impression."

"Or the right one," Sam said.

He felt her move against his chest, but she didn't raise her head.

"Violet, look at me," he said.

"I always look at you. You're not a handsome man, darling, but I like your looks."

Sam swore aloud and put his hand under her chin and forced up her head. Her pale eyes slid past him and away.

"Violet, why don't you let me help you? You can trust me."

"Of course I can, darling."

"Well?" he said.

"Well what?"

Roughly Sam pushed her away and stood up. "What about the fat man? Who is he? Why are you afraid of him? Now don't ask, 'What fat man?' or, by God, I'll strangle you."

She gave him a smile. "You couldn't hurt a hair of anybody's head, especially mine."

"Will you answer me?"

"You answered for me. I don't know which fat man you mean."

He let her have it then. "The fat man who broke into this house after you went to bed. I heard him Tuesday night while you slept, and I came down and he was in this room. He struck me with a flashlight and escaped through the window. And there was another man — a small, elderly man who held me up in my store earlier that night and demanded a

95

lot of one-hundred-dollar bills."

Her control slipped. Again, like that minute or two last night in front of the fireplace, she aged.

"Did you see the fat man, Sam?" she whispered.

"Only enough of him to know he's fat."

Violet nodded. "It must have been a burglar after your store money. I'm always telling you not to bring home — "

"And I suppose the man who held me up in the store was also a burglar?"

"I suppose so."

"My God!" he said. He strode to where she sat and gripped her shoulders. "Violet, is there any danger of your being murdered?"

She raised her eyes, and they were blank beyond their paleness. Her control was back. "What a ridiculous question! Who would want to murder me?"

"Maybe the same person who murdered Felix Skinner."

She stood up against him, and because he was so much taller he could see nothing of her face now. "Poor darling!" she said. "You've been through too much tonight. You're seeing a murderer behind every bush. I'm going to phone Ted to open the store tomorrow. You need a lot of sleep."

Fiercely his fingers began to tighten on her shoulders, then they relaxed. He felt weak and furious with frustration.

"God help both of us!" he said.

* * *

It was early afternoon before Sam got to his store. Ted Hanley, with apparently nothing to do and no customers in the store, had a copy of the New York *Courier-Express* spread open on the grocery counter. He beamed happily at Sam.

"Had a busy morning even though the register don't show it. Customers flocked in to talk about you and the murder. You see this picture?"

Sam glanced down at where Ted's chubby finger pointed. A three-column photo showed Douglas Faulcon, Senior, about to strike Sam with his cane. All that was visible of Sam was the taut arch of his back, but Faulcon's fleshy face,

97

contorted with rage, looked directly out from the page. Naomi, in profile, was hardly more than a blur.

"That's why they give the murder so much space," Ted declared, jabbing Faulcon's face. "Because the Faulcons are in it. It takes money to hit the papers even in a murder. Skinner was a nobody."

"I'm glad you're enjoying it," Sam said dryly.

Ted's head jerked up, and suddenly his face was dead sober. "The police were here this morning."

"Captain Gavigan?"

"This flatfoot was no captain. Just a sergeant. Jones, his name is. He wanted to know if Felix Skinner was here night before last. I said sure he was, and the sergeant looked kind of disappointed. I guess he figured he'd catch you up on something."

"You have a nice imagination, Ted."

"Well, he was fishing for information, that's why he was here. Like when he followed up by asking did I see you give Skinner any money. I told him I was busy with a customer and didn't see anything. I said after Skinner left you followed him outside and spoke to him for a couple minutes, so that's when you might have given him money. But I didn't say definitely one way or the other." He looked pleased with himself. "Was that the smart thing, Sam?"

"The truth is the smart thing. That was the truth."

"Sure. So then this sergeant beat about the bush for a while, and then he asked sort of casual if you was in the store all day yesterday. I said you'd gone across the street to Rickter's for lunch, but he said he wanted to know were you gone longer. I hemmed and hawed, but gee, Sam, this is murder and I could be jailed for being an accomplice or something if I didn't answer the questions straight, so I — "

"Wait a minute," Sam said sharply. "I didn't murder Skinner."

Ted flushed deeply. "Sure, Sam. Gosh, you don't think I think you did? But it was funny. When I had to admit to the sergeant that you left the store about four-thirty and didn't come back till nearly seven, he looked awful pleased, like — " He gulped. "Well, it was funny."

"Funny?" Sam said.

Ted rocked miserably against the counter. "I don't mean the laughing kind of funny." He was anxious now to change the subject. "A man phoned you three times this morning. I said you were home and gave him the number, but he kept calling here. His name is Pouch."

"How do you spell that?"

"P-o-u-c-h. He spelled it out for me."

"What does he want?"

"He wouldn't tell me except it was very important. He said you should call him back. I wrote his number on the pad."

Sam went into the back room and put on his white coat. The number on the telephone pad was the Barclay 7 exchange, which was in downtown Manhattan. He knew nobody named Pouch.

"Sam," Ted called.

He buttoned the coat and started for the front. Captain Gavigan's big bulk appeared around the refrigerator. "The guy said you were back here," Gavigan said. He looked around. "Any place we can talk?"

100

"This place will have to do," Sam told him. "I suppose you want to know where I was between four and seven yesterday."

"Do I?" Gavigan started to prowl in the crowded back room and found too many obstacles. "Okay, where were you?"

"Home. Sometimes I take off a few hours during the day."

"Anybody see you?"

"Nobody was home. My wife went to the movies."

"So she told Sergeant Jones last night," Gavigan said without interest. "Jones likes to check alibis. Personally, I've never found them to mean much one way or the other. In this case particularly they don't mean a thing. The time of murder doesn't count; we have to know when the gun trap was planted, and that's tough, if not impossible. It might have been put in the cupboard a week ago for all we know, and it just so happened that Skinner didn't go near it till last night. That's one reason I didn't bother collecting alibis from you and your stepdaughter last night. The other is that none of you three who were in Skinner's apartment when it happened would be guilty. The whole idea of a gun trap is to remove the killer far from the scene of the crime at the time it occurs."

Sam couldn't decide whether the captain meant what he was saying or whether this was his method of putting him off guard.

"What I'm chiefly interested in is the dough Skinner had on him," Gavigan went on. "You say that two days ago he came here for a loan of fifty bucks. What time was that?"

"A few minutes before eight."

"Uh-huh. And by one o'clock he had dropped nine hundred dollars at Lou's."

"You told me you found the money in Skinner's wallet last night," Sam said.

"What money?"

Sam saw his blunder. You had to be on your toes every moment with Gavigan. "Well, I mean, where could Skinner have got so much money?"

"That's what I'm asking you. He came all the way out here to borrow fifty from you. Three or four hours later he appeared at Lou's with nine hundred dollars to lose."

"Who's Lou?"

"That's a mid-town gambling joint. A poor man's dive where a guy who drops a grand is a heavy loser. Just about Skinner's speed."

"I thought gambling dens are illegal in this state."

"I'm a homicide cop. My business is murder, not gambling." He scowled at Sam. "Let's quit horsing around. Then the next evening Skinner has another grand in his wallet. You said he was dressing when you came in. He was probably going out for another fling at Lou's crap game."

Two thousand dollars, Sam was thinking. The night before last Violet had given Skinner one thousand and had told him that she had dug into the last of Ira Pram's insurance. Then the following afternoon Skinner had come again and she had had another thousand in one-hundred-dollar bills to hand out.

"Well?" Gavigan said impatiently. "What's your answer? Where did that money come from?"

"I told you I knew very little of Skinner's private affairs."

"You're a liar, Tree," Gavigan said flatly.

Sam turned to the telephone as if he had important business there. "Then there's nothing more to discuss."

"I'm not discussing. I'm asking."

"Why waste your time when you don't believe my answers?"

Gavigan pushed his hat back over his hair. "You can't be smart with the police, Tree."

"I'm willing to answer questions. Have you any more?"

"No," Gavigan clipped. He went out.

From the sounds in the store, there seemed to be many customers, but Sam did not go out to give Ted a hand. He stood there, thinking: *There's too much money. Much too much.* Violet had given two thousand to Skinner and had paid eighteen hundred for Naomi's coat and two thousand for furniture. That was well over five thousand dollars already, not counting all the money she had sent her mother and spent on other things.

The telephone jangled. He picked it up.

"Mr. Tree?" a strange voice said. "Ah, the reward of diligence. My name is Pouch. Abel Pouch, confidential investigator."

"Does that mean private detective?"

"That is the more common designation for my profession. I believe that you are interested in finding the murderer of Felix Skinner."

"It's an open secret that this city has a police force."

Pouch chuckled. "Ordinarily your sarcasm would be appropriate, Mr. Tree. I particularly stress the confidential part of my investigations. For a retainer of five hundred dollars, with the remainder of the fee to be arranged subsequently, I assure you results which — "

"I haven't the time or the money for nonsense," Sam cut in.

The voice purred across the wire. "Isn't it worth time and money, Mr. Tree, to protect your wife?"

Sam's fingers tightened on the handset. He had trouble breathing. "Protect her from what?"

"Let us limit ourselves for the time being to the mildest charge. Shall I say — bigamy?"

"What are you talking about?"

"Bigamy," Pouch said. "Married to two husbands at the same time."

"You're crazy. She divorced Skinner."

"Certainly. Very legally and properly. But I don't mean Skinner."

"What sort of nonsense is this?" Sam said hoarsely.

"I wouldn't advise you to consider it nonsense." Pouch's voice was very soft, very self-assured. "Indeed, I would advise you to call at my office as quickly as you can get here. The address is — "

Savagely Sam hung up.

7

The story of Violet Tree

MARTHA UNDERHILL'S greeting was strangely uncordial. She muttered, "Hello, Sam," and stood in the doorway looking dully at him.

"What's wrong?" Sam asked.

His words seemed to rouse her. "Come in," she said and led him into the apartment.

Tonight Martha was wearing a dress instead of one of her numerous suits. It was slate blue and rather rakish for a woman her age. Sam decided that she was better off sticking to mannish clothes. She was not the feminine type; she was too big in the shoulders and too slim in the hips.

"Are you expecting company or going out?" Sam said. "I don't want to be in the way."

"It's only Grover. He's late as usual."

She picked up a half-filled highball glass from the end table. Her eyes showed that this wasn't her first drink. "Sorry you're too moral to join me, Sam."

"I never knew you were the kind of woman who drinks alone," he said.

"I'm not. This is the first time, almost. I'm moral too, Sam." She poured the contents of the glass down her throat. "We're very moral people, we two. Why?"

He settled into a chair and looked up at her. He had never seen her like this before. "Drinking and smoking and hell-raising have nothing to do with morality."

"What sort of bachelor were you, Sam?"

"Not an interesting one."

"You can't fool me," she said. "You were the quiet, deep kind. I bet a lot of women were crazy about you. I was, you know, when Violet and I met you. I set my cap for you, but you couldn't see me for Violet. I think I'm still crazy about you."

"You're drunk, Martha," he said

She giggled. "Only a very little bit. Don't worry, Sam. I told you I'm very moral."

She started toward the foyer with the highball glass. From where he sat he could see through the foyer into part of the kitchen. A bottle of whisky and another of ginger ale were on the worktable.

"Haven't you had enough, Martha?"

"Have I?" She stopped and slowly swung to face him. All at once she looked dead sober. "The police were here this afternoon."

"About Skinner?" he said. "What did they want?"

"The detective said they were calling on everybody who knew Felix. That was the polite way he put it — 'calling on.' He really put me through the hoops for a solid hour. He struck me as being a rather stupid man."

"Then it wasn't Captain Gavigan," Sam said. "He doesn't strike anybody as being stupid."

"This man's name was Jones." She simpered, but she was no longer drunk, and it sounded forced and flat. "You know, I never actually knew anybody named Jones in all my life."

Sam said nothing.

She turned to put the glass on the table, and she spoke with her back to him. "Sam, I didn't tell Jones that Felix had been to see Violet. I didn't tell him that Felix had made Violet faint and that I'd told you about it and that you — that you — "

Sam shot out of his chair and gripped her broad shoulders and spun her around to him. "So that's why you've been drinking! I didn't murder Felix Skinner."

Limply her arms went about him. She was now what Sam had never thought he would see her — a quivering, frightened feminine woman.

"It doesn't matter, Sam. Felix wasn't any good."

"Listen to me! If I had wanted to kill him, would I do it in that cowardly way? Would I have gone there to see it happen?"

She threw her head back to look at him. "Sam, I thought — "

"You're a fool! I might have beaten him up, but where was my motive to kill him? Do you believe me when I swear I didn't?"

"Yes, Sam," she said weakly.

"And Violet didn't either. Get that into your head."

"Violet? I never said — "

"Well, don't say it and don't think it, because it isn't true."

"Are you sure, Sam?"

He took a long second before answering. "Yes, Martha, I'm sure."

They were both silent then, and he became aware of her arms tightening about him. Gently he pulled her arms away and retreated to a window. Riverside Drive was nine stories below. A doorman stepped from under the canopy to whistle for a taxi. Martha probably paid as much rent for this apartment as he did for his store. She could afford it; she had a sizable income from property in Boston which she never talked about.

When he turned back to her, she was on the couch with her legs curled girl-like under her.

"Violet has told me hardly anything about her and her former husbands," he said. "It's time I knew."

"What do you want to know?"

"Everything. Start with Ira Pram."

She studied him with curious eyes. "It

111

goes back all the way to 1923, when Violet was not quite twenty. We were all rather surprised when she married Ira Pram. We had expected her to marry Felix Skinner. Felix was one of the East Wiston boys, and Lord knows there were few enough. He wasn't anything like the way he became later. I remember him as a tall, loose-jointed boy with a very winning smile. I was soft on him myself." A trace of bitterness came into her voice. "But they always preferred Violet to me."

"Then Pram came along?" Sam said, bringing her back to what he wanted to know.

"Yes. Ira Pram met Violet when he spent a few weeks in East Wiston boating. He saw a lot of Violet, though not even Felix suspected that it meant anything. Nobody takes a fat man seriously as a lover, and Ira was very fat. He must have weighed two hundred and seventy pounds. Not the roly-poly type, though; he was a big man in every way. So when he returned to Boston, we all expected Violet to go back to Felix. But she didn't. Ira wrote her every day from Boston."

The letters Violet had burned the

other night, Sam thought. But why, after having kept them for twenty-one years? And why had she acted guilty at being caught burning them?

"Then one day Violet went to Boston. To buy clothes, she said, but I remember thinking it was really to see Felix. He was attending Harvard. She was to stay in Boston three days with an aunt. On the third day she wired her parents that she had married Ira Pram. I said we were all surprised, but we shouldn't have been. Felix, though a Harvard man, was really only a small-town boy and hardly older than Violet. Ira was a man of the world, sophisticated and apparently rich. Her father was a carpenter and had never made a good living. In all fairness to Violet, though, I don't think she married Ira for his money. He rather overwhelmed her, in spite of his fatness. After all, fat men do get married — it seems more often than thin men."

"And Felix Skinner?" Sam said.

"He was heartbroken, of course." The corners of her mouth drooped. "For a while I thought there was a chance of getting Felix on the rebound. I thought

113

if it was not me he wanted, them my father's money would — Oh, hell, I'm old enough now not to kid myself. And old enough to be perfectly frank. I haven't even been able to buy myself a man."

"Grover Langford is richer than you are and very anxious to marry you."

"Yes." She tossed her head. "To get back: Violet seemed to have made a fine catch. Her parents were very proud of their son-in-law. He rented a swanky house in Provincetown and gave Violet all the money she wanted to furnish it lavishly. About eighteen months later Naomi was born. Violet would have been quite happy except for one thing: Ira wasn't home very often. His business kept him in Boston, sometimes for weeks at a time."

"What was his business?"

"None of us was sure. Violet told us in a vague way that he was a promotion man, but I doubt if she knew what that was or cared. I was there once when she asked Ira why a promotion man's wife couldn't live in Boston. Ira replied that nobody ought to live in Boston who

114

didn't have to. He had a lot of charm and wit, and that was the kind of answer you somehow don't question, like a comeback in a sophisticated comedy. And Violet wasn't as lonely as you would think. Her mother and I and other friends visited her often. In fact, it was while I was spending a week end with her that the police came."

Martha looked longingly at the empty highball glass.

"Shall I get it for you?" Sam asked.

"You wouldn't know how." She swept up the glass and in the kitchen filled it with ice and rye and ginger ale and then returned to the couch. She drank half the highball before she spoke again.

"It was a Saturday afternoon. That morning Ira had come home unexpectedly. He brought a strange man with him — a business associate, he said. That was Earl Durand. I remember that Violet whispered to me that Durand was a bachelor and very rich and that if I played my cards right I might be able to land him. Well, I wasn't interested in any other man at that time, and even if I were — "

"Other man?" Sam said. "Oh yes, it was still Felix Skinner."

"At that time it was. But about Earl Durand. I knew him for only two or three hours, but in that time I grew to loathe him. I'm still not sure why. He was a small, mild-looking man, an inch or two shorter than myself. Beside Ira he looked like a midget. He dressed better than any man I ever knew, except perhaps Ira. His nails were polished, and I remember that he shaved so close that his jaw was blue. He was quiet-spoken and very courteous. Yet — well, I suppose it was chiefly his eyes. They were like gray ice and very cruel. And I think it was also his smile. His mouth was closed when he smiled; only the corners of his lips twitched a little, and his eyes remained cold. That man actually frightened me."

She laughed and sipped her highball. "I'm long-winded."

"No," Sam said. "You're telling me what I want to know."

"I remember that Ira was trying hard to get acquainted with Naomi," she said, swishing the ice cubes in her glass. "She was just about five, a lovely child, and shy in Ira's presence. That was his fault; he wasn't home often enough for her to get to know him. I imagine that's why Naomi became so fond of Felix Skinner later, because in Felix she found the father she had never had in Ira.

"The doorbell rang and Violet went out to answer it because the maid was busy preparing supper in the kitchen. Then Violet returned with a puzzled expression on her face. She said: 'Ira, there are three men who want — ' I remember that she never finished the sentence. Three men pushed past her into the room. Ira turned slowly, with Naomi perched stiffly and uncomfortably on one of his tremendous arms. Suddenly Ira's eyes were sick. Without knowing why, I looked at Earl Durand. His mouth twitched and he glanced at the open window behind him. Then one of the men crossed quickly over to Earl Durand and another to Ira, and the third man said: 'It's a pinch, boys.'

"Violet didn't become hysterical or anything like that. She put a hand on Ira's arm and said: 'It's a mistake, darling, isn't it?' I remember how Ira's bigness

117

filled the room, dominating everybody in it, with Violet standing so small beside him and Naomi looking like a doll on his arm. He put Naomi down and tried to smile, but the smile didn't come. He said: 'Of course it's a mistake. I'm afraid I'll have to go with these men, but I'll be back shortly.' He went to the hall closet for his hat and kissed Naomi and Violet. From the door we watched the five men get into a sedan and drive off. Then Violet turned to me. 'It's a ridiculous mistake,' she said thinly. But we both knew it wasn't."

"I understand they ran an illegal lottery," Sam said.

"All lotteries are illegal in this country. Running a lottery at all was bad enough, but they pocketed every cent they took in. They specialized on foreign national lotteries. To the French they sold French tickets, to the Spanish Spanish tickets, to the Mexicans Mexican tickets. It was clever, because the victims had been buying such tickets all along from other sources, so they suspected nothing wrong. The tickets were genuine enough, but the stubs never reached the drawing wheels, so their take must have been enormous. Ira Pram and Earl Durand got away with it for years before the police caught up with them. You know, of course, that Ira was killed while trying to escape."

"Not the details," Sam said.

Her glass was empty. She continued to hold it in both hands, studying the ice cubes.

"It was Earl Durand's fault," she said. "Ira had never been arrested before; at the most he would have received a few years in jail. But Durand had already served two sentences for fake promotion schemes, and it would have gone hard with him. He must have been pretty desperate. He was seated in front of the sedan with the driver, while Ira sat in back between the two other detectives. The police were rather careless. They later explained that they hadn't considered their prisoners criminals and so didn't take the trouble to handcuff them. They searched them for guns, but overlooked a small penknife in Earl Durand's pocket.

"It happened just outside of East Wiston. Durand slipped out his penknife and stabbed the driver in the side. He

119

couldn't have hoped to hurt him much with it, but he accomplished his purpose — at any rate, the beginning of his purpose. The driver lost control of the wheel; the car went off the road and struck a pole and toppled over on its side. It didn't do Durand any good because he was knocked unconscious. The two detectives in the back seat were shaken up. They said Ira's bulk crushed them down and somehow he managed to get out on top through the door. By the time the first of the detectives crawled out, Ira had reached the top of a sand dune. The detective pulled out his gun and shot. He said he saw Ira go down and tumble out of sight on the other side of the dune.

"When the two detectives reached the dune, they saw Ira running along the beach. They said he was wobbling as if wounded. They called to him, and when he kept running they used their guns. Ira must have realized that there was no chance of escaping by running along the beach. It was a barren stretch; there were no boats anywhere and no cover. In desperation he waded out into the bay. He was in deep enough to swim when the detectives waded in after him. All they could see of him was his head, but he wasn't far off, and they kept shooting all the time. Suddenly his head vanished, and he was never seen again."

Sam was looking out of the window. Two dark tankers were blurred shadows in the middle of the Hudson. By morning they would be mysteriously gone to join a convoy.

"What time of the day was that?" Sam asked.

"Late afternoon. The fact is that there were still a few hours of daylight left and the detectives kept watching for him to reappear. He didn't."

"Was he good swimmer?"

"A marvelous swimmer, like most fat men. But there was no doubt that he was dead. Boats arrived soon with more policemen, and the area was thoroughly searched."

Sam said: "I understand that Violet had to go to the courts to have him declared legally dead. In other words, there was doubt."

"You could hardly call it doubt. The body was never recovered, so there were necessary legal formalities before Violet could marry Felix. The tide was going out at the time; obviously his body was swept out to the ocean." She pressed the cool glass against her cheek. "What are you thinking, Sam?"

"I'm not sure," he said slowly. "What happened to Earl Durand?"

"He received a very stiff sentence — about twenty years, if I remember, chiefly because of his attack on the policeman who had been driving the car. Durand is either dead or still in jail."

"And the money?"

"For a while the police made quite a mystery of it. Ira and Earl Durand were smart enough not to put the money in banks. The police found around twenty thousand dollars in cash in Durand's place in Boston. Durand said that was only half of the loot, his share; he said that Ira had the other half. So the police searched Violet's house from top to bottom and even dug up the grounds, and they questioned Violet for days; but they never found a cent of it. I remember for a while there were ugly rumors that Violet knew where the money was. That, of course, was absurd."

With his hands deep in his pockets, Sam found himself striding back and forth in front of the couch. He checked himself because it reminded him of Captain Gavigan's prowling.

Excitedly his head jerked up. "Weren't they using the big bills then?"

"What big bills?"

"You remember that the size of paper money was larger than it is now?" he said excitedly. "What year was Pram arrested?"

"November 1929. That was just at the beginning of the depression. Would you mind telling me what you're talking about?"

He muttered, "Mind if I use your phone?" and went out to the foyer. When he got his number, he asked a single question, then dejectedly hung up. His shoulders felt tired.

Martha regarded him gravely from the couch. "I've had time to decide what struck you. If you came across a lot of large-sized bills or found somebody spending them, you'd know they were Ira's. What did you learn?"

"That the small-sized bills were issued in the summer of 1929, almost four months before Pram's arrest. By that time there were more small-sized bills in circulation than large-sized ones."

"Sam, Sam," Martha chided him. "You ought to know that Violet never had any money."

"Not even Pram's insurance policy?"

"Come to think of it, there was a policy, wasn't there?"

He went into the kitchen and stood looking down at the bottle of rye. He had seen a chance to put his mind at ease. If Ira Pram's loot had consisted of necessity of the old-style large-sized bills . . . But the fact was that the money in Violet's possession could have come from Pram's loot. Could have? It *had*.

He understood now why men got drunk. He moved on to the water tap and poured himself a glass of water to overcome the dryness in his throat.

When he returned to the other room, Martha had not stirred from her curled-up position in the corner of the couch. Her eyes followed him all the way to a chair.

"What's eating you, Sam? None of this can have anything to do with Felix being murdered. It happened so long ago."

"Why wasn't Pram's money found?" Sam said.

"Isn't it obvious? Because there never was any more than the twenty thousand dollars found in Durand's apartment?"

"Then why did Durand say there was more?"

"The police claimed that he made that statement to take some of the onus from himself — to show that Ira was in the racket as deeply as himself."

"That doesn't make sense."

She shrugged. "The police seemed to think it did. At least, that was what they implied after a while. May I have a cigarette?"

He took a cigarette from the silver box on the coffee table and brought it to her and lit a match. Over the flare her eyes continued to study him. Deeply she drew in smoke.

"Sam, don't be absurd. Do you think Violet would have taken that money?"

He flicked out the match. "I don't know."

"If she had found it, what did she do with it?"

He said: "What happened after Ira Pram was killed?"

"Violet gave up that big house in Provincetown, of course. She put the furniture in storage, and she and Naomi moved in with her parents in East Wiston. Felix Skinner, you know, lived less than a mile away with his widowed mother. He was doing fairly well as an architect, working on summer-cottage developments along the Cape, so he had plenty of opportunity to see Violet. Less than two years after Ira died, she and Felix were married.

"In those days Felix was nothing like the man you knew later. He was shy and gentle and very kindly. And very proud. I think the only argument he and Violet ever had — in those days, I mean — was about the furniture.

"His mother's house dated from before the Revolution, like many houses on Cape Cod. It had ample room, and Felix had put in modern conveniences. The furniture was shabby, though, and when Violet moved in she wanted to get rid of it and bring all her expensive furniture from the warehouse where it was in storage. Felix absolutely refused to touch a thing Ira had bought. He borrowed money to furnish the house, while Violet's furniture remained in storage. The marriage should have worked out all right. Felix loved Violet very much, and he loved Naomi, and Violet is the kind of woman who can be happy with almost any man who treats her well."

Too late she tried to catch herself. "I didn't quite mean that, Sam."

"Forget it," he said.

Martha dropped her cigarette into the melted ice in the bottom of the highball glass. "They'd married in the third year of the depression, when things really started going bad. There was no more building on Cape Cod. Then Mrs. Skinner died and Felix was offered a job with a New York building outfit. I'd come to New York a few years before, when my father died. I was alone in the world and had money and hankered for bright lights. I don't know what would have happened to Felix if he had stayed in East Wiston, but he shouldn't have come to New York.

They were hardly settled when the new outfit Felix worked for folded up. From then on, as you remember, there just weren't any jobs. For a year or two it wasn't so bad. Felix sold his house in East Wiston, and they lived on what it brought, but they had to move to a cheaper apartment and — "

"They were very poor?" Sam said.

"Very poor. That's the point. His money gave out, and then they had hardly enough for food and rent. There was no point in them going back to East Wiston, because Violet's father wasn't working either."

"I suppose that's when Skinner started drinking?"

"The gambling came first," Martha said. "Felix was pretty frantic. He couldn't get a decent job, so he tried that way. It didn't work, of course; it never seems to with poor men. But once he started, he couldn't stop. The drinking followed naturally. When that sort of man starts anything, like drinking and gambling, he goes all the way. Sometimes he didn't come home for days at a time. I won't bother with details; they're highly unpleasant. The situation became intolerable until Violet simply had to leave him. The rest you know."

"Not quite," Sam said. "What did Violet and Naomi use for money?"

"Well, Felix did send them a little when he had it. Then there was home relief."

Sam shook his head. "You're holding something back. When I met Violet in 1938, she and Naomi were living with you. They appeared to be well dressed and comfortable."

Martha found a wrinkle in one stocking and straightened it out. "Violet was my best friend. I had plenty of money. I couldn't sit by, could I?"

"In short, you supported them."

"It wasn't for long. Then Violet had the good luck to have you fall in love with her."

There was a silence. Then he said: "You are sure Violet never had any money of her own?"

"Sam, what in the world is the matter with you? You've still got Ira Pram's money on your mind. If Violet had it, don't you think she would have used some of it during those terribly poor periods? At the least, she would have used it for Naomi. You can take my word for it that there never was — "

The doorbell rang.

Martha got off the couch and brushed her cropped hair back with her hand and went out to the door. Grover Langford's plump bulk stepped into the foyer. He leaned to kiss Martha and then noticed Sam in the living room and drew back with a low laugh.

"Hello, Sam," Grover said, coming into the room with Martha. "Just the lad I have some business with."

"Police business?" Sam asked.

"Oh, that?" Grover handed his overcoat to Martha and took a ten-dollar bill out of his wallet and cleaned his rimless eyeglasses with it. "I don't think there's any reason to worry about that."

"Why should I worry?"

"Don't snap my head off," Grover said, putting on his glasses. His face was as round and jolly as a full moon. "I'm simply telling you not to worry, that's all. But the police are worrying why you gave

Felix nineteen hundred bucks."

Martha, returning from the closet, stopped to stare at Sam. "Did you give him that money, Sam?"

"Where would I get that kind of money?"

Grover clucked his tongue disapprovingly. "Don't take that line with the cops. A guy who buys expensive mink coats for his step-daughter isn't poor. You shouldn't have said you gave Felix fifty dollars. If fifty, why not nineteen hundred?"

Sam said nothing. That thoughtless mistake he had made with Captain Gavigan was plaguing him from all sides. And it had been unnecessary. He could as easily have given another excuse for having visited Skinner Wednesday night. That was what came of not being an experienced liar.

"All right, Sammy, that's your story, so stick to it," Grover said sprightly. "The business I meant was that little matter you asked me to check up on. It was a cinch. All of Ira Pram's insurance had been placed with Humanity, Inc., a Boston broker. I spoke by phone

131

to an old geezer named Warren, who remembered all about Pram because of the publicity at the time. Warren said Pram had had two policies — one a ten-thousand-dollar life and the other a ten-thousand-dollar annuity. He let both lapse — why is anybody's guess. Maybe he was planning to run out with the loot, leaving his wife and child. The life policy was, of course, worthless when he died, but Violet was able to collect something on the annuity."

Sam asked tightly: "How much?"

"Eight hundred and some odd dollars. I'll send you the exact amount if you're interested. But you must know about it, because Violet collected it back in 1931."

"She mentioned it," Sam muttered.

He felt very tired, as if all at once the weight of all the years he had lived piled up on him. Eight hundred dollars was less than half of what Violet had spent on Naomi's coat alone; less than half of what she had given Skinner in two days or spent to furnish the house. Five thousand dollars couldn't cover what she had spent in the last two years, and

132

now the amount was only eight hundred dollars.

"Sam, aren't you feeling well?" Martha asked.

Sam shook himself. "I'm all right. I'd better be going."

"The lad's just had a jolt," Grover said. "He expected Violet to come in on a fortune in an undiscovered insurance policy. Sorry I couldn't do better."

Sam thought: *But neither could Violet have had Pram's money. She would have dipped into it often during those hard years. Yet two years ago something happened to give her all the money she wanted.*

Martha was at his side, saying, "Sam, what's this about Ira's insurance?"

"Nothing. It was a brainstorm of mine."

She followed him to the door and went out to the hall with him. Cheerily Grover Langford called after them: "I'm jealous, Sam. She never goes out in the hall with me to say good-by."

Martha kicked the apartment door shut and looked up at Sam. There were harsh lines about her eyes and mouth which he did not remember. Maybe they hadn't been there before tonight.

"Sam, why did you make this trip here tonight?"

"To learn about Violet."

"I realize that," she said. "But why?"

"I couldn't get it out of Violet, and I think I've the right to know my wife's history."

She folded her hands in front of her, and her shoulders hunched. "That's not the whole answer. I'm not a fool."

"I know you're not, Martha."

"Why do you doubt that Ira Pram is dead?"

"Do I?"

"That was the point of all your questions. You think he came back for his money and that Violet gave it to him."

"No. That much I'm sure is all wrong."

"Whatever it is, you believe it concerns what happened to poor Felix." Her strong, masculine fingers reached for his hand. "Sam, I think I know what you're afraid of. You're wrong. You're terribly wrong."

A woman in a bathrobe came out of the apartment next door and put out a milk bottle with a note in it. Sam watched her until her door closed. Then he said, "Good night, Martha," and went up the hall to the elevator.

8

Abel Pouch

THERE was only one Abel Pouch in the telephone directory, and only one listing, a Chambers Street address. That meant it was in an office building. At this hour it was very unlikely that anybody would be there, but Sam tried anyway.

Surprisingly there was an answer. A male voice said: "Pouch? He that detective? I don't know where he lives. No, I don't work for him. I'm an accountant, and I have one of the offices here. I heard the switchboard buzz and I — Just a minute, here's an address book. Yeah, here's his address."

Sam had only a few blocks to walk to a brownstone house off Columbus Avenue. A drowsy, unshaven man in flapping slippers answered the bell and told Sam that Mr. Pouch lived in Room

Eleven and then shuffled back down the long hall.

Sam climbed three flights of stairs and knocked on a door. He heard feet approach and then a voice say against the door panel: "Who is it?"

"Are you Abel Pouch?"

"Correct." The door remained closed.

"I'm Sam Tree."

On the other side of the door the voice chuckled. A key turned in the lock, and Sam looked up at a great lump of sagging flesh in which merry little eyes twinkled. The rest of Abel Pouch, covered haphazardly by a faded bathrobe the size of a tent, was in proportion to his face, formless and with fat spreading in every direction. Sam was tall, but he felt insignificant beside the sheer bulk of the man.

"Come in, come in," Pouch said genially. "I am hardly so monstrous that you must gawk at me. Besides, it is hardly polite."

He stepped aside to give Sam room to pass. Sam wondered how Pouch could turn in that cramped, narrow room without knocking the walls down. It contained a bed, a dresser, a chair, and nothing else. Sam glanced at the chair but remained on his feet.

"Sit down, sit down," Pouch said.

He settled himself on the bed, which sagged dangerously and groaned, but miraculously it remained intact. A half-eaten apple lay on the rumpled cover. Pouch picked it up and munched thoughtfully.

"Frankly, Tree, I did not expect you to look me up until tomorrow. My office is more comfortable for a business deal. As you observe, I live conservatively. After all, it is foolhardy to waste money on a place where one merely sleeps. However, this room will serve the purpose if you will only sit down. I do not like to talk up to a man, and I abhor standing.

"Your continuous scrutiny embarrasses me," Pouch went on. His voice was oddly soft and small for a man his size. "I imagine you are attempting to determine what sort of individual you are dealing with. I assure you that I am an admirable poker player. Have you brought the money?"

"What money?"

"My dear man, the five-hundred-dollar retaining fee. Tomorrow we can draw up the contract in my office."

Sam said: "What am I supposed to get for my money?"

"What a private investigator has to sell information as the result of his investigations."

"What information?"

Abel Pouch bit a big chunk out of his apple and sighed. "I am in business the way you are, Tree. You sell, I believe, groceries. You expect money for your product. So do I. I trust you've brought cash. While I will gladly accept your check, I cannot consider myself working for you until it has cleared the bank."

"In other words," Sam said quietly, "you're trying to blackmail me."

Pouch laughed pleasantly. "Do you believe that you are open to blackmail?"

"No, but apparently you think I am."

"My dear man, put it this way. Everything I have learned in the past and which I learn subsequently as the result of further investigations will be kept strictly confidential between myself and my client. If you do not retain me,

I shall, of course, be forced to seek another client. That may very well be the district attorney, who will pay for my knowledge."

"Knowledge of what?" Sam said.

"I mentioned bigamy this afternoon over the telephone. I might have included murder."

"You mean you know who murdered Felix Skinner?"

The whole of the apple core disappeared in Pouch's massive jaw. "Don't try to be clever, Tree. You are not yet my client."

"Why should I part with five hundred dollars without being sure that I'm not throwing it away? You don't strike me as a particularly honest man. Chances are — "

"My dear man!"

"Chances are you read about the murder in the papers and are trying to cash in on it. You say you investigate only for money. Why should you have started this investigation for nothing?"

Pouch rose ponderously and opened the top drawer of the dresser. It was filled with apples. He selected two and handed one to Sam. "Have an apple."

Sam suppressed a shudder. "No, thanks."

"They're very good. Baldwins. No?" He dropped one apple back into the drawer. Again the bed protested as his weight settled down on it.

"I'll tell you this much," Pouch said. "I became interested in this case during an investigation I made for another client. I shall demonstrate my knowledge by briefly considering your history. You were born in 1898 in Rochester, New York. Your father was a tailor, but he managed to send you to Cornell University. At the beginning of your junior year, in 1918, you enlisted in the Army. At the end of the war you returned to Cornell, where you received your B.A. degree. For the following fifteen years or so you were a rolling stone. You had so many positions and moved around so much that your history is hard to trace, until 1937, when you opened a grocery store in Queens. You settled down then, and the following year were married."

"All right, I'm convinced," Sam conceded. "What you're really telling me is that you're the private detective Douglas Faulcon, Senior, hired to investigate my wife and stepdaughter."

"I see you're on your toes." The apple crunched under his teeth. "One thing puzzles me about you. You are a university man and obviously a high type of individual. Why would a man like you be content to be a grocer, and a very small one at that?"

"What's wrong with grocers?"

"Nothing, I imagine. My grandfather was one. But you've had good jobs in the past."

Sam said: "I don't like bosses."

"Don't tell me you're a socialist?"

"I don't like any bosses, including the state. Call me an anarchist."

Pouch moved his shoulders with annoyance. "Come, Tree, you're pulling my leg."

"Aren't we getting away from the subject?" Sam said.

"Are we? It strikes me that perhaps the best way for a man to achieve obscurity is to be an insignificant grocer in Queens."

Bleakly Sam contemplated the massive

size of the man. "I suppose you feel it essential for a private detective to have a sprightly imagination. Let's get back to Ira Pram. You haven't mentioned his name yet, but it's plain you're trying to say that you have learned that Ira Pram isn't dead."

All of the apple vanished in the maw that was his mouth. "My retainer is five hundred dollars."

"Pram was killed fifteen years ago."

"So they say." For long seconds Pouch pondered the wall behind Sam. "I was in East Wiston last week. I stood on the beach where Pram was supposed to have been killed. Several hundred feet away there is a neck of land jutting out into Cape Cod Bay. I spoke to an old-timer who said he had participated in the search for Pram's body. He told me that immediately after Pram disappeared from sight, the second detective went off to bring boats."

"The other detective still had a pair of eyes."

"One pair is not as good as two. Pram, I understand, was an extraordinary under-water swimmer, and that neck of

143

land was not impossibly far. He might have stuck his nose up for air once or twice, and even a big man's nose is not very obvious on a large expanse of water."

Sam said dryly: "You seem to know a lot about the way he escaped."

"Deduction, my dear man. Simple deduction."

"And on that you base your contention that Pram got out alive?"

Pouch smiled expansively. "No."

"What's that got to do with Skinner's murder? You couldn't have found out a week ago in East Wiston who murdered Skinner last night."

"Bigamy can be countered by liquidating the other husband."

Sam laughed with relief. "Now I'm sure you're a phony, because I know I didn't murder Skinner."

"I didn't say it was you. It was your wife who was the bigamist."

Sam stood up. The closeness of the small, airless room was gagging him. "My wife was divorced from Skinner. There'd be no reason to murder him."

"The fact is he was murdered."

"You're talking in circles that don't get anywhere."

"You would be surprised where my talk would lead to for a client of mine."

Sam went to the door and wrenched it open and slammed it behind him. When he reached the stairhead, the door opened and Pouch stuck his head into the hall. A fresh apple was on the way to his mouth.

"You'd better make up your mind fast, Tree. There's not much time."

Without a word Sam went down the stairs.

9

Blythe Brice

FROM the opposite corner Sam saw the lights in his bedroom windows go out, and that made the whole house dark. Violet had probably just gone to bed. He crossed the street. Art Carson, his next-door neighbor, was rolling his car into his driveway. Carson stopped, blocking the sidewalk, and spoke to Sam through the car window. "I see you've been hitting the headlines, Sam."

"I'm not happy about it," Sam said.

"Messy business." Carson beamed delightedly. "I saw a picture in the paper where that moneybags was swinging at you with a cane. Why didn't you smack him one? Those rich think they can get away with murder. I bet he did it."

"Who did what?"

"This rich guy Faulcon murdered this guy Skinner. Rich people either buy you out or kill you. They're all like that."

146

The bright living-room lights went on, and then somebody was pulling down the shades. Sam's watch said eleven-fifty. Why put on lights and draw the shades at this hour? It was time for bed.

Carson's voice obtruded on his thoughts. "Don't you think so?"

"What?" Sam said.

"I was saying the police always kowtow to the rich. Say you or me tried to sock a guy like Faulcon. The cops would have us booked for assault and battery before we could say boo. Murder too. If you got money — "

Carson could keep going all night. Sam said, "Good night," and walked around the rear of the car. He unlocked the front door without a sound, but the hinges squeaked when he pushed it open. In the living room somebody moved quickly.

A strange woman sat on the couch with her legs crossed. She was bringing a match up to a cigarette held rakishly in very red lips. "Hello," she greeted him brightly.

Sam was well in the room before he recognized her. Incredibly she was Blythe Brice. There was nothing left of the timid, drab woman who had been living in the house for two days. Her hair, which had appeared stringy and lifeless, was swept up from her forehead and glistened under the overhead lights. The face that had been gaunt and dull was now vivacious with the aid of much make-up. She was attractive in a somewhat garish manner.

"Anybody else home?" Sam asked.

"No. Mrs. Tree went to the movies."

"Alone?"

"I guess so," Blythe said indifferently. "She didn't leave with anybody. Naomi went straight from work to the hospital to see Doug."

She rose from the couch and undulated to an ash tray to discard her match. Her figure, too, was vastly better. She no longer looked thin. Her tight-fitting belted dress was calculated to reveal curves, and it did.

Sam said: "How long do you intend to stay here?"

"Oh, I know I'm imposing, but it's so hard to find a room."

"You found a room yesterday."

"You know what happened last night. I was all ready to leave when Mrs.

Tree heard of that terrible murder, and then Naomi came home from the police station and I thought it only right that I stay with her. When I didn't show up at the hotel last night, they gave the room to somebody else. Of course, if you're anxious to get rid of me — " She gave him a slow, intimate smile and pulled her shoulders back to outline more prominently her breasts against the tight bodice.

He wasn't sure what she was up to now. How much did her getup mean? He dropped into the easy chair at the fireplace and waited for her to make the next move. She didn't. The black raven glowered down at him from the bald skull of Pallas. The tip of the beak was white

"What happened to him?" Sam said.

"Who?"

"The raven. Somebody knocked the tip of his beak off."

Blythe studied the figure. "I'm afraid I did that. I was helping Mrs. Tree clean the house this afternoon. I felt I ought to do something for the kindness you people have shown me. I was dusting the

149

figure and knocked it over. The beak hit the edge of the mantel, but I caught the figure before it fell to the floor. It might have been smashed."

"Too bad it wasn't."

She crushed out her cigarette in an ash tray, but she didn't come closer to him.

"When are you going home to Indiana?" he asked.

"You call that home!" Her very red lips tightened. No, not red. Orange, he decided. "I've got no family. I've nothing to go back to."

She came to him then and stood beside his chair. He lifted her hand. Her nails were the color of blood. "The war will be over soon, and your husband will be back," he said.

"Then what?" Blythe dropped on the arm of the chair; her hand rested on the back of the chair, lightly touching his head, and her body was twisted so that he would be very much aware of it. "We'll never make a go of it. I never should have married him."

He knew now that he had been right. There was grim purpose behind her seductive getup.

"So you don't love him," he fed her a cue.

"I hardly know him. Two days after we met we were married." Her arm slid back, and he felt her fingers on the thick chaos of his hair. "And he's only a kid. I like older men — mature men. The trouble is the best men are already married."

She was as subtle as a burlesque show. Her acting was lousy, but she wasn't depending on acting ability. She leaned against him, and the softness of her was against his shoulder. When he turned his head to look up at her, her smiling orange lips hovered inches above his own.

"Lonely?" Sam said.

"You can't guess how lonely."

He was never sure whether he pulled her down or whether her mouth dipped to his. Suddenly they were kissing and she was on his lap. It was done, and part of him stood off, watching impersonally, wondering whether he was really being cleverer than she was. Her lipstick was perfumed and had an oily taste, and she pressed so heavily against him that he had trouble breathing. Patiently he waited for her to pull away.

"Oh, my lover!" she murmured, running her hand over his face.

Inwardly Sam squirmed. She did it so much like Violet.

"Well, where do we go from here?" he said.

"I don't know. Do you want me to stay in New York?"

"What do you think?"

Her mouth trailed along his jawbone until it reached his ear. "But you wouldn't leave a rich wife for me."

"What makes you think she's rich?"

"I was upstairs yesterday afternoon when a man came here. I heard him ask Mrs. Tree for another thousand dollars."

Something inside Sam went numb. "What else did you hear?"

"That's all, because then they dropped their voices. After he went away, Mrs. Tree fainted. When I heard about the murder of that man Skinner and read how a thousand dollars was found in his pocket, I knew he was the one who'd been here. She was married to him before she married you, wasn't she? It looks like she still — well, she'd been giving him money."

He said nothing. She kissed him again, and he forced himself to return the kiss.

"Don't you see, honey?" she said huskily. "If we two had all that money — "

"I don't know what money you're talking about."

"I've heard things. She had three husbands. The first one was a crook and had twenty thousand dollars hidden somewhere. She must have known where it was. If she could lay her hands on a thousand dollars right in this house, I bet she's got it all right here."

"Suppose I do get that money?"

Blythe continued to impose acute awareness of her body on him. "Well, if you sell your store, and with all that other money besides, we could have a wonderful time together, just you and me. Oh, honey, I love you so much!"

It wasn't flattering to be taken for a middle-aged sucker.

"So she's been double-crossing me

with Skinner?" Sam said.

"I didn't say that, but it looks like it, doesn't it?"

"Damn her!" Sam said, and he almost gagged on the words. "I've been wondering where she's been getting the extra money from. If I only knew where it was."

"It's in the house somewhere."

"What makes you sure? She might have known Skinner was coming and had the money waiting for him. If you knew a little more, so that we would know more nearly where she kept it — "

Thoughtfully Blythe ran her lips over his cheek. "Will you go away with me?" she asked cautiously.

"I'm not sure. Maybe it would be better to get an apartment for you."

"While you kept on living with your wife?"

"I don't want anybody but you," he said. Her face powder was also perfumed. He didn't like the smell of it.

"All right," she said nuzzling him. "We'll work this out together. We'll — "

Somebody was coming up the porch steps. Sam pushed Blythe off his lap and

154

stood up and straightened his necktie. Hoping that he didn't look as flustered and guilty as he felt, he glanced at her. Calmly she was adjusting her dress. A key turned in the lock.

When Naomi entered the living room, Blythe Brice was casually lighting a cigarette. Sam stood awkward and miserable, not knowing what to do with his hands. He was an utter failure as an unfaithful husband.

"Hello," Naomi said gaily, pulling off her coat, and Sam wondered at the resiliency of young people. She had taken Felix Skinner's death very hard, yet now, only a little more than twenty-four hours later, her cheeks glowed and her fine dark eyes sparkled.

"How's Doug?" he asked.

"Just fine, considering. The Army wanted to move him to an Army hospital, but Doug had enough influence to stay where he was. If they had taken him away, I wouldn't have been able to see him all the time. He'll be out in a few days, but we're not waiting. We're going to be married tomorrow morning in the hospital."

"I'm so glad!" Blythe said.

Naomi turned her head to give Blythe a smile of thanks, and the smile stopped at the corners of her mouth. Her eyes swept Blythe from neat ankles to snappy hair-do. "Well, you've certainly done something to yourself. Why didn't you dress like that before?"

Blythe drew on her cigarette. "I went to pieces when my husband left. I didn't care how I looked."

"You're very pretty," Naomi said. "Is Mother asleep? She'll want to hear the news."

"She hasn't come home yet," Sam told her. "She went to the movies."

Naomi frowned. "Without you, Sam? That's the second time in two days that she — "

Something happened to Naomi's eyes. The light went out of them. Holding her body curiously stiff, she moved closer to him, staring at his face. She stopped and looked over her shoulders at Blythe and then back at Sam. And he was afraid without being sure why.

"You two were alone here in the house?" Naomi whispered.

Blythe uttered a short, brittle laugh. "Don't tell me you don't trust him alone with a woman?"

Naomi whirled. "Get out!" she shouted at Blythe, her tall body shaking with fury. "Leave this house at once."

Sam blinked and opened his mouth, but he didn't say anything.

"What's bitten you, Naomi?" Blythe asked quietly.

"Get out!"

The two women faced each other, and for a moment Sam was afraid that Naomi would strike Blythe. He didn't know what to say, what to do. Then Blythe looked him fully in the face and her orange mouth went crooked. "I was leaving anyway," she said. Her hips swung impudently on the way to the door.

There was silence then except for Blythe's feet going up the stairs. Sam cleared his throat. "Naomi," he said.

Slowly her head swiveled to him. "You'd better wipe that woman's lipstick off your face," she said contemptuously, "before Mother comes home."

The pit of his stomach emptied. He

touched his mouth, still feeling the stickiness of Blythe's kisses. Naomi was leaving the room. He recovered, realizing the tremendous importance of making her understand. He plunged after her and caught her at the door. "Let me explain," he said.

She faced him with her broad shoulders very square and her eyes cold with distaste. "You make it sound like a cheap melodrama."

"It does sound like it, doesn't it?" He grinned in spite of the way he felt. "If I went in for that sort of thing, wouldn't I have thought of wiping my face before you entered?"

His sudden good humor softened her features with doubt. "Don't tell me she didn't kiss you?"

"She very definitely did. It was like any cheap thriller — the spy using her fair white body to obtain information."

"Spy?"

"That story about her sailor husband was a phony," he said. "She deliberately worked on you so that you would invite her to spend the night here. Then she kept finding excuses not to leave."

Gravely she studied him. "Are you sure?"

"Why else would a woman deliberately make herself unattractive and drab? She wanted to appear pathetic and inconspicuous. When I returned home tonight, I saw the lights in my bedroom go out, yet she was the only one home. Then she came down here and pulled down the shades. It's plain she was searching the house."

"But for what?"

"I'm not sure," he said, which was almost the truth. "She must have searched every opportunity she got and didn't think there would be much chance for success this time. So she dolled up, hoping that I would be the first one home, and then got to work on me."

"Your face doesn't show that you objected."

He grinned sheepishly. "I tried to outsmart her. I played along to try to pry some information out of her. It wasn't fun."

Naomi laughed heartily, and all at once he felt a lot better. "I believe you, Sam. I think you're about the only man in the world I would believe. If I could imagine you being unfaithful to Mother, it certainly wouldn't be with cheap baggage like that."

"Thanks," he said wryly.

"Did your self-sacrifice do any good?"

"Not much. You came in too soon, though probably it wouldn't have worked anyway."

Upstairs a door closed, and then Blythe Brice came down the stairs carrying her valise. They watched her from the living-room doorway.

"Good-by, Mr. Tree," she said pleasantly, ignoring Naomi.

Sam mumbled something without meaning. Blythe left the street door open. He crossed the hall to close it. When he returned to Naomi, she was leaning against the doorjamb, her eyes again grave.

"Sam, you told me very little."

"I know very little," he said.

"Did she come here to look for my father's money?"

"So you know about it?"

"I'm not a child," she said. "Sam, did you pay for my coat?"

160

"Of course."

Solemnly she shook her head. "You're a liar. That's all right. I want you to be that kind of liar. I'll lie too if they ask me. Why does Mother go to the movies alone twice in two days?"

"She's always liked the movies."

"But she hates to go alone. Do you think it's because she's worried? Because she hopes she can forget in the movies?"

"She has nothing to worry about."

Her kiss took him by surprise. It was a chaste, daughterly kiss on the cheek, and it made him happier than almost any kiss he had ever received.

"You're a swell guy," she said. "I'm sorry I made a scene with Blythe. And I suppose I oughtn't to ask questions. They might be dangerous."

"Don't say that."

"I hope Doug will be a husband like you," she said. "I'm not even going to think about this dreadful business any more. Whom was Blythe spying for?"

"I didn't find out."

"I forgot that I'm not going to ask any more questions." She sounded a little wild. She kissed his other cheek. He felt old and fatherly. "Now go up and wash your face," she said.

While he was in the bathroom, he heard Violet come home and then the excited voices of mother and daughter talking downstairs. He was in his pajamas when Violet entered the bedroom.

"Darling, isn't it glorious news about Naomi and Doug being married tomorrow?"

"Yes," he said.

She threw her arms about him. This was the kiss that counted — this and Naomi's. He was a very lucky man. He held her close to him, possessively, protectingly.

"Violet, do you think you ought to go out alone at night?" he said.

She ceased to be cozy in his embrace. She stepped away from him.

"What do you imagine could happen to me? We don't live in the wilderness."

"Are you in danger?" he pleaded. "If you are — "

That flutter of her hand stopped him. "Darling, are you going to start that all over again?"

"I suppose you have a headache?" he said grimly.

"A splitting headache. I'm afraid I need glasses. The movies always makes my head hurt."

He leaned against the dresser as she slipped her dress over her head. They were miles apart, and he couldn't get near her except physically. Ira Pram had had her first, and he had never let go of her.

"You collected only eight hundred dollars on Pram's insurance," he said.

She was at the closet. Momentarily her hand stopped as she reached for a hanger, then she resumed hanging up her dress. She said without turning: "If you keep tormenting me like this, I'm going to spend the night with Naomi."

"Don't worry," he told her. "I'll shut up till after the wedding tomorrow."

10

The Wedding

WITH his hand on the knob, Sam looked again at the name plate on the door. In the room beyond it was too quiet for a wedding party, but the card on the door read, 'Lt. Douglas Faulcon, Jr.,' so there was no doubt about it.

The hospital smell followed him into the room. Softly he closed the door, the way one always does in hospital, and was aware again of the silence. Yet they were there. Doug sat propped up in bed, and Naomi sat on the edge of the bed. Violet and Martha and an Army chaplain completed the party.

Doug's head lifted sharply to the door, and every other pair of eyes swung in the same direction. Sam had an impression that they were disappointed when they saw who he was.

"Sorry I'm late," Sam apologized. "I

can't leave Ted alone in the store on a Friday, and the union had a tough time digging up an extra clerk."

"I'm glad you came, sir," Doug said. "This is Captain Steeger."

The chaplain pumped Sam's hand, then glanced at his wrist watch. "Look, Doug, I'm due back at five. My train — "

"Let's wait a few more minutes," Doug said wearily.

The silence returned. The chaplain retreated to a window. Naomi was twisting the fingers of Doug's right hand, which was on her lap, as if they were inanimate. With his left arm in a sling, Doug lay back on the raised bed and closed his eyes. He looked sicker than Sam had expected.

Violet sat on one of the two chairs in the room and held a crumpled handkerchief to her face. She wasn't weeping. It struck Sam that he had never in his life seen her weep. For that matter, he had never before seen her so nervous, and she was obviously very nervous now.

He caught Martha Underhill's eyes,

and she came over to the side of the door where he had taken up his position. "What's the trouble?" he whispered.

"Doug's folks have been working on him. He's sick and worried, and it seems he never bucked his parents before in anything."

"Is he expecting them to come here?"

"He says he asked them," Martha whispered. "We've been waiting like this for forty nerve-racking minutes."

Suddenly Naomi released Doug's hand and stood up. Her mouth was tight, showing harsh lines of strain. "Doug, if you don't want to — "

"What nonsense!" Violet cut in. She was on her feet, holding fiercely to Naomi's arm. She sent her complacent smile at Doug. "Don't mind her. This is the most important day of her life, so naturally she's on edge."

"I know," Doug said quietly without opening his eyes. "I'm thinking I'm the luckiest man in the world to be marrying her. But we ought to wait for my mother."

"She didn't say she was coming," Violet argued.

"No, she didn't, but I asked her. Let's wait just a few — "

The door opened and a woman came in. All at once Doug was a well man. "Hello, Moms," he said.

Mrs. Faulcon was a thin woman who seemed overburdened with clothes. Her eyes swept the room impersonally. She knew Naomi and had met Violet, but she did not greet them. And she did not go to her son's bed. "How do you feel, Douglas?" she asked.

"Fine, Moms," he replied tonelessly. In the space of seconds he was again a sick man.

The door moved inward a few inches, and Douglas Faulcon, Senior's, bald pate appeared. He hesitated, then eased into the room and stood beside Sam without showing that he was aware of him. His mouth was determinedly clamped shut.

"I'm glad you came, Dad," Doug said, trying to force enthusiasm into his voice. "Do you and Moms know everybody? Naomi, of course. You've met Captain Steeger at the house. Miss Underhill is a friend of the Trees. This is Naomi's mother, and that's Mr. Tree."

The Faulcons nodded to the chaplain and to nobody else. It was going to be a very quiet wedding, Sam reflected. Too quiet.

Nobody said anything. Nobody moved. Doug sat up straighter, and his jaw jutted. "Let's get started," he told the chaplain.

It was quickly over, and Naomi and Doug were man and wife and she was bending over the bed to kiss him. Behind her Sam saw Violet's face glow radiantly. She looked more like a bride than Naomi.

Then Mrs. Faulcon said, "My boy!" and went swiftly to the other side of the bed and kissed Doug. Tightly he held his mother to him. The chaplain beamed. Naomi and Violet looked at each other with happy smiles.

"Well, that's that," Sam muttered.

Faulcon, standing near by, heard him. His hawkish eyes tilted to Sam's face. "I came here because my wife considered it her duty, but I certainly don't approve."

"You're breaking my heart," Sam said.

"The young idiot! The first swaying pair of hips that comes along — "

"Shut up!" Sam said.

His voice was too angry, too loud. Everybody in the room stared at him. Mrs. Faulcon straightened up at the side of the bed. Momentarily her eyes rested coldly on Sam and then slid past. "We had better go," she said stiffly and stalked to the door. Her husband tagged after her, leaving a wake of silence.

"I'm sorry, Doug," Sam said when the door banged. "I shouldn't have let him provoke me."

Slowly Doug separated his clenched teeth. "I know how Dad is." He looked around. "Well, what are you all so glum about? This is a wedding, not a funeral." He pulled Naomi down beside him. "Isn't she lovely?" he asked the world.

Everybody tried to be very jolly after that, but only Violet succeeded. There was a bottle of rye, but no glasses, and when the nurse brought glasses only Martha wanted a drink. They straggled out then, leaving Naomi behind with her husband.

Sam's car was parked around the corner. Because of gas rationing, he seldom used it except on special occasions like this. He drove Martha to a subway station and Captain Steeger to Grand Central. Then, alone with Violet, he headed east toward Queens.

"Well, you did it, Violet," he said. "They're married."

"What did I have to do with it? They're madly in love with each other."

"You're too modest, sweetheart. If Mrs. Faulcon were half as clever as you, she could at least have gotten the wedding postponed. She came pretty close to it at that."

"Did she?" Violet said vaguely.

"You were scared stiff. Now if Mrs. Faulcon had had reinforcements in the form of a juicy scandal about Naomi's mother — "

The car stopped for a red light on Third Avenue. Violet's face was turned toward the side window.

"Sam," she said quietly, "have you been hinting all along that perhaps I murdered Felix?"

"No."

"Then what is it?"

"They're married now," he said again. "You don't have to worry any more about scandal breaking it up. Anyway, Ira Pram was declared legally dead, so you're not a bigamist if he turns up alive."

She turned in her seat as the light changed. Her voice was unnaturally sharp. "Do you know that Ira is alive?"

"I think that would be a good reason why you paid blackmail to Felix Skinner."

"Why should I pay Felix anything because Ira was alive?"

"Because Felix Skinner threatened to make it public. Your heart was set on Naomi and Doug marrying. Doug wasn't happy about bucking his parents. A juicy scandal might have made him see things his parents' way."

"You're just assuming that Ira is alive."

"Is he?"

"Didn't the police say they had killed him?"

Sam said irritably: "Give me a direct answer for once. Is he dead or isn't he?"

"How should I know?"

"That's not a direct answer."

Her gloved hand closed over his right fist on the wheel. "Darling. I fail to see what you're driving at. If Ira were alive, you said yourself I couldn't be held responsible for bigamy."

"You could be held responsible for theft," he said bluntly.

Her hand slipped away. They were on the upper level of the Queensboro Bridge now, and she was gazing down at the rooftops below.

"Well?" he said after a silence. "Haven't you any answer to that?"

"I don't know what you're talking about."

"I'm talking about Ira Pram's twenty thousand dollars."

"That was never found. In fact, the police weren't sure it ever existed. They had only Earl Durand's word for it."

"Then what have you been using for money?"

Violet was watching him sideways. She was a great deal more composed than he was. "I don't know from whom you got your information, but — "

"Part of it from Martha," he said.

"Then Martha must have told you how

terribly poor I've been."

"What happened two years ago to make you rich?"

"All right," she said with sudden determination. "You've made me tell you. Felix had been giving me money."

"What!" The car slewed toward the white line. He yanked the wheel back.

"I suppose I shouldn't have accepted the money without telling you," she said. "I was afraid you wouldn't approve. Naturally the money was for Naomi. You know how fond he was of her."

"You didn't spend it all on Naomi."

"Well, I spent some of it on the house, and in a way it's her house too, isn't it? And I sent some to Mother."

"Was it just a gag that you objected to Naomi's seeing the man from whom you were accepting thousands of dollars?"

"One thing had nothing to do with the other."

"And how did Skinner get rich suddenly?" he asked dryly.

"Gambling, of course. He had a lucky streak these last few years. When you thought I was giving him money, I was really receiving it from him." He felt her body against his side. "You don't mind, darling, do you?"

"I mind being lied to."

"You don't believe me?" She sounded incredulous.

"No. Is Ira Pram alive?"

"How many times are you going to ask me that?"

"I'm an optimist," he said. "I'm living in hope that someday you'll tell me something I don't know already."

She shifted back to the far end of the seat and smoothed her coat. "What's the use talking to you if you don't believe anything I say? Sam, do you have to drive so fast? You almost took the fender off that taxi."

"If I had any character, I'd wreck both of us right now before you get a chance to do it your way."

"Darling, you talk like a madman."

"Behold your handiwork, madam. You ought to write a book: how to drive a husband off his nut in one easy lesson. Anyway, thanks for telling me that Pram is alive."

"I didn't tell you anything of the sort."

"Sure you did," he said. "And you told me that you're still afraid, even though you've married Naomi off safe and sound. You're afraid of Pram or of being caught as a thief or of something I don't know about yet. How far will the rest of us be dragged down with you?"

"Sam!" she cried, and what was in her voice might have been either anger or terror. "Don't talk like that."

"All right," he said. "Have you seen any good moving pictures lately?"

She said nothing.

When they reached the house, he dropped her off at the curb and tooled the car up the narrow driveway and into the cramped garage. He entered the house through the back door. Voices from the living room came into the kitchen. It was strange that anybody but Violet should be in the house, because Violet had been home only a minute or two.

Two men were with Violet in the living room. Still dressed in her hat and coat, she was pulling off her gloves while facing a small, wizened man who slouched on his spine in the easy chair.

The man's gray hat rested on one knee,

and Sam saw now that his hair was also gray. His gray muffler did not hide his mouth and nose the way it had in the store Tuesday night; it was bunched at his chin. His coat collar was up around his neck. He seemed to be cold, though the house was well heated.

The second man stood in front of the bust of Pallas. He might have been a gorilla in man's clothing. His body was hulking, his arms unnaturally long, his nose mashed flat, his brow low. He was puffing a cigar the way Sam had once seen an ape do in a circus.

"Hello," Sam said.

Violet nodded toward the seated man. "Sam, I'd like you to meet Mr. Durand. He's an old acquaintance from Cape Cod."

11

Earl Durand

THE gray little man shot a swift glance at Sam and then huddled deeper into his overcoat. His cold eyes shifted back to Violet. "Well, so Naomi was married today. The last time I saw her she was hardly out of diapers. It makes a man realize how much time has passed."

"Fifteen years," Violet said mechanically.

Sam moved farther into the room. He could see Violet's face now, and she wasn't frightened; but there was a set to her features which took most of the softness out of them, and her pale eyes were cautious.

Sam said: "How did you get into this house?"

"Through the door, naturally," Earl Durand drawled. "That's what doors are made for, I believe."

"The doors were locked."

177

"Now what do you think of that!" Within his raised coat collar Durand's head rotated to his hulking companion. "He can't know, Georgie, that locks form no barrier to a man of your talents."

The man called Georgie removed the cigar from his apish face and blew smoke at the ceiling. "It was a cinch."

"Housebreaking is minor stuff for you, Durand," Sam said. "It's nothing compared to holding up a man with a gun."

Violet removed her hat and fluffed out her hair. She remained silent.

"That wasn't a holdup," Durand said. "Call it an impulse. I heard Violet was married to a grocer. I figured that if he was anything like the grocers I knew, the sight of a gun would scare the pants off him and he'd blabber." He touched his cheek. "At that, you're lucky I haven't an itchy trigger finger." He bored deeper into the chair and looked languidly about the room. "Nice place you have here, Violet, though modest. I don't believe you've spent much of Ira's dough."

Slowly Violet removed her coat and placed it over the back of a chair. *She's*

178

sparring for time, Sam thought. Durand watched her with a smile that was not quite a smile.

"You know Ira left me only debts," she said at last.

"And about twenty grand in cash," Durand told her quietly.

A mild, soft-spoken man, Martha had said, and the cruelest eyes she had ever seen. Apparently fifteen years in jail hadn't changed Durand except to make him older.

"The police looked for that money," Violet said. "They never found it. You must have heard of that."

"I didn't hear that you didn't find it."

"Well, I didn't." Violet took the lid off the cigarette box. "Does either of you smoke?"

Georgie looked at his cigar and grinned hideously. Durand said nothing.

Violet uttered her fluttering laugh. "How about coffee and cake? My husband and I haven't had lunch yet, and we're starved."

A small, detached part of Sam could be amused. They were getting the Violet run-around, but this time she had met her match. They were too single-minded to be diverted even momentarily from their purpose. But how ruthless were they? How far did they intend to go?

"We want that dough," Georgie stated flatly.

Earl Durand sighed. "Please, Georgie, let me handle this. I was crude Tuesday evening with Tree, and it got me nowhere. Violet, we can settle this matter amicably. While the money is actually mine, I am perfectly willing to let you keep anything over ten grand."

"Does that mean ten thousand dollars?" Violet said.

She was still at it. She was too ardent a movie-goer not to know what a 'grand' was.

"It means," Durand said, "ten thousand dollars."

"That's what I thought," she said brightly. "When did you get out of prison, Earl?"

"Six weeks ago. I — " He smiled frostily. "I want that money, Violet, or I'll tell the police you stole it."

"It wasn't yours."

"No, nor yours, nor Ira's. I'm sure you don't want trouble from me or from the police. How much have you left? Perhaps if there isn't that much remaining, I'll accept less."

Sam said: "I imagine Ira Pram would want to have something to say about that."

He had half expected the bomb to be a dud, but it wasn't.

Georgie uttered a startled, "Huh?"

Earl Durand turned his cold gray eyes on Sam and searched his face. "What did you say?" he asked.

"What about Pram?" Sam said.

"What about him? He's been dead a long time."

"Are you sure?"

Durand stood up, his thin shoulders bowed in his coat, and took two steps toward Violet. "What's he talking about?"

"I haven't any idea." Her hand fluttered to her hair. "Of course Ira is dead and it was your fault he was shot by the police. If you say he had the money hidden, I suppose it's so, but he must have hidden it so well that it was never found. The police looked and looked. They even dug in the cellar."

"You bet they didn't find it," Durand said. "You got to it first."

"I didn't."

"Why kid around, Earl?" Georgie said irritably.

"Georgie is right," Durand said. "Here's the way it was, Violet. Ira and I put all the dough we made selling lottery tickets into hundred-dollar bills. Not those big-sized bills they had in those days, but those neat small ones that were just coming out. Even twenty grand made a compact pile, not too large for handling, and the denomination wasn't so big we couldn't use the bills as ready cash. Funny thing, come to think of it. Ira had a notion people paid less attention to Federal Reserve notes than to gold notes, so all our dough was Federal Reserve stuff. Turned out Ira was right, because now it's against the law to possess gold notes. Thoughtful of us to make them Federal Reserve notes, wasn't it, Violet, so now you can spend them without trouble?"

Obviously to Violet money was money.

She looked bored. "I'm afraid I don't know much about finances, Earl."

"You know enough to spend money when you get your hands on it." Durand leaned forward. "All hundred-dollar bills, do you get that, Violet? When I got out a few weeks ago, I paid a visit to East Wiston. I was wondering what happened to that dough. I found out. Your mother — Mrs. Wilson — cashes hundred-dollar bills every now and then. She's very proud that her daughter sends them to her."

"Money is easiest to send that way," Violet said.

"Easier than a check? I figured I could scare your husband — your present husband, I mean — into telling me more about Ira's dough. My method was a bit crude, perhaps, and didn't work. At the time I thought it would be safest to keep away from you, Violet. Now it's not important. I'm sure of my ground because when Skinner was murdered Wednesday night he had ten one-hundred-dollar bills in his pocket. The papers also say that the night before that Skinner had bought nine hundred dollars' worth of chips in a gambling joint, also with hundred-dollar bills. Nineteen of those bills Skinner got in two days, and he got them from you."

Violet tossed her head. "What nonsense!"

"The cops have an idea your husband gave the dough to Skinner. My own idea is you did. This Skinner was your former husband, and chances are you and he were still — "

"Careful what you say," Sam said softly.

Durand gave him his half-smile and then buried his hands deeper into his pockets and turned back to Violet. "I don't give a damn why you gave Skinner the dough, but the fact is you did and it came out of Ira's pile. I don't believe in coincidence. Every cent of Ira's money was in hundred-dollar bills; so was every cent in Skinner's possession. Do you play ball, Violet?"

"I haven't the money and I don't like your attitude," Violet said. "I think you'd better leave."

Durand's gray eyes glittered, and now for the first time Sam was really afraid. He turned toward the hall door.

"Where are you going, mister?" Durand said.

Sam kept going.

"Would you like a slug in your back, pal?" Georgie suggested cheerfully.

Sam stopped in the doorway. Georgie had transferred his cigar to his left hand. His right hand was inside his coat and under his left shoulder. He had a gun there, of course. That kind would no more go out without a gun than without clothes.

"Behave yourself," Durand advised Sam. "Georgie is very impulsive."

Violet stood very still behind a chair, gripping the back of it tightly, but her eyes were puzzled. She didn't understand what was happening, or if she did she refused to believe it. And for once she was justified, Sam thought. They couldn't gain much by getting too tough.

"I thought calling the police were one of the threats you held over Violet," Sam said. "I'm merely going to save you the trouble by calling them myself."

"A humorist," Durand said. "Are you laughing, Georgie?"

"My sides are splitting," Georgie said.

"Maybe I ought to split his sides with lead."

Violet's eyes widened. She was getting it at last. "Is that a gun you have there?"

"I ain't got my hand under my arm to scratch myself, lady."

Something in her throat broke, releasing words in shrill frenzy. "You wouldn't dare shoot. I'd be a witness, and the sound of a shot would be heard in the street, and a policeman is always on the corner, and it's broad daylight, and — well, you wouldn't dare."

Patiently Durand waited for her to run out of breath. Bowed in his overcoat, he seemed hardly taller than Violet; but all at once Sam knew that that little old man was deadlier than anybody he had ever known. Fifteen years ago he had attempted to escape from three armed detectives with only a penknife as a weapon. Now fifteen years of his life had moldered away and he was old, with nothing ahead of him except what money could buy. That money meant everything to him, and he had always been a crook and worse.

"Look at it from my point of view," Durand said mildly. "I had a share in accumulating that money. I spent fifteen years in jail because of it. I want it very badly, Violet."

"You wouldn't dare," Violet repeated doggedly. And Sam wondered whether what Violet was showing now was courage or ignorance of the capacity of men like Earl Durand or merely that complacency of hers which almost nothing could undermine.

"My dear Violet," Durand said, "Georgie has six bullets in his gun."

"Seven," Georgie corrected him. "I got my Colt .45 automatic."

"All right, seven," Durand said. "Two bullets will do for you and your husband. There will be no witnesses. We can be out the back door and blocks away before anybody realizes they heard shots."

Violet's eyes swiveled as if she were looking for something in the room, and then her eyes stopped on Sam in a wild appeal. Well, at last she was asking him for help, now that the situation had become impossible, Sam thought dully. Except that it wasn't impossible.

It struck him why he wasn't more scared. There was a basic flaw in Earl Durand's threat.

"Your gun is no good," Sam pointed out. "Shooting won't get you the money, if there is any money. In fact, you'd go far out of your way to make sure that Violet remained alive until you got what you wanted."

Violet sagged against the chair with relief.

"Now the lad is brainy," Durand said. "Are you impressed, Georgie?"

"Tell him how I like to play mumbly-peg on a guy's belly," Georgie said.

"Precisely." Durand regarded Violet sadly. "I wish you wouldn't be difficult, my dear. Your husband is right: Georgie will throw lead at you and your husband only as a last resort. But we can be very quiet if necessary. We can tie and gag you and your husband. Georgie has a knife in his pocket. It's just a little knife, but it's remarkable what Georgie can do with it."

"I can make a dummy talk," Georgie said proudly.

Out in the sunlit street an automobile

honked gaily. A boy yelled. "Hey, Danny!" and across the street another boyish voice answered, "You come over here." And in the living room there was a stillness like death.

Sam felt every muscle in his body agonizingly tight, and his stomach muscles were tightest of all. He looked at Georgie, planted solidly in front of the fireplace. Even if Georgie were unarmed, he was too big, probably too strong, and it was thirty years since Sam had fought with anybody. There was nothing he could do. It was up to Violet.

And Violet was saying: "I don't believe you."

She was afraid now. Sam could tell it by the sagging of her shoulders and the thinness of her voice. But not afraid enough, or perhaps more afraid of something else than of anything Durand could do to her.

Durand looked at Sam. "Tell her, mister, what a man will do for ten grand. I don't know whether she's being brave or stupid, but neither will get her anything."

"She told you she hadn't the money,"

189

Sam said. He was annoyed because his voice was so hoarse.

"That may be," Durand conceded. "But we'll make dead sure."

His right hand came out of his coat pocket; there was a ball of heavy twine in it. He had come prepared. "You keep them covered, Georgie, while I tie them up."

A moan started deep in Violet's throat and rose to her lips in a ragged whimper. She pushed herself away from the chair and flung her arms about Sam. "Darling, don't let him touch me!"

A hot flood of anger rose in Sam. Anger at Violet, at Durand, at Skinner and Pram — at all those living and dead who were responsible for what was going on.

"Give him the money," he said into Violet's hair.

"There isn't any. There never — "

"To hell with the money!" Sam raged. "It's caused enough trouble. Give it to him."

"If you say so, darling." She lifted her face from his chest, but remained within the circle of his arm. "It's not here."

Durand threw up the ball of twine and caught it with one hand. "Where is it?"

"Where Ira hid it. On Cape Cod."

"Provincetown, where you lived?"

"Yes!"

Georgie tossed his cigar into the fireplace. "She's lying, Earl."

"You're damn right she's lying." Durand kept tossing the ball of twine. "I think, Georgie, we'll work on her. That way we'll be sure of getting the truth."

"Sam!" Violet moaned against his chest. "O God, Sam!"

"Wait a minute," Sam said to Durand. "I can tell you."

Sam put his hands on Violet's shoulders and pushed her behind him and faced Durand. *They won't shoot*, he thought. *There'd be no sense in shooting*. The wizened little man stopped tossing the ball. His eyes started to lift to Sam's face. Sam hit him.

His fist didn't have far to travel; it landed flush on the button. Durand fell away from him, vanishing below his vision, and Sam saw Georgie moving fast from the fireplace. Georgie's long arms swung loosely; there was no gun in his hand.

Sam set himself for Georgie's charge and met it with a right to the midriff. Georgie grunted, but the blow didn't stop him. His gorilla arms wound around Sam, and Sam was crushed against a barrel chest. Distantly he heard Violet utter a strangled, mewling sound. His bones were snapping and his lungs caught fire. He threw his head back and looked directly into Georgie's hideous, sweating, straining face, and he bit Georgie in the chin and hung on. Furiously Georgie shook his head to free himself of the tenacious grip of Sam's teeth, and the pressure of his arms eased slightly. Sam jabbed his right knee up into Georgie's groin.

Sam was free then, spinning away from Georgie, pulling ragged gasps of air down his throat, and he saw that Violet was struggling with Durand. The little man had gotten up from the floor and clamped a hand over Violet's mouth to prevent her from raising an alarm. Sam started toward Durand and then hestitated. The tail of his eye caught

Georgie moving in again, sluggish now with pain, but coming. Georgie still didn't think he needed his gun, and Sam was inclined to agree. He wouldn't break that grip a second time. He backed away until his thighs touched the edge of the table, and then he twisted to sweep up the table lamp as a weapon.

That was when the doorbell rang.

Everything stopped, as if the bell had set off a fairy-tale curse which froze every living thing in the room. Then Earl Durand's voice cut the stillness.

"Use the gun this time, Georgie, if they let out a sound."

Painfully Georgie straightened up. There was no color in his face except for his fleshy lips, which were blue. His hand slid under his left shoulder. Sam turned away from the lamp and looked at Violet. Durand still had his hand over her mouth, not trusting the threat of a gun to keep her silent.

The doorbell rang again. The sound of it echoed through the house and faded. Then on the porch somebody moved.

They all turned to the two windows which looked out on the porch. A man blocked the window nearest the door; he bent over to peer into the living room.

Crazy laughter trembled in the pit of Sam's stomach. "Why, it's the detective," he said. Then he raised his voice. "Come in, Sergeant Jones. I think the door is open."

The figure withdrew from the window. Quickly Durand stepped away from Violet.

"That's no copper," Georgie whispered.

Sam heard the doorknob being turned, and then the bell rang again. Violet was at his side. "I left the snap on," she said hollowly. "The door is locked."

"I'll open it," Sam said. "Even if it weren't the sergeant, they won't dare do anything with a third person so close."

Georgie looked inquiringly at Durand, and the little gray man shook his head. Sam breathed again. He crossed the room to the hall, passing within a foot of Durand, who was rubbing his jaw. Sam saw a jagged line of blood follow the cleft of Durand's chin, and for the first time he realized that his knuckles smarted.

"Now it's become a personal matter,"

Durand said bleakly. "I don't like to be hit."

Sam turned into the hall and opened the door. "Come in, Sergeant. I'm delighted to see you."

12

Sergeant Jones

WITHIN a matter of seconds the atmosphere in the living room had changed. Earl Durand was nonchalantly buttoning his overcoat; Georgie, still white-faced from the kick, was slipping the band off a fresh cigar. And Violet came forward with a gracious smile for Sergeant Jones.

The detective snatched off his hat. "Can I have a few words with you and Mr. Tree in private?"

"Certainly," Violet said, and Sam marveled at the steadiness of her voice. "These gentlemen were just about to leave."

"Well, I'll be seeing you, Violet," Earl Durand said pleasantly.

It was all sweetness and light now. "Soon, I hope. Come on, Georgie."

In panic Sam watched them start to leave. Sergeant Jones's arrival had solved nothing; it had only provided a breathing spell. Durand wanted that money as much as he wanted to live, and Violet was the only one who could tell him where it was, and she couldn't be guarded day and night.

Sam took a quick step sideways, blocking the doorway with his body. "Sergeant, have you ever heard of Earl Durand?"

Durand stopped, and Georgie stopped behind him.

"Is that the guy who was Ira Pram's partner?" Jones said. "I been checking up on history since Skinner was murdered. What about Durand?"

"This is the man," Sam said.

Eagerness lit up the sergeant's plain features. He put a hand on Durand's shoulder. "What are you doing out of jail?"

"I've served my sentence."

"What are you doing here?"

"Mrs. Tree is an old friend of mine."

"Not a friend," Sam said. "And he didn't act like a friend. He came here to threaten my wife, and I had to hit him. Look at my cracked knuckles and look at his jaw."

Jones looked and grinned. "And I broke it up, eh? I guess that's the yell I heard as I was coming up the porch. That's why I looked in the window when nobody answered the bell. Well, I'll tell you, Mr. Tree. I'm Homicide and this isn't my district anyway, so if you'll call the local police precinct — "

"Wait!" Violet said. "My husband doesn't want Mr. Durand arrested."

Durand took his smile out of the icebox. "You're damn right he doesn't. It was Tree that hit me, as you can see."

"No," Violet said. "Earl Durand tried to — " She bit her lip. "I think it's best that we forget the whole thing." Her eyes appealed to Sam.

Of course, Sam thought bitterly. If he had Durand arrested, too much might come out in court, and that would be as harmful to Violet as anything Durand could do to her. Violet was still making him play her game, even though he didn't know what it was.

"I don't want them arrested," Sam

said, "but I want something clearly understood. Durand came here to extort money from my wife. He threatened to kill us both. Sergeant, if anything should happen to my wife, you'll know that Durand and this other man are responsible."

Durand huddled his small form deeper into his coat. "He's nuts. I came here for a social call, and we got into an argument and Tree clipped me in the jaw." His bloodless mouth twisted. "Tree's very brave. He doesn't outweigh me by much more than forty pounds, so — "

"Hold it!" Jones cut in. "I'm getting some sort of run-around. Mrs. Tree, what sort of money did he want from you?"

"Just money," she said vacantly. "He said he was broke, and because he had been my husband's partner — my first husband, of course — he thought that I should give him money."

"Is that right, Tree?"

"Yes." In a way Sam was beginning to hate Violet for making him do such things.

"Does that make sense to you,

Sergeant?" Durand asked scornfully.

Jones poked a finger into Durand's skimpy chest. "I'll decide what makes sense. You're an ex-con, so your word don't mean a thing to me. And I don't like the looks of your pal either. What's your name, fella?"

"Georgie."

"Your whole name."

Georgie flicked cigar ashes on the carpet. "Jones."

"Jones, eh?" The sergeant flushed angrily. "That's my name."

"A couple of people can have the same name, especially like Jones."

"He has a gun," Sam said. "He threatened to kill me with it."

"Well, now, that's interesting," the sergeant said happily. "A phony name and a gun. I like to bring in mugs on concealed- and illegal-weapon charges." He stepped up to Georgie. "Lift your arms."

Georgie obeyed. Expertly the sergeant passed his palms over his big body and then frowned. "He's clean. Did you see a rod?"

Sam felt like a fool. "Not exactly. He

kept his hand under his shoulder as if he had a gun there."

"I was just kidding him," Georgie said.

"Yeah?" Jones stepped back and scratched his skull. "Something fishy. Damn fishy. Okay, you lugs, beat it. And God help you if anything happens to Mrs. Tree or Mr. Tree. Do you get that?"

"Yes, Sergeant," Durand said meekly.

Sam stepped away from the doorway to let them pass.

When they were gone, Sergeant Jones crossed over to the fireplace and glumly contemplated Pallas and the raven. "This thing gives me the heebie-jeebies," he decided. "What's that bird doing on the guy's head?"

"Poe liked the sound of the name Pallas, so he put the raven on her head."

"What?"

"It's a poem," Sam said.

"Oh, a poem." Jones lost interest. He watched Violet settle down on the couch with a compact to renew her make-up. "What dough was Durand after, Mrs. Tree?"

"Any money, as long as it was money."

"Not Ira Pram's dough, by any chance?"

Sam went to the couch and sat down beside Violet and took her hand. Her flesh was cold, but there was nothing wrong with her eyes. It was only recently that Sam was learning what a remarkable woman she was.

"He did mention that Ira had owed him some money," she said.

Jones twirled his hat carelessly. He didn't look particularly bright, but that could be protective coloration. "I told you I've been digging up history. Heard Pram was supposed to have a lot of dough hidden somewhere. You didn't find it, Mrs. Tree?"

"Don't be silly."

"Guess it would've been spent years ago if you did. Not my business, anyway. I'm interested in who killed Skinner." He dropped into one of the easy chairs. "Funny how Skinner got all that dough suddenly."

"He could have won it gambling," Sam pointed out.

"Nuts. A dozen cops have been

checking. Skinner liked to stick to a couple of places, mostly a joint called Lou's. For a long time he'd been gambling with peanuts. Then about three weeks ago he shows up at Lou's with two grand."

Violet's fingernails dug into Sam's palms. His eyes swirled to her face, and he saw that she was genuinely startled.

"Funny thing about gambling," Sergeant Jones was musing. "It happens to me in poker. A bad streak starts, and sometimes it's weeks you don't win a single decent pot. Skinner had a streak like that starting with the first two grand. He dropped it in one sitting at the crap table. Don't know why he favored dice; it's a sucker's game, but I guess all guys like Skinner are born suckers. Anyway, a week later Skinner comes back to Lou's with two more grand, and the dough goes the same way as the other. Another week passes, and Tuesday, the night before he's murdered, he's there again. This time he drops only a measly nine hundred bucks, but next night we find another grand in his wallet. Here's a guy who's dead broke all the time, yet can lose five grand — four thousand, nine hundred dollars, to be exact — in three weeks, and be on the way to drop the sixth grand when he's killed. You folks got any idea of an answer?"

Violet had curled up on the couch during the sergeant's monologue, and her cheek was pressed against Sam's arm. Looking down at her, he could see only the top of her head.

"What denomination was all that money in?" Sam asked.

"Well, we found ten hundred-dollar bills in his pocket, and he had nine of the same in Lou's the night before."

"I mean the first four thousand dollars Skinner lost. Do you know?"

"Do I know?" Sergeant Jones appealed to the ceiling. "I'm a cop, ain't I? It's my job to find out things. When Skinner showed up at Lou's three weeks ago with the first two grand, he had it in tens and twenties. Nothing bigger. Lou says it was a roll could choke a horse, but not a bit of it remained by the time he left. Two grand exactly to the dollar. Same when he showed up with the second two grand."

Sam's sigh was almost audible. It was

likely that Violet hadn't given him that first four thousand dollars. Likely, but not certain.

"Would gambling debts be paid off in comparatively small bills?" Sam said.

"That's it, Mr. Tree. Say Skinner won the dough at the races or somewhere, would they hand him that much in chicken feed? And if they did, how come it was just two grand every time? Last time it was nineteen hundred, but he could've spent a hundred of it. In three weeks he gets two grand three times. What does it sound like?"

Jones waited for an answer. Sam refused to give it.

"Like somebody gave him the dough," Jones declared. "And what sounds crazy as hell — pardon me, Mrs. Tree — what sounds crazy is all along he was broke. He was way behind in rent up to the minute he died. He left a flock of bills and personal debts all over Greenwich Village. And that time at headquarters he had to borrow a quarter from the Skipper for coffee."

"What time at headquarters?"

"Oh, you don't know? Didn't you hear

about it, Mrs. Tree?"

Violet seemed to wake from a bad dream. "About what?"

"Of course it hadn't anything to do with the murder or anything," Jones said. "Seems Skinner was out on one of his drinking parties, and a pal of his — a guy named James Artill — was driving him home. They tore down West Eleventh Street like a bat out of — well, witnesses say he was doing fifty, if a mile. Some kids was playing in the street, and the car killed one of them."

"Was Skinner driving?" Sam asked.

"No. I said it was Artill's car. Artill was cockeyed drunk, so it was open-and-shut manslaughter. I went out for Homicide and took Skinner back as a material witness. He was pretty sober by then. While the Skipper was questioning him, he said he was hungry, so the Skipper sent out for coffee and cake. That's when Skinner couldn't find even a quarter in his pocket."

Eagerly Sam leaned forward. "What happened to Artill?"

"He's out on bail. His trial comes up next week."

"And Skinner was the witness against him!"

Jones laughed through his nostrils. "That would be neat, eh? Artill bumping off the key witness. There's nothing in it."

"I'm talking about blackmail," Sam persisted. "Skinner might have been holding Artill up for money. How long did the accident occur before Skinner lost the first two thousand dollars?"

"A week. No, less. Five days."

"Why can't that be it? Artill paid four — I mean six — thousand dollars and then got tired of paying and decided to get rid of his blackmailer."

"It sounds good, don't it?" Evidently the sergeant was enjoying Sam's excitement. "Only one thing wrong. Skinner was a witness, but not the only one. Several people were in the street when the kid was killed. We know Artill was drunk, and we know he was driving. Skinner couldn't help or hurt Artill one way or the other."

Sam sank back, feeling like a starved man who had had a loaf of bread snatched away from him. Violet's head moved with his shoulder. She was being unnaturally quiet.

Jones dug into his vest for his watch. "Got plenty of work ahead. What I came here for, Mr. Tree: why, with Skinner getting his hands on six grand in three weeks, would he travel all that way to borrow fifty bucks from you?"

"I've been asked that several times."

"Sure. You'll be asked till there's an answer. Remember, a couple of hours later he had nine hundred bucks to lose in a crap game. What do you know about that dough and the other dough he had?"

"Nothing," Sam said. "It's likely that he didn't expect that other money when he came to my store Tuesday night to hit me up for a loan. Then, after he left me, he somehow got his hands on nine hundred dollars or nineteen hundred or whatever it was."

Violet's cheek stirred against Sam's shoulder. He patted her hand to assure her that he wouldn't give her away.

Skeptically Jones pursed his lips. "He wasn't borrowing fifty from you when he could get a lot more any time he wanted."

"Skinner didn't find it easy to bring himself to blackmail. He did it only as a last resort."

"You singing that tune again? I told you it couldn't be James Artill. Who was it then?"

"Ira Pram," Sam said.

"You kidding? Pram's been dead a long time."

Again Violet moved. Sam waited for her to speak. She didn't.

"But if Ira Pram isn't dead," Sam said, "he would have been an excellent victim for blackmail."

"If!" Jones slid off the arm of the chair and started to put on his hat. "Have you any information Pram is alive?"

"No. But if we assume that he is — "

"Assume!" Jones snorted. "I want facts, and you're not giving me any. Instead I waste my time telling you stories and listening to harebrained ideas of yours. You're trying to put me off the track, that's what!"

"What about Earl Durand?" Sam suggested. "Maybe he was being black-mailed by Skinner."

"Don't teach me my business." The

sergeant was annoyed now. "I'll check on Durand, all right, and on you and on everybody else." He said good-by and left.

They listened to the hall door close behind him and to his feet going down the porch steps. Then Violet found her voice.

"What would have happened, darling, if the sergeant hadn't arrived when he did?"

"Georgie would probably have used his gun," Sam said.

"But he didn't have a gun."

"That's right. Durand is too clever to bring weapons around the first time."

"You were very brave, darling." She hugged his arm. "A woman can live with a man for years and not suspect how brave he is."

He pushed her away from him and stood up. "I wasn't brave. I was scared stiff, but I was even more scared of what they were going to do if I did nothing."

"You foolish man," she said airily. "Couldn't you see they were just bluffing?"

He looked at her as if seeing her for

the first time. For a little while her complacency had shown cracks, but now she again exuded that placidity of hers which was an indomitable armor against him and the rest of the world.

"If reality becomes too unpleasant, you simply refuse to believe in it," he said. "You don't believe that Durand and Georgie meant business. You don't believe that Skinner was really murdered and that the police are after his murderer."

"Darling, is that philosophy?"

He took a jerky step toward her, then turned aside to the hall.

"Sam, where are you going?" she called after him. "You haven't had lunch yet."

"I've lost my appetite," he said.

13

Martha Underhill

THE sun lay along the broad avenue with unseasonable warmth. Cars weaved and darted and swooped, fighting for parking space. Shoppers made walking difficult. Absently, as he approached his store, Sam noted that Ted had piled empty egg cases in front of one window. Time and again he had told Ted to take them down to the cellar as soon as they were empty.

"Oh, Sam!" a breathless voice said in his ear.

Again he did not recognize her immediately. She looked younger in a violent red-and-brown-checked cloth coat and with a tam worn rakishly over her brow. In the sunlight her orange lips glistened.

"Don't stare at me like that, honey," Blythe Brice said with a gay laugh. "You saw me dressed up last night."

Bosher, the tailor, was standing in the doorway of his store looking at them. Sam felt himself flush guiltily. "What are you doing here?" he asked Blythe.

"Why, to see you. I could hardly come to your house after last night, could I, honey?"

"Don't call me that," he said testily.

"Of course, they know you on this street." She stood very close to him, with both her hands gripping her handbag in front of her. "Can't we go somewhere?"

"No."

"I mean for a soda or a beer. We didn't have much chance to talk things over last night."

"There's nothing to talk over."

Rouge appeared conspicuously on Blythe's cheek as her natural color receded. "You can't mean you've changed your mind?"

Mrs. Witlow almost ran them down with her baby carriage. Expertly she swung it around Sam. He nodded to her; she was a very good customer, and once she and her husband had been over to the house for bridge. Mrs. Witlow's gaze was fixed with wide-eyed curiosity on Blythe.

"Sam, honey!" Blythe said anxiously and touched his arm.

"For God's sake!" he whispered. "Not here."

"Then let's go somewhere."

Bosher was smiling broadly. It seemed to Sam that everybody in that crowded street was watching him.

"Listen," Sam said. "Why go through the farce of kidding each other? You were trying to play me for a sucker last night, and I was trying to pry information out of you."

"Is that all it meant to you?" She was either a very good actress or that was actually her bruised soul he saw in her eyes.

"Didn't you come to my house to search for the money?"

"I admit I did at first. But Sam, honey — " Her body became a bow, with the arc of it touching him. "Honey, there was nothing phony about last night. I'll go with you anywhere you say."

"Provided I take twenty thousand dollars along with me."

"No. I've been thinking. Even if you haven't a cent."

He should have been flattered, but he wasn't. Ted came outside and looked at him and Blythe and then went back into the store. She was standing too close to him. Sam took a step backward.

"I don't want your money," Blythe was saying. "Honest. I want you."

"Well, I don't want you," he told her brutally. "I've too much to do to stand here talking."

He heard her say hoarsely, "Sam!" and he brushed by her. A few strides took him to Bosher's store. He should have known that there was no hope of getting past the tailor.

"Getting warm, ain't it?" Bosher leered. His myopic eyes were looking past Sam. "That's a nice number. She's been walking up and down here since one, waiting for you, I guess."

In spite of himself, Sam glanced over his shoulder. Blythe hadn't moved. He looked away quickly to avoid meeting her eyes. "Some customers have nerve," he told Bosher. "She wants me to give her stuff without ration stamps."

"Do they ration that now?" Bosher chuckled. "Don't worry, I won't tell your

215

missus. Like I always say, why shouldn't a man have some fun?"

Sam went on. He looked back when he reached the entrance to his store. Blythe was picking her way across the street against a red light. For the first time he noticed that her legs weren't nearly as nice as Violet's, although she was considerably younger.

There was one customer in the store, and the new clerk was waiting on her. His name was Mac something. He was a bowed old man who hardly seemed able to stand on his feet. One had to be satisfied with almost any kind of clerk these days.

Ted Hanley followed Sam into the back room and rocked on the balls of his feet while Sam got into his white coat.

"There's a woman been asking for you," Ted reported. "She was in three or four times. Hot stuff. I'd like to date her up myself."

"What do you mean, yourself?" Sam rapped.

"Gee, you get sore quick, Sam. I didn't mean a thing. She wouldn't say what she wanted or leave her name."

"I saw her outside."

"Oh, you did?"

Sam said savagely: "You know damn well I did. You saw me. Now try taking your nose out of my business."

"Boy, what a temper!" Ted blew his nose mightily. "That clerk stinks. You going to keep him?"

"Till tomorrow, anyway. Stop nagging me and get out."

Ted shook his head dolefully and moved his bulk. Almost at once Sam was contrite. He had no right taking out on Ted the way he felt.

For the next few hours Sam was in work up to his neck. These days, with rationing and priorities and scarcities, a grocer was enmeshed in red tape, and he had been neglecting the business since the day before Skinner's murder.

As he counted ration stamps in the back room, his eyes fell on the barked knuckles of his right hand, and he looked at them in wonder. Back in the familiar surroundings of the store, it did not seem possible that he had knocked down one man and fought with another, for his life, perhaps, and for Violet's life, and that all the other unaccountable and abnormal things that were happening could happen to a man like him.

All at once terror possessed him. He shouldn't have left Violet home alone. Durand and Georgie might come back, or somebody else might come, like that mysterious prowler of Tuesday night. He snatched up his telephone and called his home. There was no answer.

Probably Violet was at the movies again, he thought bitterly as he hung up. He felt tired, helpless. What could he do to protect her? He couldn't stay with her day and night. Perhaps he ought to hire a private detective.

Like Abel Pouch? What about Pouch? He was a very big, fat man, and Ira Pram had been, or was —

Ted's head appeared. "It's very busy," he announced.

Sam nodded and went front to give the two clerks a hand. The five-o'clock rush was jamming the store, and the new clerk wasn't much good. Waiting on customers, Sam could forget a little, relax a little, and he discovered that he was hungry. He stuck cheese between a roll and took a bite of the sandwich whenever he was behind the dairy counter.

Then he saw Martha Underhill standing near the front of the store. He called to her, and she waved the cigarette in her hand. The customer he was waiting on was a crank who took a long time over every item. When he was finished with her, he went over to Martha.

"What's up?" Sam asked.

Martha Underhill crushed the cigarette under her toe. "Earl Durand came to my apartment this afternoon."

"He did?"

"You don't seem surprised."

"He was at our house when we got home."

"Oh." Martha lit another cigarette. He saw now that she was very much disturbed. Her eyes were bloodshot; she had chewed most of the red off her lips. "What did he want?"

A flock of customers pushed into the store. They swirled around Sam and Martha.

"How'd you like to have a bite with me across the street?" he said.

"Fine."

"As soon as I get rid of some of these customers. Do you mind waiting?"

"I have nothing else to do."

He went back behind the counter. Gradually the customers thinned out. He told Ted he was going out for supper and tossed his white coat into the back room and started across the store to Martha.

She was looking out of the store window, and he saw her back tense as she leaned forward to peer into the darkening street. She took a frantic step forward, as if to avoid an invisible assault, and she bumped against Sam. He saw her face then, and color was draining from it.

"What's the matter?" he asked.

Her hand flapped limply to indicate the street. "Sam, why are they coming here?"

Captain Gavigan and Sergeant Jones had alighted from a car at the curb. The sergeant was pausing under the street lamp to light his pipe, and Gavigan waited for him.

"To see me, I guess," Sam said. "They're policemen, you know. You told me Sergeant Jones had been to see you."

"Is that other man also a detective?"

"He's Captain Gavigan."

The two men crossed the sidewalk to the store.

"Martha, is anything wrong?" Sam whispered. "Are you afraid of the police for any reason?"

"What an absurd notion!" Her laughter was strained, mirthless. "Don't mind me, Sam. I've had a fine case of the jitters since Felix was killed. Durand's visit didn't help."

The door opened. Sergeant Jones said something to Gavigan, and Gavigan looked at Martha.

"This is luck," Gavigan said. "Jones tells me you're Martha Underhill. I was going to stop off to see you after I was finished here."

The four of them were bunched at the farther window, out of the crush of customers at the counters, yet part of the swirling hubbub of a busy store. Ted Hanley came around the counter for a can of tomato juice from the floor display and lingered in the hope of overhearing something interesting.

Martha muttered: "I told Sergeant

Jones everything."

"Let me decide that, please," Gavigan said. "Can I have a talk with you now?"

Martha started to bring a fresh cigarette up to her mouth, then changed her mind and let it slip to the floor. "Here?"

"Say I drive you to wherever you want to go. Is that all right?"

Martha's shoulders squared, and she threw a tenuous smile at Sam. "I'm afraid we'll have to postpone our eating date." And Sam thought: *She's afraid of the police. What happened between her and Durand?*

Gavigan said to Jones, "Wait here till I come back," and cupped his big palm lightly on Martha's elbow and steered her out to the street. They got into his car. In the gathering twilight Sam saw him strike a match and hold the light to her cigarette and then to his own.

"What does he want with her?" Sam asked.

Jones shrugged. "Search me. The Skipper is close-mouthed. You never know what he's up to. Like when I reported Earl Durand being in your house, he got all excited and dashed over here."

Behind the dairy counter Ted was whispering to Mac, and the new clerk gaped at Sam and the sergeant.

"How long will Gavigan be?"

"You never can tell," Jones said.

Captain Gavigan wasn't gone long. He came in briskly, plucked the sergeant's sleeve, waved Sam to the rear, cut between two customers, and made the back room without breaking his impatient stride.

"What about Earl Durand?" Gavigan flung at Sam.

"I told the sergeant."

"Tell me."

"He was in my house with that friend of his when we returned from my stepdaughter's wedding," Sam said. "He asked my wife for money; said he needed a stake to get back on his feet. I told him to get out, and he insulted my wife, and I hit him."

"Just like that?"

"In broad outline. Do you want a blow-by-blow account?"

"Save it for your memoirs. Martha Underhill didn't want to come back. She asked me to drop her off at the subway station. Did she come to see you for any special reason?"

"She's a very close friend."

"What scared her? She was nervous all the way to the station."

"I suppose she isn't used to policemen," Sam said.

"Did she tell you that Durand visited her this afternoon?"

"She was starting to when you arrived."

"She claims he called on her for old times' sake," Gavigan said. "How well did she know Durand?"

"You'll have to ask her."

Gavigan pushed back his hat in annoyance. "I did. She says she met him once twenty years ago. That would hardly establish a firm friendship. Skinner, I understand, knew Pram. I wonder if he also knew Durand."

"I wouldn't know," Sam said.

The excited slap of Sergeant Jones's palms sounded like a pistol shot. "Say, why couldn't Durand have bumped Skinner off?"

"Why couldn't seven million other people in the city?" Gavigan growled. "Or somebody who visited New York just for the purpose." He regarded Sam as if looking for something in his face. "So you think Pram is alive?"

"I think he might be."

"You told Jones you know he is."

"No. I said he might be."

"That's right," Jones put in. "He said it was just an idea of his."

Gavigan turned to prowl and realized again that the place was too cramped. "What gave you the idea?"

"Well, Pram's body was never found," Sam said. "Skinner suddenly got his hands on a lot of money. If we assume Pram's alive — "

"Is that all you have, an assumption?" Gavigan cut him short.

"I haven't any facts, if that's what you mean."

"Have you got rumors? Has anybody said they saw him or heard he wasn't killed?"

"Well, no."

"Hell!" Gavigan said. "I can scare up my own ideas and assumptions without traveling out here." He looked at his watch. "After seven. Don't cops ever get time off? Come on, Jones."

When they were gone, Sam at last had a chance to go to the restaurant across the street for his first real meal of the day. He was hungry, but he found himself leaving most of the food. For the first time in his life he seemed to be having trouble with his stomach.

It was eight o'clock when he returned to the store. He sent Ted and Mac home and locked the door and took cash. Tonight the register was sixteen dollars short. There was no doubt now that Ted Hanley was stealing from him and doing it clumsily. The only thing Sam could do about it was to fire Ted, but that would tie him to the store twelve hours a day, and now more than ever in his life he needed freedom of movement. Let Ted steal for a few days longer. What were a few dollars compared to twenty thousand?

The telephone rang. Sam at once recognized the voice which purred over the wire.

"Tree? This is Abel Pouch. I'm

surprised you didn't call at my office today."

"I'm not," Sam said.

"I'd be willing to reduce the amount of my retainer. If we come to terms by tomorrow, three hundred dollars would be all — "

Sam hung up. It was almost eight-thirty. He took everything but the small change out of the register and let himself out of the store.

The only light on in his house was a living-room floor lamp. Going up the porch steps, Sam thought of the time four nights ago when that one lamp had also been on and he had seen Felix Skinner coming out. *I oughtn't leave her alone*, he thought as he entered the hall. And it was still the way it had been Tuesday night, for Violet sprang up from the fireplace when she heard him. But tonight she was not burning Ira Pram's old love letters. She had a heavy automatic pistol in her hand.

Sam stopped dead just inside the doorway. His eyes lifted from the gun to her face. And for a moment, like Tuesday, she was older than her years.

"Sam!" she whispered. "I was going to make a fire, and in the ashes I found this — this gun."

She was afraid. The hard feel of the gun could not be dismissed with a vague word or a placid smile.

"Now you realize that those men meant business," Sam said.

"It's that Georgie's gun. I wasn't watching him when you went out to the hall to admit Sergeant Jones. He must have tossed it into the fireplace."

"He didn't want to be caught by a cop with an illegal weapon on him."

Gingerly Violet held the gun between her thumb and second finger. She stared down at it in horror. "He might have shot you!"

Sam moved toward her. Her defenses were down. Now was his chance to smash his way through to the truth, to make her tell him —

A key turned in the street door.

Violet stiffened. "That's Naomi. She mustn't see this gun. There's no sense frightening her."

Sam swore under his breath. In the hall the telephone rang. He ignored it, watching Violet turn quickly to the mantel above the fireplace and stick the automatic behind the bust of Pallas.

He heard Naomi answer the telephone. "Hello? . . . Hello? . . . Who's this, please?" He listened intently then, the way people always do when a telephone is answered in the house and there is a wait to hear for whom it is. "I can't hear you . . . What? . . . Can't you speak more distinctly?"

Sam went out to the hall. Naomi, her mink coat back over her square shoulders, looked up at him with a puzzled frown. "It sounds like a child. She keeps asking for her mother."

"It must be the wrong number."

Naomi shook her head. "She sounds so queer. That voice — " She handed the handset to Sam. "See if you can understand."

"Hello?" Sam said into the mouthpiece.

Music drifted over the wire, forming a noisy background to a thin muttering in which there were no words. "Hello?" Sam said again. He would have thought the wire was dead if not for the radio playing at the other end. Probably whoever had made the call had left the telephone without replacing it on its cradle. He was about to hang up when the muttering returned, gathering volume like a sluggish motor striving for life.

"Ma," a far-away voice wailed like a lost child. "Ma — "

"This isn't your mother. Whom are you calling?"

"Sa . . . " the voice gasped. "Sa . . . Sa . . . "

His blood ran cold. "Sam? This is Sam speaking."

"Sa . . . Sam . . . Ma . . . Ma . . . "

"Martha!" he cried. "Martha, is that you? What's wrong?"

An unctuous voice was clearly audible, advising women on the proper soapsuds to use for laundering dainty underthings, but there was nothing else on the wire. Sam looked up in terror. Violet had come out to the hall; he saw her only as a blur. Naomi was close, clawing at him.

"Did you say Martha?" Naomi said. "Why did she sound so — "

He shook Naomi off. "Martha, are you there?"

As from a far distance the closer,

smaller voice at the other end of the wire gathered strength, piercing through the spiel of the radio announcer. "I . . . I . . . " Her voice ebbed.

"Martha, for God's sake!"

Her voice exploded. "Pram! Ira Pram! He . . . he . . . "

Then there was nothing at all on the wire, not even the radio.

"Martha!" he pleaded. "What happened to you?"

Violet and Naomi were hurling frantic questions at him. He waved them silent, pressed the receiver furiously against his ear. "Martha, this is Sam. I'm listening. What are you trying to tell me?"

The radio band struck up an insane clamor, but it was not so loud that he would not have heard a voice speaking directly into the mouthpiece. And he did not hear it.

He pressed down the bar and dialed the operator. Violet and Naomi were suddenly silent, and their eyes were glazed buttons watching him. After a small eternity the operator's voice came on.

"Give me the police," Sam said.

In the hall Violet screamed.

14

Strychnine is hell

ON the Queensboro Bridge a cop stopped him. Sam's hands tried to snap the wheel of his car in two as he waited for the beefy motorcycle cop to lumber leisurely over from his motorcycle.

"Trying to murder somebody with your car?" the cop said nastily.

Impatient words of explanation tumbled from Sam's lips.

"Wait a minute," the cop said. "You trying to tell me somebody was murdered and then phoned you?"

"Yes. No, of course not. She had enough life left in her to reach the phone."

"Why didn't you phone the police?"

"I did."

"Then what's your hurry?" The cop's eyes narrowed. "Let's see your license."

It was maddening, but there was no help for it.

"I'm following you up, Mr. Tree," the cop said after he had written down Sam's name and address. "And take it easy."

A crowd was gathered before the apartment house on Riverside Drive. At the curb an ambulance and a number of police radio cars were parked haphazardly. Sam had to go half a block back to West End Avenue to find room for his car. The motorcycle cop stuck to his tail.

"I guess you're right, Mr. Tree," the cop said as they walked to the entrance of the house. "You're coming up with me."

"Of course," Sam said.

There were policemen in the lobby and one in the elevator, and they crowded the seventh floor. A couple of them were planted at the door to Martha's apartment.

"Who's in charge?" the motorcycle cop asked.

"Lieutenant Croon. He's inside."

The motorcycle cop opened the door and nudged Sam in ahead of him. At the farther end of the foyer the telephone table lay on its side; the two parts of the telephone were scattered on the floor. A man in plain clothes rose from his knees; a second man was getting a camera set to take a picture of that section of the foyer. Sam and the motorcycle cop moved around them to the living room.

The air was already thick with smoke and heavy with the breathing of many men in a closed space. Martha wasn't anywhere in sight. Sam looked back into the foyer and saw that the door to Martha's bedroom was closed.

The only one in the room who seemed not to be occupied at the moment was a patrolman trying not to show that he was studying a print of Boucher's 'Three Graces' on the wall. Sam went over to him. "Is Miss Underhill alive?"

"Last I heard she was." The cop eyed him suspiciously. "Say, you ain't a reporter? The lieutenant says no reporters — "

"I'm not a reporter." Sam turned from the cop and saw Grover Langford seated on the couch.

In the crowded room the plump lawyer was curiously isolated and alone.

Mechanically he was wiping his rimless glasses with his handkerchief. His head lifted. He looked straight at Sam and did not see him. His eyes did not seem to see anything.

Sam started toward him. A heavy hand grabbed his arm. "This is the man, Lieutenant," the motorcycle cop said. "His name is Samuel Tree."

Lieutenant Croon had a dour horseface and suspicious eyes. "So you're the one called the police? I sent a man out to your house."

"I'm here," Sam said.

"I can see that. Why did Miss Underhill call you instead of the police?"

"My wife and I are her closest friends."

"What did she say?"

Sam wet his lips. "She managed to gasp out her name, but that was about all."

"Then how did you know somebody had poisoned her?"

"Poison!" Sam said. "I didn't tell the police she had been poisoned. I said she sounded as if she was dying."

Lieutenant Croon's sour scrutiny lay flatly on Sam's face. "I'm told you used the word 'murder.'"

"I don't remember, but I suppose I did."

"Why?"

"Because of Skinner."

"Skinner?"

"Felix Skinner. He was murdered Wednesday night. He was a friend of Martha Underhill."

"Is that right?" Excitement edged Croon's voice. "Say, Cohen, get Captain Gavigan here."

A plain-clothes man nodded and left the apartment.

"Will she live?" Sam asked.

"Strychnine," Croon said as if that were its own answer. "It's hell." He waved toward the couch. "Do you know that man?"

"Very well. He's Grover Langford."

"What about him and Miss Underhill?"

"They're close friends."

"Humph," Croon said. He touched Sam's elbow and steered him to the couch. "Think you're fit to talk now, Mr. Langford?"

Dully Grover raised his head. This time his eyes focused on Sam. "God,

I saw her, Sam!" he moaned. "She was lying there in the hall by the overturned telephone table, and she was twitching all over and her mouth was open, but we couldn't hear anything except that damn radio blaring."

"That's the question I've been asking," Lieutenant Croon said. "When the police came here in response to Mr. Tree's call, they found you in the hall, ringing the bell. How long had you been there?"

Grover fumbled with his glasses. His hands shook so that he had trouble getting the earpieces adjusted. "Hours, it seems now. I guess it was only a couple of minutes. I rang and rang, and she didn't answer."

"Why didn't you go away then?"

"I — well, I heard the radio."

"People sometimes forget to shut off radios when they leave the house."

Grover shivered. "We had a date for nine o'clock. I was sure she was home. Then the two cops came, and they had a pass key and unlocked the door and there she was. Sam!" His voice rose stridently. "She was all tied up in a knot on the floor, twitching and writing, and that

237

radio blaring all the time."

"Take it easy," the lieutenant said.

Sam's legs were wobbling under him. He dropped down beside Grover on the couch. The room was not as crowded as it had been a few minutes ago. The motorcycle cop was gone, and so was the patrolman. A man was scattering dust over the coffee table. The photographer came in from the foyer. Another plain-clothes man, who had been parked in the middle of the room, stepped aside, and Sam saw that he had been protecting a highball glass which lay on the floor near the legs of the coffee table. The photographer got down on his knees to take a picture of it.

The glass which had contained the poison, Sam thought hollowly. Where was the other glass?

The powerful bulk of Captain Gavigan appeared with such whirlwind impatience that he gave the impression of crashing into the room. For a fraction of a second he paused at the doorway to sweep the room with his eyes, then he propelled himself furiously to where Lieutenant Croon stood. His triangular face was taut with urgency. Sergeant Jones tagged meekly after him.

"Can she talk?" Gavigan demanded. "Did she say anything?"

Croon shrugged. "You know strychnine, Captain. It raised hell with her nervous system, like it always does. Even when they're conscious, they often can't speak."

Gavigan's shoulders drooped. "I hoped we'd get a break."

"She's not dead yet," Croon pointed out. "They're giving her belladonna now. It might help. How'd you get here so quick? I sent out a man for you a couple of minutes ago."

Gavigan became aware of Sam and Grover Langford on the couch. "Quite a party, I see." He turned back to Croon. "Jones stopped off at my place to pick me up. He was at headquarters when word came that a woman named Martha Underhill was poisoned, so he figured that our district came in because of Skinner."

"Think there's a connection?" Croon said.

"Perhaps. I wouldn't be surprised if Miss Underhill expected something like this to happen. Something was bothering her when I questioned her a few hours ago, but I couldn't get much out of her."

Sergeant Jones snapped his fingers. "Earl Durand! Miss Underhill said he was up here to see her this afternoon."

"Why didn't he kill her then?" Gavigan said. "If she was afraid of him, why did she drink with him?"

"Anyway, we should pick Durand up and that other guy — that mug with the phony name, Georgie Jones. You want I should go send out an alarm for them?"

"Go ahead, Jones."

The sergeant picked his way across the room.

"Durand didn't poison her," Sam said. "Ira Pram did."

The couch creaked as Grover sat upright.

Gavigan brushed his hat back from his broad forehead. "That's what you said this evening in your store. Another assumption?"

"Now I'm sure," Sam said quietly. "Martha told me."

"Told you how? Before she took the poison? Anyway, how come you happen to be here?"

Lieutenant Croon answered for Sam. "She managed to crawl to the phone and call him. Here's the way I figure it, Captain. Miss Underhill was drinking with the killer at that low table there. He slipped strychnine into her drink. About the only thing strychnine is soluble in, you know, is alcohol. Even then it has a bitter taste, but most whisky tastes bitter anyway, so she — "

"I'm impressed with your knowledge," Gavigan interrupted irritably, "but get down to facts."

"Well, the killer washed his glass and — "

"How do you know he washed it?"

"There's only one glass around. It's still there on the floor where she dropped it."

Gavigan's brow corrugated. "Maybe we've been on the wrong track. Maybe it's suicide."

"With strychnine?" Croon said. "Strychnine is hell, Captain. It's about the worst way to die I can think of."

"Suicides aren't always particular."

"I guess that's so. But if it was suicide, why would she crawl out to the hall and pull over the table so she could get to the phone and call for help?"

"She might have changed her mind about wanting to die."

"Then why would she call Mr. Tree? She'd call for an ambulance. And then the radio was on as loud as it could go. The killer turned it on so nobody in the room could hear her screams, if any. Then he washed his glass, like I said, and went out. We're checking up on who was seen coming in and out of the building this evening, but it won't be easy. Close to fifty families live in this building, and there are two pairs of fire stairs and a side door out, and the killer — "

"For God's sake, get to the point!" Gavigan shouted. "You said she phoned Tree. What did she tell him?"

The lieutenant scowled down at Sam. "He told me she didn't tell him anything. Now he says — "

Sam said: "She managed to blurt out a name. The name was Ira Pram."

"What did she say about him?" Gavigan asked.

"Just his name."

"Damn it, is everybody trying to drive me crazy? I want the exact words."

Sam looked at his knees, knowing that he would never in his life forget that voice over the wire. "She said her name and then mine, and it came out very slowly, almost incoherently. Then she gathered herself for a final effort. She said, 'Pram! Ira Pram!' Then she said the word 'he,' as if to start a sentence about him, but she never got any further."

"Just that name, eh?"

"Isn't that enough?" Sam said. "It's obvious that she was telling me who her murderer was."

Gavigan prowled to a window and looked out at the Hudson River and came back. Every policeman in the room watched him.

"Screwy," Gavigan decided. "Is it your idea that Pram also murdered Skinner?"

"Yes."

"Why?"

"Blackmail," Sam said. "Pram is living under another identity. It would mean a very stiff jail sentence for him if he were discovered."

Gavigan snorted. "Was Miss Underhill blackmailing him too?"

"She must have discovered that he was alive, or perhaps she had known all along that he had not been killed. In either case, she knew that he had murdered Skinner, so he had to get rid of her."

"You have all the answers, haven't you?"

"I've been thinking about them," Sam said.

Lieutenant Croon's sour face turned acid. "Is this a private conference, Captain, or can I find out what it's all about? After all, this is my district."

"You'll get the low-down in good time," Gavigan said gruffly. He brooded down at Sam. "Try thinking about this. Would Miss Underhill, knowing Pram was a murderer, invite him up here and calmly drink with him?"

"Perhaps she wasn't sure he had murdered Skinner. She might have been trying to find out."

Grover Langford snapped out of his coma. "That's it!" he exclaimed, and all the attention in the room shifted to him.

"That's what?" Gavigan asked.

"Martha phoned me tonight at about seven-thirty," Grover said. "She asked me to come here at nine o'clock. I had a business appointment; I said I couldn't make it, but Martha insisted. She sounded quite excited."

"Excited over what?"

"She didn't say. She said she needed me, but that I mustn't come before nine. I couldn't refuse her. It was shortly after nine when I arrived, and — and — " Grover's voice started to break.

"He was ringing the bell when the prowl car got here," Croon explained to Gavigan.

"So?" Gavigan massaged his pointed chin. "Are you in love with Miss Underhill?"

"I have asked her to marry me."

Captain Gavigan took three strides to the center of the room and then back. He tapped Croon's chest. "You know something? How do we know Langford was trying to get into this apartment? Maybe he was leaving. When he got out to the hall, he saw the police coming and he did some quick thinking and turned back to ring the bell."

"Right, Captain," Croon agreed enthusiastically. "I had the same idea."

The couch creaked. Sam did not want to look at Grover. There was too much mixed up in the way he felt — too much pity and sorrow and horror and anger.

"Are you implying that I poisoned Martha Underhill?" Grover's voice had become clear and strong. "Why, I'm mad about that woman. I love her. Isn't that so, Sam?"

"Yes," Sam muttered.

"So what?" Gavigan said. "Some men murder women because they don't love them, some because they do. And you — " His mouth clamped shut and opened slowly. "Hello, Doc."

Dr. Slocum, deputy medical examiner, had entered from the hall. Immediately he was the focal point of all eyes. "You here, Captain?" he said heartily. "Isn't this a bit too far uptown for you?"

"Is she talking, Doc?"

"Miss Underhill? No." Dr. Slocum drew in his lips. "She's gone, Captain."

Every emotion washed out of Sam except anger. He was so angry that he was shaking with it, burning with it as with a fever. Beside him on the couch he heard Grover sob like a woman, but he did not feel sorry for him. There was too much anger in him to allow room for anything else.

Captain Gavigan was saying, "She didn't speak at all, Doc?"

"We tried our best. Brought her back to consciousness several times, but I'm sorry we did. Convulsions of a tetanic nature. The poor thing couldn't utter a sound. It wasn't nice."

"Strychnine is hell," Lieutenant Croon said dismally.

Grover's sobs ceased. He put his head back against the couch and removed his glasses. "How long ago did she take the poison, Doctor?"

"How should I know? Death is supposed to occur in from one to three hours with strychnine — sometimes sooner, sometimes later, depending on a lot of things."

"Would you say she was poisoned before eight-thirty?" Grover persisted.

Dr. Slocum looked at his watch. "Ten-forty now. Two hours ago? Could be. When was she found? After nine? Say between eight and nine. That will have to satisfy you at present."

"That doesn't satisfy Langford," Lieutenant Croon sneered. "He's trying to show that she got the poison too early for him to give it to her. You'll have to try something else, Langford."

Grover stood up. His glasses dangled from one hand; his round face showed no sign that he had been weeping. He was a lawyer fighting to protect a client, and the client was himself.

"Sam, what time did Martha phone you?" he said.

"Close to nine o'clock. I'm not sure."

"That's about right," Croon agreed sourly. "Mr. Tree phoned the Queens precinct at nine-five." He turned his head to a man in a police sergeant's uniform. "What time did you get here, Bill?"

"You mean get the radio call?"

"I mean what time did you get up here in the hall outside and see Langford ringing the bell?"

"Nine-fourteen," Bill said.

"Then that's that," Grover said triumphantly. "Martha couldn't have called Sam while the murderer was in the apartment. Say she phoned Sam at five to nine, or even exactly at nine. Say it took her no time at all to crawl out to the foyer and knock down the telephone and get the number after the murderer left. That would still leave ten or fifteen minutes before I arrived. If I were the murderer, wouldn't I have left at once instead of hanging around? Besides, the elevator operator knows me. He'll tell you that he brought me up after nine."

Grover replaced his glasses, and his eyes gleamed behind them. Sam's anger reached out to include him. *Damn all lawyers!* he thought. *They prefer mental gymnastics to decent grief.* That wasn't quite fair, he knew, because Grover was fighting for his life, but Sam wasn't in the mood to be fair.

Captain Gavigan had moved away, prowling with that nervous aimlessness which rasped Sam's nerves. He returned to the couch. "You could have forgotten something and come back."

"Or you were handing yourself an alibi

by returning up the elevator," Croon put in.

Grover's face creased in a scornful smile. "Isn't it obvious what happened? As Violet's closest friend since childhood, Martha had known Pram well. As Sam suggested, she might have been aware all along that Pram was not dead. She had an appointment with him tonight. Obviously she was up to something. Perhaps she was trying to find out if Pram really murdered Felix Skinner, as she suspected. That was why she was so anxious to see me after Pram left. I was her — well, we were practically engaged to be married. Besides, I am an attorney who could advise her. But Pram, while drinking with her, slipped the poison into her drink, and when I arrived — "

He dropped down on the couch, abruptly the grief-stricken lover replacing the calculating lawyer.

"So we're back to Pram," Gavigan said. "Where's the proof?"

"Martha's phone call to Sam."

"That's no proof. That's only — "

A detective appeared in the foyer doorway. "A woman who says she's

250

Mrs. Tree is on the phone. She says she wants to speak to her husband."

Sam rose.

"Wait!" Gavigan snapped. "How does she know you're here?"

"She was at home when Martha called."

Gavigan muttered, "Okay," and Sam went out to the foyer. The telephone table had been replaced upright.

"Sam?" Violet's voice came shrilly. "Naomi and I are going crazy here. We've been calling and calling, but the line was always busy."

"Martha is dead," he said.

"O God! How did she die?"

"Ira Pram poisoned her."

She was silent so long that he thought she had hung up. Then she said: "Did they catch him?"

"Nobody knows where Pram is. Do you, Violet?"

"I swear I don't."

"All right," he said. "I don't know when I'll be home."

He hung up and returned to the living room. Grover was off by himself on the couch; again he was absently cleaning his glasses. Captain Gavigan and Lieutenant Croon stood near the foyer doorway.

"I don't advise it," Gavigan was saying. "Langford is a lawyer and a damn shrewd one. He'll hogtie you with writs."

"Maybe Miss Underhill was cheating on him with somebody else," Croon said. "She had dough and this swell apartment. Those kind of dames always — " He saw Sam listening in and scowled. "I'll be ready for your statement in a little while."

"I made my statement," Sam said.

"Not in writing."

Sam started toward the couch, then turned to Gavigan. "Do you intend to look for Ira Pram?"

"Still got Pram on the brain," Gavigan said wearily. "Naturally we don't pass up any angle. What did he look like?"

"He was a very big man. Tall and fat. Close to three hundred pounds, I'm told, though that was in 1923. He was dark. The Massachusetts police might have a fairly complete description of him."

Gavigan passed his fingers through his hair. "So we look for a man who's big and fat — "

252

"And about fifty years old."

"And about fifty, who's been dead for fifteen of those years."

"He's alive," Sam said.

"You sound pretty sure."

"I am sure," Sam said.

15

Portrait of an angry man

SOFT weeping came from the living room when Sam entered the house. He knew that it was Naomi. *Violet never weeps,* he thought in bitter anger.

They had waited up for him. They sat opposite each other in front of the dead fireplace, flanking the black and hideous raven on the mantel. Now more than ever it looked like a bird of evil omen. Naomi lifted her face from her handkerchief and tried to talk, but no speech could get past her sobs. This was her wedding night, and her husband lay wounded in a hospital and the woman who had been a second mother to her was dead.

Violet was dry-eyed, but when she looked at him he understood for the first time that she had her own ways of weeping. What he saw in her face frightened him. For a moment compassion overlapped his anger, but only for a moment.

"Go to bed, Naomi," he said.

Surprise stopped her sobs. He had never before spoken to her like that. "I — I'm all right," she mumbled irrelevantly.

"Go to bed."

Violet frowned at him. "She's not a child, Sam. You've no right to order her like — "

"That's all right, Mother." Naomi got to her feet and tried to smile through her tears. "He wants to speak to you alone. Isn't that right, Sam?"

"Yes."

Naomi went out quickly. Her sobs broke again as she ascended the stairs. Violet sat small and crumpled in the easy chair, looking up at Sam in a kind of terror.

"Did she suffer much, Sam?"

"She's dead. That's all that matters." He took a breath. This wouldn't be easy, but more than his anger was making him do it. "You killed her, Violet."

"Sam, you're mad! I was home all the time. You know I was."

"I don't mean you gave her the poison." He was speaking slowly, carefully. "I thought perhaps you had murdered Felix Skinner. It was hell. Now I know you didn't, because Skinner's murderer murdered Martha, and that person is Ira Pram."

"Then why did you say — "

"Martha would be alive now if you had been honest with me."

"No, darling! Dear God, don't say that!" She was shaken more than he had ever thought she could be. "What could I have done?"

"You could have told me from the beginning that Ira Pram was alive. If he had been arrested for Skinner's murder, he could not have gotten at Martha."

"But I couldn't have helped." She was begging him to understand. "I don't know where he is, what name he is using, how to find him. I learned that he was alive only when Felix told me."

"Didn't you ask him for proof?"

"Felix said he could take me to him, but I didn't want to go. I was afraid. Ira might cause trouble; there would be court complications about having two husbands. He was dead; he had to stay out of my life."

"And so you believed Skinner?"

"Whatever Felix was, he wasn't a liar."

"Only a blackmailer," Sam said.

"Yes, he was driven to that finally. And I had to give him the money. Don't you see, darling, that I couldn't have a scandal? It was so important that Naomi and Doug be married before his leave was over, and anything at all might have stopped it."

Sam let his exhausted body sink into the chair Naomi had occupied. He said musingly: "Tuesday night Skinner came to me first for money. I suppose even he did not find it easy to blackmail the woman who had been his wife. He must have rationalized it to himself: try me first, and if he couldn't shake anything loose from me, it would serve me right if he got it from you." He looked up. "Why did you burn Pram's letters after Skinner left?"

"So you know about that too! You can imagine how upset I was. I wanted to get rid of everything I had of Ira's."

"And you were afraid to leave samples

of his handwriting around which might conceivably be compared with his present signature."

"I've got to make you understand, darling." Her body was bent forward, her hands clasped as if in supplication. "You think I should have known that Ira murdered Felix. But why? Felix knew all sorts of unpleasant people. I've read of gamblers being murdered because they don't pay their gambling debts. It could have been almost anybody. And I was afraid. If I said anything at all, it might have come out that Felix was blackmailing me, and the police would have believed that I had killed him. Even you did, darling."

"I tried not to believe it."

"But you did."

He believed her. He knew now what she had gone through, and his anger melted.

"This afternoon you had proof that Pram was most likely the murderer," he said. "When Sergeant Jones told us about that other four thousand dollars, it was plain that Skinner had been blackmailing Pram also."

"Yes. But by then you knew that too. I had no more information than you did."

He started to rise, to go to her and comfort her and tell her how much he loved her. Then he sank back in the chair, realizing that so far she had told him nothing he did not already know.

"The real reason you couldn't confide in me," he said, "was that then you'd have to tell me about the money."

"What money?"

He was back on the merry-go-round. It had made a complete turn and was starting over again. Anger rose hot in his throat.

"Pram's money, of course," he shouted. "You knew I suspected you of murder, but you didn't tell me then what you've just told me. You kept fighting me, and you're still fighting me. What about the money?"

She curled deep in her chair and said nothing.

"You're afraid I'll make you give it back because it's not your money," he said. "Because it's a stolen money." He strode to her chair and stood over her in quaking rage.

She put up a hand in a helpless gesture of defense, then let it drop to her lap. "Darling — " she said and stopped.

"Where is it?"

"Darling, there's no money."

"Violet, why don't you trust me?"

She opened her mouth and closed it without a word. He stood watching her, waiting for her to make up her mind. And when he saw her defenses go up in the form of that protective placidity of hers, he knew that he was once more licked.

"I don't know what you're talking about, darling." She stood up. "I'm going to bed."

"Another headache?" he sneered in angry helplessness.

"It's very late, darling," she said. "You'd better come too."

For a little while after she was gone he stood where he was. *I ought to search the house*, he thought. Yesterday he had searched casually, under mattresses and all the other usual and obvious hiding places. The money must be extremely well hidden, or Blythe Brice would have found it. She had had plenty of time and opportunity.

His eyes fell on the red brick fireplace, and all at once excitement stirred in him. Why not? A loose brick was traditional and close at hand.

Five minutes later he rose from the fireplace, dusting his trousers. There was no loose brick. He went to bed.

* * *

Rain beat against the windows. Sam lay listening to it and wondered what time it was, and he thought: *She said Cape Cod*. For a bewildered moment it meant nothing to him, and then he remembered. It was a thought that had struck him between waking and sleeping some time during the restless night in bed.

Violet had told Ira Durand that the money was somewhere on Cape Cod. At the time Sam had dismissed the statement because it had sounded like another of Violet's glib evasions. But why not Cape Cod? She had visited her mother recently and on her return home had had money to give to Felix Skinner. And she had made a trip there a couple of weeks before she had bought the mink coat for Naomi.

He reached for his watch on the bedside table. Ten to seven; the rain had delayed the dawn. The store opened at eight. There was no hurry, and he liked to linger in the soft warm curve of Violet's body. But not this morning. He slipped away from Violet and out of bed and put on slippers and bathrobe. Violet stirred fitfully, but she did not awaken.

Naomi heard him open the door to her room. Dawn was pushing through the curtain of rain, and Naomi was a blurred shape rearing up from the cover. She snapped on her lamp.

"Sam, is anything wrong?"

"It's seven," he said. "I thought I'd look in to see how you were sleeping."

"I've hardly slept." She sank back. "Martha has always been so good to me. And Felix too. And I keep thinking that my father killed them. At least that's what you told Mother over the phone."

"Did she tell you that?"

"She refused to talk about it, but I was standing next to her when she phoned you at Martha's, and I heard you."

He sat down on the bed and lifted her hand between his palms. "Do you remember your father?"

"Not at all. That's odd, because I was five when he died."

"He wasn't home often."

"I suppose that's it. You're sure he's alive?"

"Yes."

"But where is he?" she said. "What does he call himself?"

"I don't know. It's even possible that he's somebody we've seen and spoken to."

"But that can't be. Mother would have recognized him."

He watched rain slide down the window. "That's so. I guess he's a stranger then."

"Sam, what you mean is that Mother knows who he is and won't tell." Her fingers became hooks between his palms. "You're wrong."

"I didn't mean that."

Naomi brushed her wild, dark hair

263

from her face and turned her head to watch the rain also. "I promised not to ask questions or even think thoughts. I know you wouldn't hurt Mother for the world. I'm sure whatever you do will be to protect her."

"Yes." He patted the back of her hand, straightening her fingers on his palm. "What did Violet do with the furniture she and Ira Pram bought when they were married? I understand that Felix Skinner refused to have it in his house. Is it still in storage?"

"She gave the furniture to Grandma."

"So it's in East Wiston?"

"Yes. Mother took the furniture out of storage shortly after she and Felix were separated. She was far behind in rent, and the storage place was going to sell it at auction. I was about thirteen then, but I remember Mother worrying about it. She had held onto the furniture all those years, though it was probable that she would never be able to use it. Mother is like that about her possessions. Even then, when we were so very poor, she hated to let the furniture go. Finally Grandma solved it by saying she would pay what was due the storage warehouse in return for the furniture, so Mother let her have it."

That had been seven or eight years ago, yet Violet had started to spend a lot of money only in the last two years. But that could be explained. She hadn't come across the money until two years ago.

Naomi was eyeing him curiously. "Why didn't you ask Mother? She knows much more than I about the furniture."

He couldn't tell her that he didn't want to put Violet on guard or that he couldn't trust Violet to tell him the truth. He avoided an answer by asking a question. "Did you know that Felix Skinner was involved in an accident several weeks ago?"

"You mean when that poor boy was killed?" she said. "Felix wasn't involved. He merely happened to be riding in the car. I went to the movies with him a few days later, and he mentioned it. He said they kept him in the police station half the night."

"Was he upset about the accident?"

"Naturally. He was a very sensitive man. He was very nervous telling me about it, though a few days had passed since it happened." She frowned. "Sam, what's the reason for all these questions?"

"You said you believe I know what I'm doing."

Gravely she nodded. "Sam, the doctor said Doug will be able to leave the hospital Sunday morning. His leave was extended, of course — sick leave. He's going to stay here at the house for a while."

"That's fine." He patted her hand, feeling much like a sentimental old father, and stood up. "Try to get some sleep."

Sam went downstairs and dialed Ted Hanley's number. The bell rang a long time before it awoke Ted.

"Ted, I want you to open the store again this morning. And I won't be in today at all."

"On a Saturday!" Ted exclaimed incredulously.

"You'll have Mac to help you."

"He stinks."

"You'll manage," Sam said. "And don't be surprised if I'm not in Monday either. I might be gone for a few days."

"You're taking a trip?"

"Yes."

Gray daylight seeped into the bedroom while Sam dressed. He fetched Violet's little overnight bag from the hall closet and tossed in a change of clothing.

"Are you leaving me, Sam?" Violet asked quietly from the bed.

He had not known that she was awake. She was propped up on one elbow, her pale eyes solemnly watching him.

"I wouldn't run out on you now, though Lord knows you deserve it." He dropped a comb and toothbrush into the bag, then added: "Even if I didn't love you."

"Then where are you going?"

"I need a rest." He snapped the bag shut.

"Sam, answer me."

"How do you like not getting answers?" He straightened up and looked at her, wondering if he should kiss her good-by.

"Don't tell me it's another woman!" That was supposed to be said mockingly, but Violet didn't quite bring it off. Her voice sounded as if it were stuck in her throat.

"It might be." His anger lay between them; for the first time in his life he did not want to kiss her. "Don't expect me back for a couple of days."

As he closed the bedroom door behind him, he expected her to call after him. She didn't.

He was out on the porch when he remembered something and returned to the house. Georgie's automatic was still behind the bust of Pallas where Violet had put it last night. He slid back the magazine. There were only five cartridges, not seven as Georgie had said. He opened the bag and pushed the gun between a pair of pajamas and a shirt.

16

A Study in Ethics

HATLESS and without an overcoat, Sam walked in the drizzle to a restaurant across the street from his bank and breakfasted leisurely. When the bank opened, he deposited the store receipts of the day before and then withdrew six hundred dollars in fifty-dollar bills. His store was only a block away, but he did not stop in.

One hour and forty minutes remained before his train departed from Grand Central. He had counted on that. He took the subway to Chambers Street, walked two blocks east, and entered one of the shabbier and smaller office buildings.

Part of the seventh floor was chopped up into cubbyholes, each individually rented by struggling lawyers and accountants and such, sharing a common switchboard and stenographer. The haggard girl-of-all-work left her typewriter in the lobby and plugged in the switchboard. "Mr. Pouch says you should go right in. It's the fourth door on the right."

Swinging his bag, Sam walked down the narrow, windowless hall. Black letters with gilded borders on the fourth door read: 'ABEL POUCH, CONFIDENTIAL INVESTIGATIONS.' He pushed the door open, and all of the cubbyhole appeared to be filled by Abel Pouch. A skimpy desk stood in the middle of the room, yet Pouch was squeezed, with no room to spare, between it and the window at his back. A second chair and a steel letter file completed the furnishings; there wouldn't have been space for anything else.

Pouch did not rise to greet Sam. His little eyes twinkled in their fatty sockets. "I am not a betting man, Tree," he cooed, "but this morning one would have got anybody ten that you would be here before noon." He indicated four newspaper clippings on his desk. "You see, I am on my toes. These clippings are from the morning papers, and they concern the tragic murder of Martha Underhill."

270

"I read them all," Sam said, "and they give little information."

"Very little," Pouch agreed. "The murder occurred too late for complete coverage by the morning papers; besides, there is important war news today. It is obvious, also, that the police are not eager to give out information. There is no mention that this murder and the murder of Felix Skinner are connected. Indeed, there is a strong hint that Martha Underhill committed suicide."

"The police know better."

"Of course, but they like to provide themselves with an out. If the murder is not solved, they can write it off as suicide and keep their record clean. Do the police suspect that she was murdered by Ira Pram?"

"Do you?" Sam said.

The loose folds of Pouch's face gathered themselves into a vast smile. "Suspect is a mild word." He dipped a hand into a pocket; it came up with an apple. "Sit down, sit down. Make yourself comfortable."

A woman's cloth coat was thrown over the back of the chair, and a handbag lay on the seat. Pouch rose quicker than Sam had imagined a man his size could and sidled around the desk and gathered up the coat and handbag. "Ah, that girl, that girl," he muttered vaguely as he placed them on the desk.

Sam sat down. She must have been in here when the switchboard operator had announced him. The hall was a dead end, so likely she hadn't left the building. Behind him a door connected this cubbyhole with the next one.

The apple crunched between Pouch's massive jaw. "You have the money, of course?"

Sam counted out six of the fifty-dollar bills and dropped them on the desk. Pouch separated them with a thumb and then leaned back in his swivel chair against the sill of the window at his back.

"That is only three hundred dollars."

"You came down to three when you phoned me last night," Sam said.

"That was before Martha Underhill was murdered. It complicates the case. I shall want a six-hundred-dollar retainer."

Sam placed four more fifties on the desk.

"That's better," Pouch beamed. "Five hundred it is." He gathered up the money and stuck it into his wallet, which he replaced in his inside jacket pocket. "Now you're my client."

"What about a contract?"

Pouch brushed the notion aside with his hand. "Give me what you think my investigation is worth when I submit my final report. Precisely what happened last night in Martha Underhill's apartment?"

"Wait a minute," Sam said. "I'm the one who's paying for information. Who is Ira Pram?"

"That, of course, remains to be investigated."

Sam stared hard at him. "So you don't know?"

"I never said I did."

"Not in so many words, but you — " Sam sat back, checking his temper. "What's your proof that Ira Pram is alive?"

"I had a talk with one of the detectives who made the arrest back in 1929. A man named Thomas Marvin, who is now living on his pension near Lynn. He was rather evasive as to just what happened when Pram was ostensibly killed. It was extremely simple for me to deduce what actually took place. I have mentioned that policemen like to have an out in order to keep their record clean. Put yourself in the position of those detectives. They had allowed a man to escape; the consequences to them would be serious. What easier way could they clear themselves than by stating that they had shot him dead?"

"So you think they lied about shooting him and seeing him go under the water and not coming up."

"I am convinced that the detectives were very far from certain that Ira Pram had not escaped unscathed. I go so far as to doubt that Pram ran into the bay at all. We have only two detectives' word for it, and under the circumstances their word is not to be taken."

The little office was growing dark with the sweep of rain between tall buildings. Pouch sat in semi-shadow, his hips spilling over either arm of the swivel chair.

"In other words," Sam said, "you don't know a thing. You got that five hundred dollars out of me on a bluff."

Pouch looked grieved. "I am just at the beginning of my investigation. Pram is not an easy man to locate. He was never arrested, you know. There are no fingerprints of him. As far as I could learn, no photographs. Your wife hasn't one by chance?"

"No. What makes you sure Pram is the murderer?"

"Did I say that? I distinctly remember my words. I asked if the police suspect if Pram is the murderer. Incidentally, so far I have not brought up the matter of a certain twenty thousand dollars."

Sam plucked at a corner of the woman's coat on the desk. "What about it?"

"I have learned that Earl Durand's share of the loot, which was found in his place in Boston, consisted wholly of one-hundred-dollar bills. I have also learned that Pram's share was never found. Finally, I have ascertained that some weeks ago a certain Mrs. Tree, of your address, purchased a mink coat from a New York furrier and paid for it with eighteen hundred-dollar bills."

"You get around," Sam said dryly.

Pouch grinned modestly. "I try to satisfy my clients. Mr. Douglas Faulcon, Senior, paid me well to investigate Mrs. Tree. That included such matters as the purchase of an expensive coat for her daughter. Those eighteen one-hundred-dollar bills interest me profoundly."

"Why?"

"Oh, come now, my dear man. I recognize what you are up against. It was, of course, a crime to withhold Pram's loot from the police. But there are ways out. To find those ways and means is why you have hired me. Needless to say, I am helpless without your complete confidence."

"Why should I tell you?"

"Because you need my experienced help." He reached into his pocket for a second apple and purred: "It should be obvious that that much money can provide adequate motivation for murder."

Sam fought his anger. "Aren't you trying blackmail too early in your game?"

"My dear man — "

The window behind Pouch was open

a couple of inches from the bottom, and a sudden gust of wind swirled rain on his back. Ponderously Pouch rose and pushed his chair into a corner to give him room to get at the window. It stuck.

Sam stood up, staring across the dim office at Pouch's great spread of hips and buttocks as he bent over to force down the window. There had been hips as broad as that bending over another window Tuesday night. But that other room had been dark except for the glow from a distant street lamp, and Sam had been groggy from a blow on the head, and Abel Pouch was not the only big, fat man.

The window closed with a bang. Pouch wiped his brow with the back of his hand and sank into his swivel chair. "I wonder why somebody doesn't invent windows which do not stick?"

Sam stepped in front of the desk and flipped over the woman's handbag which lay beside the coat. Silver initials on the other side read: 'B.B.' But that was not surprising, and he still could not be sure about Pouch.

"The windows of my house also stick," Sam said.

Pouch brought his apple slowly up to his teeth. "Windows are doubtless a fascinating subject, but we have more important business to discuss."

"Windows are important," Sam said. "Especially my living-room windows, which squeak. I'd also like to talk about flashlights used as clubs."

"I — " Pouch looked across the desk at Sam and shrugged. "So you recognized me? I did not think you had a good look at me that night."

"I didn't." Sam laughed with an anger that was somehow exhilarating now. "You're a hell of a detective. I wasn't sure it was you until you just now told me."

Pouch clucked appreciatively. "A nice piece of work, Tree, if I say so myself. No hard feelings, I trust. After all, I was working for Mr. Faulcon at the time. It proves what a thorough investigator I am."

"You'd finished working for Faulcon by Tuesday. You were on your own then." Sam fingered the cloth coat on

278

the desk. "I thought I recognized this coat when I came in. I always had an idea that Blythe was tied up with the prowler. Did Blythe duck into that adjoining office when the switchboard girl told you I was outside?"

Pouch's teeth came down hard on the apple. "Blythe? I know of no — "

The door to the adjoining cubbyhole swung open. "Stow it, Abel," Blythe Brice said. Three steps took her to Sam. She tucked an arm through his and leaned intimately against him. "You've got me wrong, Sam, honey. I meant every word I said."

Her face was tilted up, her orange lips not far from his own. The grayness of the room took the garishness out of her make-up. Her tam sloped saucily over one eye. She was, at that moment, considerably more attractive than yesterday in the sunlight.

"Isn't Pouch your boy friend?" Sam said.

"That fat slob!"

"Now, Blythe!" Pouch protested with ruffled dignity. "There's no need to be insulting."

279

"He's just a broken-down shyster I do odd jobs for," Blythe told Sam. "I helped him investigate your wife for Faulcon."

"Nice work," Sam commented. "It includes outraging people's hospitality and searching their homes and making love to any man from whom you think you can pry useful information."

"Don't say that, honey. I was just telling Abel what a sweet man you are and that he should lay off you. Wasn't I, Abel?"

"I would say you've made a conquest, Tree."

Sam yanked his arm away from her and put both hands flat on the desk. "You weren't interested primarily in that retainer, though it's money and you like any kind of money. You're after Pram's money, if it exists. It's stolen money to begin with, and if it's stolen again whoever had it couldn't very well complain to the police."

With pudgy fingers Pouch massaged the uneaten half of the apple. "Do you imagine that I am so absurd as to believe that an appreciable sum of that twenty thousand dollars would remain after fifteen years? Or that you would leave such a sum around in the house loose for the taking?"

Sam stood erect and wet his lips. Pouch had something there. Or did he?

"That part came later," Sam said. "You'd finished your job for Faulcon. During it you got the notion that Pram might still be alive. Or maybe all along you knew more about Pram than you pretend."

"Just what do you mean by that last remark?"

"Let it ride for the present. Let's say you merely suspected and that it would pan out nicely if you proved to be correct. I owned a house and a store; I looked like a good victim. You sent Blythe into my household to keep her eyes and ears open. But you're thorough, as you boasted, or perhaps you didn't trust Blythe completely. Even while she was on the way, you decided to have a look for yourself. There might be letters or something. What do you crooks call it — casing the joint?"

"My dear man, I won't sit here and listen — "

"You'll sit and listen," Sam said. "Blythe overheard Skinner asking my wife for money. Your field broadened when Skinner was murdered that night. There were several angles for you to play. And if I became your client, I might confide in you. Blackmail would be subtle; you'd call it a fee for keeping information confidential. When that didn't work out, you instructed Blythe to make love to me."

"I think," Pouch purred, "I shall sue you for defamation of character."

Blythe laughed harshly. "His character can't be defamed. Most of what you said, honey, is right, though not all of it. And he had nothing to do with what happened between us the other night. I swear it."

"I see," Sam said. "You decided to work on your own."

"No, honest. Maybe at first, but yesterday I realized I couldn't be away from you. That's why I hung around your store, waiting for you. I don't want money or anything. All I want is you."

Sam looked into her face and saw with a shock what he had seen yesterday in the street — that she probably meant it. He was annoyed and mildly disgusted with himself for being partly responsible. He said: "You knew what Pouch was sending you into my house after."

She swayed toward him, as if her body were reaching for his. "This investigating business is all spying anyway, except that Abel is worse than the others. And I'm not saying I'm any better." Her perfumed breath was on his cheek. "You're the first real thing that ever came into my life. Don't believe anything, but you've got to believe that."

"A very touching scene," Pouch observed, popping the remainder of the apple into his mouth.

Sam's watch said that he had thirty-five minutes to make his train, and it would take at least twenty minutes to get up to Grand Central. He leaned pugnaciously across the desk toward Pouch. "I want my five hundred dollars."

"My dear man, a retainer is a retainer."

"You got it through a bluff."

Pouch shrugged. "You misunderstood. You thought you could purchase information from me. You may dispense with my services if you are so inclined, but ethically the retainer — "

"My kind of ethics demands my money back."

Pouch thumped his vast belly. "Blythe, I would appreciate it if you would remove yourself from my office with your swain."

Sam pushed Blythe aside and went around the desk. His shoulders were hunched forward, his head down, and his accumulated rage was centered on the man overflowing that chair like an obscene idol. Pouch's small eyes widened in terror. He started to rise, and as he did so, he pulled open the top drawer of his desk and dug a hand inside. Before Pouch was all the way on his feet, Sam hit him in the jaw. Pouch sat down again. His rear caught only the edge of the swivel chair, and it rolled away from under him to the wall, and Pouch kept going down all the way to the floor. The office shook.

Momentarily Sam's arm was numb with the jolt of the blow. He said savagely: "That was for socking me on the head with your flashlight." His glance stopped at the open desk drawer at his right arm. A snub-nosed automatic pistol lay there.

"I wasn't going to shoot you," Pouch whined. "It was only to hold you off." The mass of him was wedged on the floor between the desk and the side wall, and his back was against the chair. Both his hands held his jaw. His eyes blazed with malice, but carefully he kept it out of his voice. "You have a sweet wallop there, Tree. I didn't think it of you."

"I didn't either," Sam muttered. In two days he had knocked down two men, a little one and a big one, and he had fought a third. Twice in that time he might have been shot, and that was only part of what was happening to a man to whom nothing dramatic had ever happened before. He said again: "I want my money."

"This is outrageous," Pouch protested thickly. "Blythe, phone for a policeman."

She laughed. On the other side of the desk she stood completely relaxed now, and she smiled at Sam. "You're quite a man, honey."

Sam sucked his split knuckles. He was

only a middle-aged grocer who wanted to be let alone, and nobody would let him alone. He turned back to Pouch and bent over him. Pouch shrank against the chair, trying to make himself small. He clawed feebly as Sam ripped open his jacket. Sam slapped him sharply. Pouch's hands fell away; he blubbered like a child. Sam extracted the wallet and then went back to the front of the cubbyhole.

"This is robbery," Pouch wailed.

There were three singles in the wallet beside the ten fifties. Sam removed the fifties and dropped the wallet on the desk and picked up his bag.

"Honey, if you'll just let me talk to you in private — " Blythe's fingers dug into his arm.

Roughly he shook her off and went to the door. Pouch was lumbering up to his feet. His face was formless gray putty. "We haven't seen the last of each other," he said heavily.

"We definitely haven't," Sam said.

Blythe was picking up her coat and handbag. Quickly Sam closed the door. Through it he heard Pouch bellow: "Get out of here, you dirty little double-crossing sneak!"

"You couldn't keep me here, you — "

Blythe said more, but Sam lost her voice as he hurried along the hall.

17

East Wiston

A FLUFFY layer of snow added to the picture-postcard effect of the house. Its gabled whiteness glistened in the late afternoon sunlight. Distantly, between scattered houses, a blue-gray patch of Cape Cod Bay was visible.

Sam opened the gate of the white picket fence. Above his head a sign, bearing the one word, 'TOURISTS,' swung squeakingly from a post. That, too, was authentic Cape Cod.

It had ceased snowing only recently, yet the walk between the gate and the porchless front door was trodden hard by many feet. Sam lifted the knocker. There was no immediate answer, so he stepped into the parlor. The heavily curtained windows blocked out all but a trickle of light. In another part of the house he heard Mrs. Wilson say: "Poisoned!

288

I can't believe it!"

Sam put down his bag and went through the arched doorway into the dining room. His mother-in-law was speaking into the telephone. She looked over her shoulder and said to him, "Why, Samuel, it's you!" and then into the mouthpiece, "I'll call you back, Clara," and hung up. She peered past Sam. "Where's Violet?"

"Home."

"You came alone?"

"I hope I'm welcome even without Violet," he said good-humoredly.

"What a thing to say, Samuel! Of course you're welcome." Mrs. Wilson's head cocked birdlike; there was much of the bird about her. She was as short as Violet, but much thinner, with the bony hardness of age, which made her tiny. Her movements were quick and impulsive, her eyes bright and inquisitive and almost always excited. "Samuel, is there anything wrong?"

"I've been working too hard in the store," he told her, "and Violet suggested that I come here for a short rest. Violet had to stay home to help look after the store."

Her lips compressed, disappearing against each other. "That was Clara Atkins on the phone. She told me that poor Martha was poisoned. She said it's all in the East Wiston *Post*. It can't be true."

"I'm afraid it is," he said.

"Poor Martha! She was a fine girl. I can't see why she never got a husband." Her tone sharpened. "Though I can't approve of my own daughter's choices — except, of course, you, Samuel. You're a respectable, upstanding businessman. But first Ira Pram and then Felix Skinner! My daughter having married two men who were shot! It was enough of a disgrace when that terrible thing happened to Ira. And now people are talking about nothing but Felix."

Her flow of words washed over Sam without being quite heard. He was looking at the dining-room set. He had seen it a number of times before, but this was the first time he really looked at it. It was expensive bird's-eye maple. How does one hide money in furniture? By unscrewing the leg of a table or something similarly melodramatic? Two hundred one-hundred-dollar bills would take up considerable space

"Samuel, are the police keeping Violet in New York?"

"What?" he said. "Violet has nothing to do with the murders."

"Of course not. What ever put such an idea into your head?"

"You were the one who said — "

Mrs. Wilson's mind was like the rest of her, in constant impulsive movement. "What did Violet ever do to deserve husbands like Ira and Felix?"

"It was just bad luck."

"Why should it happen to Violet? Like I was saying to Mr. Darrow — he's a guest who came this morning — such a nice quiet man, though I can't say I like that other one, Mr. Smith — he's so big and ugly — "

"Isn't this the wrong season for tourists?" Sam said.

"It's not like the summer, of course, when I have both upstairs rooms and the hall room filled all the time. These two men who came this morning have both upstairs rooms. You'll have to sleep in the hall room, which used to be the storage room until I started taking in tourists after Martin died. Of course it isn't as comfortable."

"That's all right," he said. "Is this the furniture which used to belong to Violet?"

"Every scrap of it. There was so much that I had to get rid of everything I had in the house. Most of my own furniture was shabby, but there were some nice pieces, like my gorgeous mahogany whatnot and my — "

A step sounded on the stairs. Mrs. Wilson turned to the hall at the rear, where the staircase ran down from the two bedrooms in the upstairs half-story. Sam felt his muscles bunch. *It can't be*, he thought.

But it was. The gorilla form of Georgie Jones, or whatever his real name was, entered from the hall. He looked at Sam and removed his cigar from his mouth.

"Are you going out, Mr. Smith?" Mrs. Wilson said. "I'd like you to meet my son-in-law, Mr. Tree. He's from New York."

Georgie nodded once, mechanically, his squat face impassive. He walked across the dining room and into the parlor. They heard the front door close behind him.

"Aren't you nervous staying alone in the house with strange men?" Sam said.

"Why should I be? I never yet saw a man I was afraid of."

He knew now where Violet got her stolid refusal to recognize menace. The Wilson women lacked imagination.

"And I practically know those two men," she was saying. "They stayed here one night last week."

"Where's the other guest?" Sam asked.

"He left an hour or two ago in his car. I'm forgetting. You must be famished. I've a fish chowder on the stove. You wash up."

Sam fetched his bag from the parlor. When he returned to the dining room, he heard Mrs. Wilson bustle in the kitchen. The guest register lay on the buffet. He opened it. The last entry read, 'G. Smith,' and the one above that, 'E. Darrow.' E. for Earl and Darrow for Durand. They said they came from Boston.

Last week they had been here and

learned that Mrs. Wilson received occasional one-hundred-dollar bills from Violet. Why were they back?

He left the bag in the hall and went upstairs to the two bedrooms. The roof sloped so sharply that he could not stand erect close to the walls. There were no bags, no extra clothing of any sort, nothing in the dresser drawers. He stood in the doorway connecting the two bedrooms and studied the charming maple bedroom furniture. Once he had read a story about a hiding place in the hollow leg of a brass bedstead; but these beds were all wood, and there was nothing that could be unscrewed. He searched both mattresses, knowing that he was wasting time; and he was.

Fifteen years ago the police had searched all this furniture, with a lot more time and skill and tools. They had found nothing — yet the fact remained that two years ago Violet had somehow stumbled across the money.

"Samuel," his mother-in-law called, "the food is on the table."

She was speaking through the closed door of the downstairs hall room. When she heard him coming down the stairs, she gave a startled little jump. "Those rooms upstairs are taken. I said this will have to be your room."

"I forgot," Sam muttered. "I'll be right out."

He went into the hall bedroom and took Georgie's automatic out of his bag. After making sure that the safety catch was on, he practiced bringing the gun up quickly and then sighting it out of the single window and then contracting his hand gently on the stock the way he had been taught so many years ago. It was all rather foolish, because if they wanted to shoot him they wouldn't give him a chance, or if they did give him a chance, he would be slow and awkward compared to either of them.

He dropped the gun into his pocket. It bulged out the material and sagged the pocket, but there was no other way to keep the gun on his person. He joined Mrs. Wilson in the kitchen and sat down opposite her at the porcelain-top table.

Over the fish chowder Mrs. Wilson kept up a running dialogue, asking questions and then, before he could answer, flitting to reminiscences of Felix Skinner and Martha Underhill, so that it was easy for Sam to tell her very little. While she was serving coffee and her delicious homemade apple pie, Sam managed to get in a question of his own.

"You said you were speaking to Mr. Darrow about Martha's murder. What did he have to say?"

"It wasn't about Martha. This was right after lunch; Mr. Darrow and Mr. Smith had arrived at about eleven this morning. I didn't know about Martha until Clara Atkins — " The coffee pot froze above his cup. "How did Mr. Darrow know this morning there were two murders?"

"What do you mean?"

"We were talking, and once he said: 'The town must be quite excited over two former residents being murdered.' I said: 'Did you say two?' He laughed and said: 'You must have misunderstood.' I didn't give that a second thought, but if I only found out a little while ago about Martha, how did he know this morning?"

"He might have read it in one of the

296

city papers," Sam suggested.

Mrs. Wilson's bright eyes glittered with excitement. Much of her life was lived with the melodramatic radio plays which filled the air, so she was on intimate terms with mystery. "Then why didn't he tell me about Martha being murdered? We talked a long time, and he didn't mention it once." She screwed up her bony little face and poured the coffee.

"Did he ask you many questions?"

Mrs. Wilson sat down at her place. "Now why would he ask questions?"

"People are curious about murders."

"Did I mention that Mr. Darrow was one of the people who had bought those lottery tickets from Ira Pram? Well, he was, so he knew all about that terrible thing that had happened years ago. He said it was a tragedy the way my daughter had been fooled by Ira Pram. I said she'd been fooled again by Felix Skinner. I said if only she had married right off a decent hard-working man like you, Samuel, who has a good business and doesn't smoke or drink or go in for any other foolishness — "

"What did Mr. Darrow want to know

about Violet?" Sam broke in gently.

"I didn't say Mr. Darrow wanted to know anything about her. But we were talking about her, and he wanted to know if she still had her house in Provincetown. I said Violet had refused to go near Provincetown since that awful thing happened. He asked did she ever come here to see me. I said, of course, Violet had always been a devoted daughter. And we talked about — "

Her coffee spoon clattered on the table. "Samuel, Mr. Darrow is a policeman!"

"What gives you that idea?"

"Of course," she said determinedly. "You were right — he was always asking questions. And he knew all about Martha in the morning." She drew her lips into her mouth. "Now why would policemen come here and pretend they're somebody else? It's about those terrible murders."

Sam hardly heard her. His attention was fixed on a spaced series of faint crunchings outside, like somebody carefully putting his weight down step by stealthy step on the pebbles under the snow. Then, without the feet — if they were feet — departing, there was silence.

298

Sam pushed back his chair and started quickly toward the side kitchen window over the sink.

"Samuel, where are you going?" Mrs. Wilson asked loudly. "You haven't finished your pie."

Feet crunched again, hurrying this time. By the time Sam leaned over the sink and got the window up and poked his head outside, he had only a glimpse of a blurred shape turning the front corner of the house. Mrs. Wilson's voice had warned whoever had come to listen in on their conversation. Sam slammed the window down and crossed to the kitchen door.

"Samuel, your pie!" Mrs. Wilson said.

"I'll be right back," he told her.

Outside moonlight lay brilliantly over the whiteness of the snow. Sam went through the gate and stood in the middle of the narrow dirt road which curved in from the highway. Ahead somebody was walking at the side of the road. He seemed to be a big man — as big as Georgie, if not Georgie — but moonlight was deceptive, and Sam could not be sure. Over the soft pad of snow

Sam strode after him.

About him the lights of near-by houses twinkled cheerily, warmly. The gun in his pocket seemed a vulgarism in the peace and charm of the countryside, but his hand was tight on the stock of it. If the man ahead was Georgie or Earl Durand, there would be nothing he could do. Even if he were Ira Pram —

Suddenly the man he was following was gone. Sam blinked, wondering if the moonlight was playing tricks before he realized that the road angled into the highway at that point. He hurried to the intersection. There was nobody walking on the highway, no car going or coming in either direction. On the left toward the bay a single house stood; on the right scrub-covered dunes rolled away. It was impossible to tell which way the man had gone.

Sam removed his hand from the gun and was aware of cold wind sweeping across the cape from Nantucket Sound. He should have had enough sense to bring an overcoat to this place. He turned back to his mother-in-law's house and then turned once again toward the lights of a gas station at the edge of the town.

In the gaily painted little wooden shack Bob Britt's spare body lounged in front of a coal stove. When Sam entered, Britt dipped the copy of the East Wiston *Post,* which he had been holding in front of his face. Sam saw a photo of a handsome young woman occupying three columns. For a moment Sam didn't recognize her as Martha Underhill; the picture must have been taken many years ago.

"Been reading about Martha Underhill," Bob Britt said. "Say, I knew her when she was just a tot. Sunday mornings she and Violet Wilson would come past here all dressed up to kill. The boys hung around outside and whistled at 'em, but the girls never once turned their heads. Felix Skinner was there too, but he never whistled." His head bobbed on his skinny neck. "Say, don't I know you, mister?"

"I'm Mrs. Wilson's son-in-law. You put a new transmission in my car a couple of years ago."

"Sure," Britt said. "Violet's husband. I never forget a face. Well, like I was saying to Emmy at supper tonight, it don't seem it's healthy to be married to Violet. She married three men, and two was shot dead."

"That's not funny."

"I guess it ain't to you," Britt conceded without embarrassment. "You visiting with Violet?"

"I ran up alone on business."

"That so?" Britt rubbed his unshaven jaw. "Say, you ain't running away from the police?"

"Would I come to this place and then walk about openly?"

"I guess not. Only I'm wondering what New York cops are doing around East Wiston."

Sam stretched his palms toward the warmth of the stove. "What cops?"

"He didn't say he was a cop, but he couldn't fool me none. A little man, speaking so quiet and polite, but sharp as a whip, like that police inspector they have on the radio — the one who solves all them mysteries. From New York; has a New York license tag on his car. Was here last week too. Bought gas that time, but not tonight."

"Did he say he was a cop?"

"Not him. Too cagey. But he asked all kinds of questions, like they always do. Last week he asked: was Mrs. Wilson well off and did her daughter send her money from New York and did I ever change a hundred-dollar bill for Mrs. Wilson? Me, I never saw more'n a twenty in my life, I guess. Tonight he asked: where was Ira Pram killed? Why'd he want to know that?"

"It happened near here, didn't it?" Sam said.

"Just four miles up the road. They was driving down from Provincetown, you know. I helped look for the body. Had an old catboat those days, and me and Joey — that's my oldest boy — they just took him in the Army, though he's thirty-seven and has three kids and a wife who never — "

"What happened when you searched for Pram's body?"

"Nothing happened. It never came up at all. The tide was going out, so it took the body along. I guess the fish had themselves a meal."

"How long ago was the man here?" Sam asked.

"The New York cop? Maybe half an hour ago; maybe twenty minutes. Told him just where the place was, and he drove off."

Sam withdrew his hands from the stove. His right wrist struck the hardness of the gun in his pocket. Bob Britt was looking at him from beneath beetling brows.

"I'd like to have a talk with that police officer," Sam said. "Can you lend me a car for a short while?"

"There's a Chevy outside you can use for ten bucks."

"I only intend to do six or seven miles."

Britt picked up his paper and settled back in his chair. "Ten bucks. On account of you're Violet's husband, I ain't even asking no deposit."

"All right," Sam said. "How do I find the place where Ira Pram was shot?"

Britt took the money from Sam's hand and stuffed it carelessly into his vest pocket. "You know something, mister? I don't believe you. I don't believe that cop either."

"You don't believe what?"

"Just don't believe, is all. I should've charged you twenty bucks and you'd paid it, but being you're related by marriage to Mrs. Wilson — " He pulled a mackinaw off a hook and got into it. "Car's right outside."

Sam followed, acutely aware of his gun pulling down his pocket.

18

Mrs. Wilson's Furniture

A DARK coupé was parked in front of the boarded-up refreshment stand which Bob Britt had described. The feeble headlights of the rattletrap car Sam drove sprayed on the New York license plate.

This, according to Britt, was where the police car had gone off the road fifteen years ago. There had been no refreshment stand then and no house within a mile. Ira Pram had raced toward the nearest of the dunes between the road and the bay, and he had made the top of it before one of the detectives had extracted himself from the wreck and shot at him.

Sam pulled up behind the New York car and walked across the road and up the dune. His shoes were already damp; icy moisture seeped through his socks as his feet sank through the thin layer of snow and into soggy sand underneath. The wind was bad here, but he kept his head alertly high, and his hand was tight around the gun in his pocket.

Earl Durand was not in sight when Sam reached the top. No living thing was in sight. A lower dune rolled away from this one, blocking out the beach directly ahead. Beyond it the blue-black surface of Cape Cod Bay in moonlight was disturbed by silver ripples raised by the wind. Toward the east the shore curved sharply, forming a cove in the bay. Abel Pouch had suggested that Ira Pram might have swum to land that way, but it was a good three hundred yards.

"Looking for Pram's ghost?" a casual voice asked.

Sam's finger stiffened on the trigger of his gun, but he kept the weapon in his pocket. Earl Durand had come over the rise of the dune from Sam's right, and he was standing a little below Sam. His coat collar was up above his ears; the gray scarf muffled him up to his chin. Both his gloved hands were in view — empty. He looked like a harmless old man.

"You didn't have to ask the way from

Bob Britt," Sam said. "You were here before."

"It was a long time ago, and I was unconscious a couple of seconds after I reached the place." Durand's gloved hand pointed east toward the curving shore. "Do you think a man can swim that far under water with just sticking his nose up now and then to breathe? I'm not a swimmer. Pram was a fish."

"It was daylight, and the detectives were watching, and they said he was wounded."

"I see." Durand dug both hands into his coat pockets, and Sam tensed. "So that was just bluff, telling me Pram was alive? You thought you could scare me off with that."

"No," Sam said. "I think the detectives never saw which way he ran and never shot at him. I think that by the time they managed to get out of the car he was out of sight and they did not know to which side of the road he had gone."

"Your idea is the coppers were giving themselves an out?" Durand nodded. "Could be. They're like everybody else — why get into hot water with headquarters if they can get away with cooking up a fancy yarn?" He laughed through his nostrils. "Am I going wacky letting you talk me into it? Pram is dead as a herring."

"But you're worried," Sam said. "You came here to make sure."

Durand moved up the dune until he stood level with Sam. His old face twisted. "I'm up here for my dough. I spent plenty of time in jail for it. Violet said it's here. She said Provincetown to try to put me off, but it's here all right. Mrs. Wilson likes to talk. She says Violet visits her a lot. Violet was here just before Skinner got that fistful of hundred-dollar bills."

"Why shouldn't she visit her mother?"

Durand's hands came out of his pockets, and Sam's lungs skipped a couple of breaths. The hands were still empty.

"If the money's here, I'm getting it," Durand said. "If it's somewhere else, I'm getting it. If you have any sense, you'll advise Violet not to drive me too far."

The wind whipped Sam's clothes and enveloped him in an icy blast. He huddled low without dropping his head. Durand clicked a snap on his glove and started to descend the dune.

Sam said: "If you go near Violet again, I'll kill you."

The violence of his feeling shook him more than the wind. And he knew with remorseless certainty that he meant it — that this was a man he could kill and be glad he killed.

Languidly Durand turned. His chin lifted from his muffler to look up at Sam. His face was a frozen white splotch, and his voice was frozen too. "I'm not forgetting that you smacked me the other day."

"I haven't forgotten why I did," Sam said.

Durand's laugh was frozen too. "So Violet's grocer is talking tough? You terrify me, Tree. I really know how to be tough, and you don't. Remember that."

Snow and sand crunched under Durand's feet. With his ears between his shoulders, Sam watched him go all the way down. Durand turned his car and headed back to East Wiston. Slowly

310

Sam's fingers loosened from around the gun in his pocket.

★ ★ ★

The front door opened before Sam reached it.

"Well, I declare!" Mrs. Wilson said in outrage. "You run out in the middle of your supper and walk around in the cold without a hat and coat."

Sam stepped into the house and closed the door. He shivered in the sudden warmth. "I wanted to find out if Mr. Darrow was really a policeman, so I went out to telephone New York."

"Why didn't you use the phone in the house?"

"Isn't that odd!" Sam said. "I forgot you had one."

He had learned in the last few days that he was a bad liar, and this was as feeble as the one to the police about Skinner having borrowed fifty dollars. But Mrs. Wilson's excited mind was jumping too far ahead to linger over the lie. She said eagerly: "He is a policeman, isn't he?"

"No. The New York police said they never heard of him. They said there was no reason why they should send a policeman to East Wiston."

She was relieved at the same time that she was disappointed. "I'm glad to hear that. It made me nervous to think I had a policeman in my house. Come finish your supper, Samuel."

She meant the pie. He tagged after her into the kitchen and accepted a second slab of pie and a second cup of coffee. The coldness left most of him except in the region of his stomach. Not often in his life had he had occasion to be greatly afraid. Now he knew that it was like physical sickness.

"Did Smith come back?" he asked. He had not seen Durand's car outside.

"Mr. Smith is up in his room. The reason I was waiting at the door for you, Samuel — that man makes me uneasy."

"I thought you'd never seen a man who frightened you."

Her eyes were less bright now. He wondered if she, too, was afraid. "Oh, Mr. Smith doesn't frighten me, but

there's been so much murdering — "
She giggled stridently. "Anyway, Samuel,
I'm glad you're spending the night."

So am I, he thought.

When he finished his pie and coffee,
they retired to the parlor, where Mrs.
Wilson listened to the radio. Her chair
was close to the loud-speaker so that
she would not miss a word of the
heart-rending drama on the air. Sam's
gaze moved about the room and settled
on the piano.

"Was that piano among Violet's
furniture?" he asked.

"I told you — every stick in the
house."

"Violet doesn't play."

"Ira Pram was the kind of man who
bought everything he laid his eyes on."

Sam went to the piano and ran his
fingers over the keys. He had never had
lessons, but he liked to improvise. Several
of the keys stuck; the rest were very much
out of tune.

"Does anybody ever play it?"

"Who is there to play?" She waved her
head toward the radio. "Shh! She's going
to shoot her husband."

The bowels of the piano were roomy enough to hide a lot more than twenty thousand dollars. Tonight, after everybody was asleep, he would have a look — if Durand didn't try to beat him to it. Pram couldn't have kept his money there, because doubtless the police had searched it thoroughly, but later Violet might have transferred the money to it.

The radio play ended with the heroine reconciled in the loving arms of her husband. Mrs. Wilson switched off the radio and looked at Sam, seated at the piano.

"I didn't want that piano," she complained. "It takes up too much room, but Violet said it would cost too much to move it to New York. Violet took hardly any of the furniture when it came from the warehouse except a few little things she could put in Martha's car. Has Martha still got her car? I wonder who she left it to? And her money. She has a cousin in Yarmouth, name of — "

Sam swung sharply from the piano. "What did she take?"

"Martha? I said Martha's money — "

"I mean Violet. You said she took

some of the stuff which came from the warehouse."

"Oh, it was hardly anything," Mrs. Wilson said. "There were some ash trays and cigarette boxes I hadn't any use for, and some figures I didn't want."

"Figures?"

"Especially that big statue I couldn't stand the sight of. It had an ugly black crow sitting on top of a woman's head. Who ever heard of anything so silly? Violet said it was supposed to be about a poem."

"'The Raven.'" Sam found it hard to breathe.

"That's what Violet called it. Well, it looked like a crow to me. I said I had no use for it and didn't know to whom to give it. Martha had her car here, so Violet took it along."

"Was that two years ago?"

"No, that was back in 1937, a few weeks after all the furniture arrived from the warehouse." Mrs. Wilson's head cocked. "Why are you so interested in the furniture? I hope you're not trying to get any of it back."

"Of course not."

Suddenly his breath burst loose in ironic laughter.

His mother-in-law frowned at him. "Have I said something funny, Samuel?"

His laughter trailed off, but it continued to quiver inside of him. "It was home all the time and I didn't guess. Violet was clever. She didn't — " He caught himself.

"What are you talking about, Samuel? What was home?"

"Nothing," he said quickly.

Mrs. Wilson's eyes moved past him to the dining-room doorway. "Can I help you out, Mr. Smith?" she said.

Sam stepped across the room. Georgie was in the dining room, pulling the stub of an unlighted cigar from his lips.

"I'm looking for the bathroom," Georgie said. Carefully his eyes were not on Sam.

"It's back there in the hall," Mrs. Wilson told him.

"I forgot."

Georgie's weight made his steps heavy as he retreated to the rear of the house. But he had been silent enough coming down the stairs and into the dining

316

room, Sam reflected. How much had he overheard? And how much did whatever he had heard mean to him?

Weakly, as if exhausted from a long run, Sam sank into a chair. If Georgie had guessed, it wouldn't make much difference. Sam would know when Georgie and Durand left, and a train would beat a car to New York. If absolutely necessary, Violet could be phoned to seek protection.

A car pulled up to the house, and then Earl Durand entered. He nodded briskly to Mrs. Wilson. "It's a raw night," he said politely.

"I keep my house nice and warm for my guests," she said. "You can keep your hat and coat right in the hall closet, Mr. Darrow."

"Thanks." Durand moved toward the arched doorway and stopped in front of Sam's chair. His hands were deep in his overcoat pocket; his chin was sunk in his muffler. "So you're still here?"

Sam's wrist lay against the hardness of the gun in his pocket. "For at least as long as you are."

"I wouldn't bet on it," Durand said softly.

He disappeared into the dining room. Sam heard him open the closet door and then go upstairs.

"Samuel." Mrs. Wilson was on her feet. With her hands folded limply in front of her and her shoulder curved forward, she reminded him of Violet, except that her bright eyes were frank with excited curiosity. "Do you know Mr. Darrow?"

"I met him in Bob Britt's gas station. I told him I didn't know how long I would stay in East Wiston." Practice made lying come more easily.

"He looked so oddly at you, Samuel. I had a notion — " A clock in the dining room struck once, and Mrs. Wilson's mind flitted. "Gracious, is that ten-thirty? I seldom stay up this late. Will you remember to put out the lights?"

"I'm going to bed too," he said.

In the hall bedroom Sam moved noisily about without doing anything. He was still fully dressed when he pulled the drop light chain. The house was silent. If there were any minor sounds, they were obliterated by the wind moaning around the house and rattling the windows.

Standing in darkness, Sam opened the door several inches. The night light was on in the hall. Through the crack in the door Sam could see halfway up the staircase. A mumble of voices drifted down to him. Durand and Georgie were talking to each other; his straining ears could not catch words.

Sam went to the foot of the stairs. The voices were no clearer. Under his wet shoes the first step creaked. It was a small sound, probably inaudible as far as the stairhead, but he froze. His finger curled around the trigger of the gun in his pocket. The second step he mounted more gingerly, and the wood remained quiet.

When he was halfway up the stairs he paused. Still there was no meaning to the muttering upstairs. They must be in the farther of the two rooms.

In the dining room the telephone rang.

Upstairs the voices ceased. Even the wind seemed suddenly hushed, and Sam could hear the thumping of his heart. Again the telephone rang. Sam turned and started down as soundlessly as he had ascended, but the last few steps he found himself hurrying. He was slipping back into his room when he heard Mrs. Wilson come out of her bedroom, which was in a wing off the dining room.

"Who is this?" he heard Mrs. Wilson say. Her voice was worried. People like her did not receive telephone calls at eleven at night unless there was bad news.

And Sam felt his heart contract. Was the call from New York? He shouldn't have left Violet alone.

"Mr. who?" Mrs. Wilson said. "Durand, did you say? . . . There's no Mr. Durand here. You must have the wrong number . . . Yes, this is Mrs. Wilson speaking . . . Yes, there are two guests tonight, but there's no Mr. Durand. There's Mr. Darrow and — . . . Oh, you mean Mr. Darrow. I though you said another name . . . I think Mr. Darrow is asleep."

Upstairs a door opened. "Is that for me?"

"Just a minute, please," Mrs. Wilson's voice said. Through the narrow opening in the door Sam saw her come into the hall. She was wearing a faded bathrobe. "There's a man wants to speak to you, Mr. Darrow."

"Who is he?"

"He didn't say."

Upstairs Georgie muttered something. Durand said to him, "I'll be damned if I know," and then raised his voice, "Did he say he wanted to speak to Darrow?"

"I said he did," Mrs. Wilson said testily. She was impatient to return to bed. "First he gave another name. He spelled it out: D-u-r-a-n-d. Then he said he meant Darrow."

"I'll be right down."

Mrs. Wilson withdrew. Sam heard her bedroom door close. There was a brief silence before Earl Durand came down the stairs. Sam eased the door shut, opening it again when he heard Durand in the dining room. There was another silence, as if Durand were hesitating to pick up the telephone. Then his voice came low and puzzled.

"Hello . . . What's that? . . . First you tell me who this is . . . What! . . . Is this a gag or something? . . . Nuts! It was so long ago — . . . What?"

Long seconds ticked off, during which Durand evidently listened without interruption. When he spoke, his voice was hoarse. "Maybe I do and maybe I don't, but you've got to show me . . . That's just what I intend to do . . . Right now? . . . I guess you're right . . . Five minutes. Maybe ten . . . Right."

Sam closed the door as Durand returned to the hall.

"What's it all about?" Georgie called from the foot of the stairs.

"I'm going out for a little while."

"What for?"

"None of your damn business!" Durand snapped.

Sam heard him take two steps in the hall, and Sam stood very still in the darkness of the little room, his hand sweating on the gun. A door in the hall opened. Sam's nerves eased somewhat; Durand was getting his hat and coat out of the hall closet. The closet door closed. Durand's feet moved to the front of the house.

19

A Dead Man's Face

SAM stepped into the hall and looked up the stairs. Georgie had returned to his room. The front door of the house opened and then closed behind Earl Durand. Sam went the few feet down the hall to the back door and unlocked it and slipped out into the biting wind. Only the length of the house separated him from Durand, but if Durand used his car there would be no chance to follow.

Over the powdery snow Sam moved along the back of the house. Cautiously he peered around the corner. Durand was not in sight; his car stood dark and isolated just off the moonlit road. By this time Durand should have reached the car. Did that mean that Durand did not intend to drive to his appointment? Sam turned the corner and hurried up the side of the house.

Suddenly Earl Durand appeared past the front of the house. Sam was not ten feet away then. He stopped dead, in the moonlight as conspicuous as if it had been broad daylight. His right hand dipped into his pocket.

Durand did not see him. His back was to Sam, his small figure huddled deep in his coat. His head turned up the road and then down it, and Sam knew that he had also paused warily like that at the front door. With his head down against the wind, Durand made for his car.

"Earl!"

The warning voice cut high above the wind. Durand whirled, his eyes lifting. Without thinking, Sam also looked back and up. Georgie's head was poking out of a second-story window.

"There's Tree," Georgie shouted. "He's tailing you."

Durand's eyes had already lowered. They lay flatly on Sam. Across ten feet of moonlit space they faced each other. Sam thumbed off the safety catch of the automatic in his pocket.

Then Durand spoke in a voice which rose cold and harsh on the wind. "I warned you to keep out of my hair. Now, by God, you will!"

Sam fumbled for words. "I was just — I happened to be out here." The wind was against him and hurled his voice back into his teeth.

Durand planted his legs apart, as if to prop himself against the wind, and started to unbutton his overcoat. *He's got a gun there*, Sam thought. *He's going to kill me*. And his own gun came out of his pocket.

At the window Georgie yelled. At the sight of Sam's gun, Durand's head bobbed in surprise. "That tough, eh?" Durand said tightly as his fingers ripped his coat open all the way. His right hand disappeared inside the coat.

That was when Sam shot the first time. The gun jerked so violently that he felt the wrench in the socket of his arm. He had forgotten how badly a heavy pistol could kick. Grabbing the gun with both hands, he steadied it against his stomach and squeezed. Durand grunted and bent forward from his waist. His left hand pressed against his left hip.

"Now stop it!" Sam said shrilly.

Durand's face tilted up at Sam. In the moonlight it had changed into brown cracked leather. There seemed to be no life in it except for the slit of mouth which opened and closed without sound. And wildly Durand's right hand fumbled inside his coat.

Sam found himself moving in on Durand, holding his gun away from his body now, knowing that if Durand made him shoot again the next shot must count. "Stop it!" Sam was saying. "Stop it or I'll have to kill you!"

A gun sounded. For a dazed moment Sam thought it was Durand's gun, but Durand was stumbling forward in the snow. Then he thought that it was his own gun, but that couldn't be. Then he remembered Georgie at the upstairs window, and he looked back and up. Georgie's head had vanished. That gun, which was neither Sam's nor Georgie's, cracked a second time.

Sam's head twisted back to Durand. He was on the ground now, lying face down in the snow — a dark, immobile splotch against the whiteness. And from the front corner of the house a man approached with long, nervous strides. His face was a shadowy blob under the brim of his hat, but the black automatic in his hand was visible enough. Sam brought up his own gun.

"Take it easy, Tree," the man said quietly. "I'm Gavigan."

Sam's arm flopped to his side. "I think you killed him," he muttered.

Captain Gavigan dropped to one knee at Durand's side and turned him over on his back. The mouth was open, the eyes staring; the face seemed to have shrunken so that the leathery skin hung in wrinkled looseness from the jaw.

"Dead all right," Gavigan grunted. "Is this Earl Durand?"

"Yes."

"I thought so. Looks like the description of him we got from Boston. You wounded him."

"In the hip," Sam said.

Gavigan nodded. "I saw it from the gate. Lucky I got here when I did. What were you waiting for?"

"He was wounded. I couldn't shoot down a wounded man."

"No?" Gavigan pulled the dead man's

coat wide open. "Take a look at this." His gloved finger pointed down at the small pearl-handled revolver clutched in the lifeless right hand. "More than a slug in the hip is needed to stop guys like Durand. You don't take chances with them."

"I guess not," Sam said. He looked down at Gavigan closing the coat over Durand's hand and gun. "The Marines to the rescue. How did it happen?"

Gavigan stood up and brushed snow off his knee. "Luck. I was having you tailed, you know."

"I didn't know."

"You weren't supposed to," Gavigan said. "When I learned you'd bought a ticket to East Wiston, I figured there might be something doing here. I spent an hour talking to local people and the district attorney. Then I thought it wasn't too late to pay a visit to your mother-in-law."

"She's asleep."

Gavigan looked at the house. "Shooting doesn't seem to disturb her."

Very close to them an automobile motor sprang into life.

"Georgie!" Sam cried. "I forgot about him."

Durand's car was already bouncing onto the road, roaring in second speed. Gavigan frowned. "Who did you say?"

"Georgie Jones, the man who was with Durand."

"Hell, why didn't you tell me?" Gavigan ran toward the road, yelling something that was lost in the wind. He threw a quick shot, but the car had made too much distance. Gavigan leaped to the middle of the narrow road and raised his gun. The car swung out of sight onto the highway. Shrugging, Gavigan put up his gun and returned to Sam.

"He won't get far," the captain said. "An alarm will be sent out for him, though I'm not sure yet what charge can be clamped on him. Probably he helped Durand murder Skinner and Miss Underhill."

Stretching toward the bay, there were houses within two hundred feet on both sides of the road, yet they remained dark and silent. Shots were not recognizable as shots unless you expected them. It was simpler for sleepy people, suddenly awakened by loud noises, if they were awakened at all, to dismiss them and go back to sleep.

Sam said: "Durand didn't murder them."

"No? Then who did?"

"Ira Pram."

Gavigan brooded down at that dead face which looked as if it had never lived. "What are you doing in East Wiston?"

"I thought Ira Pram might be here."

"Like hell!" Gavigan lifted his eyes to Sam's face. "You're after Pram's dough."

"I thought it might be hidden in Pram's furniture," Sam admitted. "The stuff Pram bought when he was married has been in my mother-in-law's house for the last seven years." It was a relief to be able to tell the truth again — at least part of it.

"Was the money there?"

"I couldn't find it. Neither could Durand. That's what he and Georgie came here for. When I arrived, I found Durand and Georgie registered as tourists under false names."

Gavigan prowled a short distance from the body. He pulled his coat collar up against the wind and his hat down lower and returned. "Where'd you get the gun?"

"It's Georgie's. He'd tossed it into the fireplace of my house when Sergeant Jones arrived. I found it later."

"Yeah?" Gavigan looked as if he were determined not to believe anything Sam told him. He removed the automatic from Sam's fingers and dropped it into his coat pocket. "Where's your overcoat?"

"I don't wear one."

"That's right, you told me that the other day. Did you come out here to meet Durand on the field of honor?"

"I followed him," Sam said. "A couple of minutes before, he'd received a phone call from Ira Pram."

"Huh? You're sure of that?"

"It sounded as if it came from Pram. Durand didn't suspect that Pram was alive, but over the phone Pram convinced him that he was. Durand made an appointment to meet him somewhere near here."

"So you're saying that Pram is in East Wiston?"

"Yes."

"Did you hear Durand mention Pram's name on the phone?"

"Not exactly."

Gavigan's triangular face, framed by his hatbrim and raised coat collar, twisted in disgust. "Not exactly! You've never seen him. You haven't given me a shred of proof he's alive. As far as I'm concerned, you came up here and solved me a couple of murders."

Durand's dead eyes were staring directly up at Sam. Sam wished that Gavigan hadn't turned him over on his back. "So you insist Durand was the murderer?"

"Hell, isn't it plain?" Gavigan said. "He figured you were wise to him, so he tried to kill you. Guys like that don't go around popping slugs at everybody they see for the fun of it. They kill when they think they have to."

"Pram's in East Wiston," Sam persisted. "At least you ought to look for him on the chance that I'm right."

"You forget I have no jurisdiction here. It's up to the local police."

A strident voice cut across the night. "Samuel, is that you out there?"

With the parlor light at her back, Mrs.

Wilson was standing at the front door in her faded cotton bathrobe.

"I'll be right in," Sam called back.

Captain Gavigan ran his palm across his face. "I'll have to straighten this out with the local law and have an alarm sent out for Georgie. You haven't much to worry about. I'm a witness that you shot at Durand in self-defense."

"I did," Sam said.

"That's what I said." Gavigan started toward the road, then turned. "Don't suddenly have an idea to start back to New York before you get permission." He walked briskly to the highway.

Sam headed across the snow to the house. His feet were frozen; wind knifed through his flesh. Though his back was now to the dead man, he could still see that face staring up from the snow.

Mrs. Wilson had closed the door against the cold, but she was waiting just inside the house for him.

"Your voices didn't let me sleep," she complained. "Why did you stand out there talking? Wasn't that Mr. Darrow out there with you? Why doesn't he come in?"

"Didn't you hear shots?"

"I heard some loud noises. I thought they came from the bay." Her head cocked. "Samuel, was somebody shooting? Has anything happened to Mr. Darrow? I heard him leave the house right after he received a phone call."

"He's dead," Sam said. "The police shot him. And his name wasn't Darrow. It was Earl Durand."

"Durand?" Her bright eyes glittered. "That was the name the person who called him on the phone said, but I didn't connect it with Earl Durand. That can't be the man who was Ira Pram's partner? Earl Durand!" Her head bobbed in excited agreement with herself. "He's the identical man, I'm sure. Why did he come here of all places?"

"The police aren't sure."

"Gracious!" Mrs. Wilson said.

20

Nevermore!

WHILE the state police were removing the body, a deputy called for Sam and drove him to the home of District Attorney Rufus Modley.

In the library Captain Gavigan was prowling along the bookshelves with a cup of coffee in his hands, pausing only long enough to introduce Sam to Modley. The district attorney was a bright young man who wore a flaming dressing gown over silk pajamas. Heartily he shook Sam's hand.

"I knew your father-in-law well," Modley said. "He built this house for my father. How are you?"

"Shooting at men doesn't agree with me," Sam replied.

Modley revealed a perfect set of teeth. "Nobody objects if you confine yourself to rats like this Durand. Captain Gavigan

335

put in the finishing touches, but some of the credit goes to you."

"I don't want credit," Sam said.

"It's yours all the same. Coffee?"

There was a huge electric percolator on the library table. Modley poured a cup for Sam and refilled his own and Gavigan's cup. "Now to business," Modley said cheerfully.

Business consisted of three men swapping stories over endless cups of coffee. It was all so amiable that Sam wondered if Modley and Gavigan were laying some sort of trap for him. On the other hand, with Durand assumed to have been the murderer of Felix Skinner and Martha Underhill, Captain Gavigan had triumphantly solved a tough case and Modley would be spared a headache in his own district.

Sam refused to let them get away with it. "Are you going to look for Ira Pram? He's somewhere in the neighborhood — if he hasn't been scared away."

"Of course I'll have a look into the Pram case," Modley said indifferently. "It's very old stuff by now, and there's not an iota of evidence that Pram is alive.

What do you think, Captain?"

"All Tree has is a hunch. I don't believe in hunches."

"Precisely," Modley agreed. "It's likely, however, that it might come down to a matter of Pram's money. After all, there's your motive. Skinner must have been the one who found it. He used to be a local boy."

"Uh-huh," Gavigan said. "Only if Skinner found the dough, it happened recently. That explains how he got his hands on all that cash. Durand wanted him to fork it over. When Skinner refused, Durand killed him. Miss Underhill learned that Durand had murdered Skinner, or else she and Skinner had gotten their hands on the dough together. Like you said, they both came from these parts. Whatever it was, Durand had to kill her also to save his hide."

Sam kept quiet.

"And then Durand came to East Wiston to find what was left of the money," Modley said. "And you, Tree — " His hand stopped in the midst of a flourish. His face sharpened. "You were after that money too."

"Merely looking for money is no crime," Sam told him.

"More coffee, Mr. Tree?" Modley asked. "No?" He beamed at Gavigan. "If you ask me, Captain, Ira Pram is a red herring. How deep do you think Mr. Tree is in these murders?"

Gavigan bent forward from his broad hips to place his cup on the table. "That's what I can't decide."

"Well, that's your job, Captain, when he returns to New York. I'm concerned with the shooting of Earl Durand, and that, at least, was self-defense." He shifted his beam to Sam. "I'll want you in my office early tomorrow morning to sign a statement."

Sam glanced at the typewriter on the desk. "Why not get it over with? I can type."

"You're pretty anxious to leave East Wiston."

"I'm anxious to get back to my wife," Sam said. "She'll worry when she reads about myself and Durand."

Modley waved at the typewriter. "Go ahead. There's paper in that drawer. You write what I tell you."

Sam tried to keep his fingers steady on the keys, but it wasn't easy.

★ ★ ★

Shortly before noon of the next day Sam was back in New York. He had been gone only twenty-five hours.

At Grand Central Terminal he bought the Sunday papers and read them on the subway. There was not a line about the death of Earl Durand; he had gotten himself killed too late and too far away for the Sunday papers. Tomorrow, probably, the palmers would carry the news that the shooting of Earl Durand had solved the murders of Felix Skinner and Martha Underhill. The police would have a closed case, and everybody else concerned would be happy about it, including Violet. Except that he did not intend to let Violet be happy about it.

With the newspapers under one arm and the week-end bag swinging from the other hand, Sam strolled the three blocks from the subway station. The day was brightly brisk; Sunday languor lay over the street of identical gray brick houses.

His next-door neighbor, Art Carson, was in the gutter polishing his car. Carson waved a rag at Sam over the hood of his car. "Hi, Sam." He started around the front of the car with a conversational glint in his eyes.

Sam said fearfully, "See you later," and hurried on to his house. At the bottom porch step he hesitated. The shades of the two living-room windows facing the porch were drawn. The sun never came in past the porch roof; the shades were drawn only at night to block the eyes of passers-by.

So what? It was Sunday, and they were probably sleeping late and had not yet been in the living room.

The door was locked. His hands were cold on his keys as he selected the right one. He unlocked the door and took a single step into the hall and stopped. In the living room somebody was speaking in whispers. Yet the shades were drawn.

"Come in, Tree," a voice said. "It's your house, ain't it? We been waiting for you."

Georgie's gorilla bulk appeared in the living-room doorway. His left hand rolled a fat cigar between his lips. His right hand held a gun as heavy as the automatic he had tossed into the fireplace, except that this one was a revolver. He leaned against the doorjamb so that both the living room and the hall would be in view.

Sam closed the door behind him, thinking, *I should have guessed. Georgie was in flight, but he could flee in this direction as well as any other*. He put down his bag and placed the newspapers on top of it and moved past Georgie into the living room. Georgie turned, his gun covering everybody in the room. The place seemed crowded, and it was dim because of the drawn shades.

"Darling!" Violet came out of nowhere and flung her arms about him and kissed him.

Over Violet's head he saw Naomi on the couch, huddled like a frightened child in the circle of Doug Faulcon's good right arm. Sam remembered that Doug was to be discharged from the hospital this morning; he must have arrived here only a short while ago. It was a hell of a honeymoon.

Ruefully Doug glanced down at his left

arm in a sling and then grinned tightly at Sam. "He wouldn't have gotten away with this, sir, if I had the use of both hands."

"This is no time for heroics," Sam said.

"You tell him, brother," Georgie said without taking his cigar from his mouth.

And Abel Pouch was there. The great loose flabby bulges of him were rooted in front of the fireplace. He was mopping sweat from his face with a pocket handkerchief.

"Another of your operatives?" Sam asked Pouch, nodding toward Georgie.

"No, no! It was sheer accident that I was here when he arrived."

Violet said: "This man is a private detective. He showed me his credentials. He said you had hired him to look after me while you were away." She looked up at Sam. Lines of strain were about her eyes and mouth, but essentially her face told him nothing of what she felt or thought. "You didn't really hire him, darling?"

"No." Sam unwound her arms and crossed the room to Pouch. "So you're still up to your old tricks, Pouch? You don't give up easily." Without taking a breath, Sam whispered: "Have you a gun?"

Pouch shook his head. The lumps that were his face flowed together into a formless mass. He was more afraid than anybody in the room except perhaps Sam. Like Sam, he knew the capacity of men like Georgie.

"All right, the party's started." Georgie took two steps into the room, but no more, keeping everybody within his range of vision. "Now for the dough."

"You'd better give it to him, Violet," Sam said.

He knew that she would start talking about something else. She said: "This terrible man made me call Mother in East Wiston. He stood there with the gun while I spoke to her. He wanted me to find out where you were, and when Mother said you had started back home before daylight, he said we would all wait in here for you."

Georgie ran a thick thumb affectionately along the barrel of the revolver. "She still says she don't know where the dough is.

Maybe, but you know, Tree. I heard you tell Mrs. Wilson it's here. Now give."

Everybody but Violet stared at Georgie's gun. Violet concentrated on words. "And Mother said the police shot Earl Durand right outside her house. And she said this man — "

"Cut it out!" Sam snapped. Sweat ran down from his arm-pits. "Can't you understand that this is no time for raising a fog with words? Give him the money."

Her hands folded loosely in front of her; her body relaxed into that studied, placid pose of hers. "I'd be glad to give him money if he would go away. I offered him everything I had in my handbag, but he refused to take it."

Deep in his throat Georgie made a sound more animal than human. The cigar in his mouth bobbed with his words. "I can't deal with no woman like that, except with lead. It's up to you, Tree."

"Yes," Sam said slowly. "Yes, it is."

He went to the fireplace and waved Pouch aside. Pouch stepped to the end of the couch, watching Sam with greedy intensity that was stronger than his terror. Naomi sat up erect on the couch; Doug leaned forward. Sam took Pallas and the raven off the mantel. He heard Violet gasp: "Oh no, Sam!"

The figure was heavy, but not as heavy as he had thought. Like all plaster casts, it was hollow, and there was an opening in the base. He placed the figure on its side on the hearthstone and poked his fingers into the opening. He felt the base of the armature.

"Hold it!" Georgie barked.

Sam withdrew his fingers. "The money is in here."

"Yeah? Maybe a gat or something." Georgie came forward, waving his gun. "Get over to that couch. You too, lady."

Sam and Violet joined the others. She reached for his hand, and her palm was moist and hot. She was not looking at Sam or at the cast or anywhere.

Facing them and keeping his gun up, Georgie squatted behind the figure. His hand pushed into the opening at the base, but only his fingers could get past the armature. He rose, lifting the figure under his arm, and dropped it on the hearthstone. The raven twisted around to the back of the skull, its claws taking part of Pallas' helmet with them, but it did not come off. It hung limply askew. And nothing at all happened to the bust.

Georgie's eyes did not leave the two on the couch and the three standing at the side of it as he reached for the fire tongs. His barrel chest rose and fell with the heaviness of his breathing. He tossed the cigar into the fireplace and then smashed the tongs down on the bust. The plaster chipped and cracked up to one ear, but the bust did not come apart.

Furiously Georgie kept driving the tongs down. Bits of plaster came apart, but did not fall off, adhering tenaciously to the burlap lining on the inside of the mould. The ruggedness of an ordinary plaster cast was amazing.

Georgie was sweating when he dropped the tongs and pulled a clasp knife out of his pocket. Always watching the five at the couch, he slashed the burlap. Large chunks of plaster came off now, revealing the lead pipe which was the armature.

With an exultant cry, Georgie dug his

hand in among the shambles. A one-hundred-dollar bill was pinched between his fingers. "Here's one of 'em!"

The vise about Sam's heart loosened. Would Georgie go now that he had the money? He might kill one witness to his theft, but he couldn't kill five. Not even Georgie could kill five.

"What the hell is this?" Georgie said hoarsely.

He was on his knees again, slashing with his knife the burlap between the cracked plaster. Nothing of it remained but the lead pipe running into the bowels of the raven. And amid the chaos of plaster and burlap Sam could see no money.

"Just that one C," Georgie said. "That means you got the dough, all right. It was here once, but it ain't now."

Sam looked at Violet. Her face was turned away from him.

"Try the raven," Sam said. "That's also hollow."

Georgie had learned the method. He broke the plaster with the tongs and cut the burlap with the knife. There was no more money.

The silence that came then hurt physically. Doug's wry voice broke it. "'Quoth the raven, Nevermore!'"

Dully Sam glanced at Doug. An amused grin was starting on his freckled face. He was young and not easily frightened and he did not understand. Abruptly Doug's grin died. His eyes receded; his good arm tightened about Naomi.

Sam turned back to Georgie, who stood on the hearthstone amid white and black plaster and burlap. Not even Doug had been able to doubt the utter savagery which now possessed all of that gorilla face.

"Get this, Tree." The gun shook in Georgie's hand with sheer animal fury. "I ain't hanging around much longer. I go with the dough or leave with a slug in your wife's belly. Which do you like better?"

"Isn't that strange!" Violet muttered, staring down at the hearthstone. "How ever did that one hundred dollars get into that figure?"

"Violet!" Sam pulled her hard against him. "Did your mother tell you that I was the one who shot Earl Durand first?"

"You, darling? Mother said the police."

"They came in on the gun fight. Durand tried to kill me, but I shot first. Now do you understand what kind of man he was? And Georgie is worse because he's not smart. He's not here to play games."

"You tell her, brother," Georgie said. "I got nothing to lose. The coppers are after me. I need that dough for a getaway. If you got it, sister, you have one minute to fork it over. I think I'll plug your husband instead of you. Then you'll talk."

"The — the shot will be heard outside," Violet whispered weakly.

"You think that'll make the lead in your husband's belly feel better?"

Violet sagged against Sam. Fear had broken through her complacency now in all its naked ugliness. "Oh, darling, I can't!" she moaned.

"Why not?"

"Because — because — " Lifting her head, she looked at Naomi and Doug, sitting still and tense on the couch, and then at Abel Pouch, towering over her, and then up at Sam. "It's in the cellar," she murmured.

Georgie laughed harshly. "Now we're getting places. I'll go last. If anybody tries to make a break, so help me, I'll plug the nearest one. And no more horsing around. A cellar's a good place for shooting."

Sam and Violet led the way. Her feet dragged, and Sam had to support her with an arm about her waist. *Does the money mean so much to her?* he thought bitterly.

The cellar stairs led down from the square little vestibule at the back door. Sam switched on the light at the head of the stairs and let Violet go down first because there was no room for two to walk abreast. She had to hold onto the railing to keep herself erect. A wave of pity for her swept over him. When a woman like Violet broke, she broke completely.

Then all five of them were bunched in the cellar, with Georgie standing a short distance off and holding his revolver against his hip. "Okay, I'm in a hurry now," he said.

Doug removed his good arm from about Naomi's waist and stepped to Sam's side. His face was drawn now as it had not been before. "It just occurred to me, sir — "

"Don't keep calling me sir." Sam's frayed nerves were at the snapping point. "My name is Sam."

"Why, sure." Doug looked startled. "I mean, this mug is just bluffing. If he shoots anybody, the rest of us will be witnesses. That ugly face of his is easily recognizable. He knows the police will be able to pick him up at once."

Pouch breathed, "For God's sake!" and ran his sleeve over his brow.

"Don't be a fool, Doug!" Sam said.

Cautiously Georgie stepped back to the foot of the stairs. His revolver moved out from his hip. "Try it, sport," he warned, "and see what you get."

"I believe I will," Doug said evenly. With careful deliberation he started toward Georgie.

Naomi shrieked and flung herself at Doug. Sam gripped his shoulder.

"You young idiot!" Sam shouted. "Save your heroics for the battlefield or where women can't get hurt."

"But if he shoots, I'll be the only one — "

"Damn it!" Sam said. "There's not enough money to risk any of you getting hurt." He swung toward Violet. "Give him that money before something happens."

Mechanically she nodded. There was no resistance left in her. With eyes strangely expressionless, she moved past the oil furnace to the little potbelly coal stove which was used to heat water in the summer when the furnace wasn't going. She opened the coal door and dug her hand in among the cold ashes and brought out a small bundle wrapped in newspaper.

Pouch wheezed in Sam's ear.

"Open the paper so I can see if it's the dough," Georgie said hoarsely.

Violet shook ash dust from the package and unwrapped it. Amid the crumpled paper the money lay in a neat pile.

21

The Money

EAGERLY Georgie moved forward from the stairs. Both his hands were outstretched, one holding the gun and the other reaching for the money. He passed so close to Doug that Doug did not have to move at all to crack the side of his good hand down on Georgie's wrist. At the same time Doug kicked him in the ankle.

The revolver went limp in Georgie's fingers. Howling with pain, he wheeled toward Doug, bringing his left hand around to help his right hand raise the gun. That took time. Doug kicked him again, in the kneecap, and that leg folded, tilting Georgie off balance.

Sam was on him then. He clamped both hands around Georgie's gun wrist, turned the muzzle against Georgie's own body. Doug's blow must have damaged something in the wrist, because Georgie had no power in that hand. He screamed louder than Violet and Naomi were screaming.

Violently his body was yanked back. His voice choked off; his left hand flew up to his throat. Above his contorted face hovered an even beefier face, with teeth bared and eyes popping with strain. Abel Pouch had come up behind him and hooked one arm about his neck and was strangling him.

"The gun!" Pouch gasped. "Get his gun!"

Doug pressed against Sam, sliding his good arm in among the swaying bodies. He stepped back. "Okay, I have it."

They released Georgie, and he sat heavily on the cellar floor as if props had been knocked away from under him. Gingerly rubbing his right wrist and then his knee, he cursed in a voice ragged with pain and hate.

Naomi's voice sank to a whimper. She was clinging to her mother. Violet was silent now, her face as set and still as a death mask.

Sam felt empty, washed out. No money was worth all that had happened. "That was foolish," he told Doug. "One of us could have been killed."

Standing there in his spruce uniform with Georgie's revolver held expertly against his hip, Doug looked competent, self-assured. "I had to, sir. After he got the money, there was no telling what he would do. If he simply walked out, we'd phone the police a moment later, and he's too conspicuous to make an easy getaway. It seemed to me that the logical thing would be for him to take one of the women along as a hostage until he had made good his escape."

Sam shivered. He'd been too tired to think it through. "And if you didn't succeed, you were the only one who would be shot. You had only one hand, yet you took that chance."

"There wasn't so much danger," Doug said without heroics. "I was in the Rangers, you know, before I was transferred to artillery. That was where I learned that trick of disarming a man by paralyzing his hand. I never thought I'd have any use for it."

Naomi left her mother and came over to Doug and slipped an arm about him.

She was as tall as Doug, but somehow she looked helplessly feminine beside him. Georgie had grown quiet. Nursing his wrist, he looked around with sick eyes at the one-hundred-dollar bills scattered on the floor. The money had fallen from Violet's hands at the beginning of the fight. She seemed unaware of it.

"You'd better call the police, sir," Doug said. "I'll hold him down here with his gun."

Sam said dully: "I'm going to let him go."

Georgie's head snapped up. Pouch, mopping his brow with his handkerchief, chuckled softly.

"But you can't, sir," Doug protested.

"My name is Sam."

"Well, you can't," Doug said. "He's a crook and worse. He scared the daylights out of us. It's our duty — " He stared at Sam. "Why don't you want the police?"

"I think I know what I'm doing."

"But he's dangerous. He might come back."

"No," Sam said. "He knows that the money will be out of this house in a short time. He'll have nothing to come back for." He dropped his eyes to Georgie on the floor. "What will you do if we let you go?"

"Make tracks," Georgie said ardently. "Head for the West. I swear you'll never see me again."

"That money," Doug muttered. He was studying the scattered money as if he had never before seen one-hundred-dollar bills. "What was it doing in the stove? Whose is it?"

"Doug!" Naomi said. "Please do as Sam says." Her tone softened. "Do it for me, darling."

Doug transferred his gaze to his wife's face. "Do you know what this money and all the rest is about?"

"I know that I trust Sam to do the right thing. I want you to trust him too."

"I do, but — " Doug moistened his lips. "All right, sir. He's your baby. And I suppose you want me to keep quiet about whatever happened?"

"Yes."

Doug slipped out of Naomi's embrace and stood over Georgie. "On your feet, mug. I'll show you out." He added with his lips tight: "Through the back door."

Georgie had trouble walking, but he was anxious to get out of that house. He limped up the stairs. Gun poised, Doug followed at his heels. Naomi trailed a dozen steps behind.

They were hardly out of sight when the front doorbell rang upstairs. Sam went to the foot of the stairs. He heard the back door close and then feet hurry across the kitchen floor overhead. Naomi was answering the door. Sam turned back to the cellar and saw Abel Pouch down on his knees picking up the money. Without interest, Violet was watching him.

"Let that alone," Sam said.

Pouch smiled up at him from the floor. "It has occurred to me that you are presenting me with this money."

"Am I?"

"Naturally. You would hardly want me to tell the police that you helped a desperate criminal escape."

Sam sighed. "Don't heels like you ever give up trying blackmail? Give me that money."

Pouch lumbered up to his feet. "I am a reasonable man. For only half of it, I am willing to close my eyes and mouth."

"You've a glass jaw," Sam reminded him. "Do I have to hit you again?" He stepped forward and Pouch cringed, making no protest when Sam pulled the money from his hand.

Pouch's bloated lips drew back over yellow teeth. "You'll be sorry, Tree."

"You're bluffing," Sam said. "If you went to the police, I'd have to go into detail about the ethics of a licensed private detective. Now get out."

Pouch looked at the money and then at Sam, and he seemed on the verge of tears. Then he moved to the stairs.

Only a few of the one-hundred-dollar bills were left on the floor, and the bundle of them in Sam's hand felt pretty thin. He counted them rapidly. Not many more than thirty, and there had once been about two hundred.

"Just a minute, Pouch," Sam barked.

Halfway up the stairs Pouch paused. "What now?"

"I want the money you put in your pocket."

"You have every cent I picked up. Did

you see me pocket any of the money, Mrs. Tree?"

Violet stirred without moving from the spot where she had been standing for a long time now. "What?"

"How much money did you put into the stove?" Sam asked her.

"Forty-one hundred dollars," she muttered.

On the cellar stairs Pouch whistled. "Sixteen grand spent! What was left wasn't worth the effort."

"Get out!" Sam flung at him. He felt sick all the way down to the core of his being.

"Certainly, certainly." Pouch continued up the stairs. When he opened the door, Sam heard voices in the front part of the house. Then he heard Pouch go out through the back door.

Sam picked up seven more bills from the floor and then counted them all. Violet was right — there were forty-one of them.

"How much was there originally?" he asked.

"Eleven thousand, three hundred dollars."

He looked at Violet. "Was that all?"

"I knew you wouldn't believe me," she said tonelessly.

Naomi came down the cellar stairs. The light caught her face, and it was radiant.

"Doug's parents are upstairs," Naomi said excitedly. "They want to be friends with me and you and Sam, Mother. Isn't that wonderful?"

That was one of the things Violet had wanted, but her voice was flat, almost indifferent, when she said: "I'm glad." She shuffled past Sam to the stairs. "What made them change their minds?"

"Well, Doug is their only son, and he'll be going abroad as soon as his wound is healed and — oh, I don't know or care. All that matters is that it's making Doug so happy." Gaily Naomi's voice went on as she preceded her mother up the stairs.

Stuffing the money into his pocket, Sam tagged after the two women.

In the living room Doug's mother, still dressed in coat and gloves and hat and veil, occupied the easy chair as if it were a throne. She greeted Violet and Sam with a tight, formal nod. "We just dropped in for a minute," she announced.

The hearthstone was clean. Sam saw that Naomi had swept what was left of Pallas and the raven into the fireplace.

Reluctantly Douglas Faulcon, Senior, pushed his dumpy self toward Sam. "I don't like misunderstandings, Tree. I realize I shouldn't have raised my stick to you in the police station."

"That's all right," Sam said. "I understand how you felt."

Doug grinned delightedly. "You two will like each other a lot when you get to know each other."

Like hell! Sam thought. Aloud he mumbled: "I'm sure of it."

Then nobody had anything to say. It was Violet's fault. Ordinarily she could have kept up a sprightly conversation with a mummy, but now she had lost her flow of words or the desire for them. Something seemed to have died within her when she had been forced to give up the money.

Desperately Naomi suggested tea. Her mother-in-law dismissed the notion with an imperious wave of her hand and rose to leave. Violet did not urge her to remain. The senior Faulcons had come for their reconciliation at precisely the wrong time.

When they were gone, Sam remembered that he was hungry and went into the kitchen. There was boiled ham in the refrigerator. He made two sandwiches. While eating them, he scribbled figures on the back of an old envelope. He washed the sandwiches down with milk and then went up the hall and looked into the dining room. Doug sat in the easy chair, and Naomi sat in his lap. Sam turned to the staircase.

Violet was in the bedroom, sitting at a window and looking down into the street. She did not seem to hear Sam enter. He dropped down on the edge of the bed.

"I believe you, Violet," he said gently.

Her head moved. "What do you believe?"

"That you found only eleven thousand, three hundred dollars in the figure."

"Do you, Sam, or are you only saying that?"

"It's the only explanation I can believe

for your actions," he said.

Life flowed back into her pale eyes. "Darling, then you do understand?"

"Yes."

Violet came quickly to the bed and sat beside Sam. She took his hand between her two hands.

"I found the money about four years ago," she said. "I was cleaning the figure, and one of the bills dropped out. I knew, of course, it was Ira's money. I got a stick and worked the rest out; it wasn't far up. There were only one hundred and thirteen of those bills, and there were supposed to be about two hundred. I kept poking with the stick, and that's all there was. You can imagine how I felt. Earl Durand had said there was twenty thousand dollars; the police were looking for that much. All along there had been a suspicion that I had found the money and kept it. Don't you see what the police would have thought if I had turned over nearly nine thousand dollars less to them?"

"They'd think you'd stolen it."

"Of course they would. I was afraid, darling. So I stuffed the money back into the figure and left it there."

He said bitterly: "Couldn't you at least have confided in me?"

"I couldn't take the chance, darling, that you would think me a thief. I was afraid that you wouldn't believe me. Would you have?"

"I don't know," he admitted in all honesty. "But then you decided that you might as well become a thief in fact."

"Yes." She was twisting his fingers. Though it hurt a little, he let her. "Look at it this way, darling. For two years I knew that money was in the figure, and I did not dare do anything about it. Several times I thought of burning the money. I was always afraid that somebody would find it and then perhaps I'd go to prison. But in a way that money was mine because it had been my husband's. Oh, I know he stole it, but they would never find the people to whom he had sold the lottery tickets. Then, about two years ago, I needed a little extra money I didn't want to ask you for. I took one hundred dollars. Then, a little later, I took another bill. Then I wanted to refurnish the house and you didn't have ready money, and

there it was in that figure and I — "
Her face pressed against his shoulder.

"The fact remains," he said, "that you
didn't tell me about the money even after
Felix Skinner was murdered."

"I didn't trust you, darling." Quickly
she added: "I mean, I didn't trust you
to keep quiet about it. You're so moral.
You'd have made me take what was left
of the money back to the police. There
would have been a scandal. It wasn't
only that I would be arrested and lose
you. Naomi might have lost Doug."

"You continued to hold out on me
after Naomi and Doug were married."

Violet spoke against his shoulder.
"There were so many reasons all mixed
up. On top of all the other things I was
afraid of, I was afraid of being accused of
murdering Felix. If I gave up the money,
it would come out that I had paid Felix
blackmail. You already suspected me
of murdering him. What would the
police think? They would jump to the
conclusion that I had murdered Felix to
keep from paying him any more money."

"When did you transfer the money to
the coal stove?"

"After you told me there had been a thief in the house. I had a terrible time of it, darling, even though I didn't show it."

Gently he stroked her hair. "I suppose it's worse when you have to keep acting all the time."

"Especially when Earl Durand was here and then that terrible Georgie a little while ago," she said. "It was so hard pretending that I wasn't afraid and that I didn't know what they were talking about. Because if I gave them the money, you would see how much was missing and hate me."

"I could never hate you."

"It's sweet of you to say so, darling, but you can't tell beforehand. And only four thousand dollars wouldn't have satisfied Earl Durand or Georgie. They wanted at least ten thousand dollars. Earl said so. Giving them the money wouldn't have saved us."

"They would have taken what they could get."

"Would they? I didn't know." Defiantly her face lifted from his shoulder. "Anyway, they had no right to that money."

Sam laughed then. It was good to be able to laugh again without restraint. "You're precious, sweetheart. Now stop worrying about the money."

"I feel so much better now that I've told you. We'll give that four thousand dollars to some war charity."

"We'll turn it over to the police," he said.

"Sam!"

"We'll hand over exactly the amount you found in the figure."

He took out the envelope on which he had written in the kitchen. "You've spent in all seventy-one hundred dollars. Is that correct?"

"Exactly seven thousand," she said listlessly. She was sitting forward on the bed, staring down at the floor.

"We're one hundred short." He scowled at the envelope. "I have only — " Suddenly he was laughing again. "Say, we let Georgie get away with that one-hundred-dollar bill he found in the figure. Oh well, it was worth it to get rid of him. In short, I have to raise seventy-one hundred dollars. I worked it out downstairs. It will be a tight squeeze, but I can get a three-thousand-dollar mortgage on this house and borrow the rest on my insurance. We'll have to economize for a couple of years, but business is good these days, and I — "

"And I will go to prison," Violet said, rising from the bed. She stood with her bowed back to him.

He leaped up and put both hands on her shoulders and his cheek against hers. "Don't talk like an idiot. Do you think I'll ever let any harm come to you?"

"But the police won't believe that I didn't steal the rest of the money."

"I told you not to worry," he said. "When Ira Pram is found guilty of murder, I'm sure he'll admit that that's all the money he'd left behind in the figure."

Slowly she turned under his hands. Her eyes were wide. "You know where Ira is?"

"Yes."

There was a knock on the door.

"Are you in there, sir?" Doug's voice said.

"What is it?" Sam asked.

"I've hidden that gun under the couch.

I thought you'd want to know."

"Get rid of it," Sam said, holding Violet close to him. "Throw it down a sewer or something. I've no more need for guns."

22

Ira Pram

ON Monday Sam spent little time in the store. By late afternoon he had completed arrangements for borrowing seven thousand dollars. Then he telephoned Alvin Banderson, the district attorney of New York County.

The next morning Sam awoke with the thought that it was Tuesday again and that only a week had passed since the evening Felix Skinner had come into his store. He lay flat on his back, looking up at the ceiling.

All at once Violet was shaking him. "Sam, it's eight-thirty."

"That's all right," he said. "Ted's opening the store this morning. I'm not going in today."

She subsided beside him. "You leave Ted alone too much. You said yourself he's stealing from you."

"Then he'd better take all he can

get today," Sam said. "Tomorrow I'm cracking down on him. We've an appointment with the New York district attorney at eleven o'clock this morning."

She was silent. Then she said in a small voice: "Do I have to go?"

"I'm afraid so. Whatever I say or do, don't interfere. Will you remember that?"

"Yes, darling," Violet said meekly.

Sam drove the car to Manhattan, and he had to go to the outskirts of Chinatown before he could find a place to park. It was twelve minutes after eleven when he and Violet were shown into the district attorney's office. Four men were in the room.

A man with a beaked nose and jutting jaw came around a big desk and introduced himself as District Attorney Banderson. Captain Gavigan left off prowling along a line of windows long enough to nod to Sam. Sergeant Jones politely pushed up a chair for Violet. A natty man with a Hitler mustache sat obscurely at a smaller desk; evidently he was a stenographer.

Banderson returned behind his desk

and looked pointedly at his watch. "I'm a busy man, Mr. Tree."

"Not too busy to catch a murderer, I'm sure," Sam said.

"So you said over the phone yesterday. Because you've been an important witness from the first, I — " Banderson leaned forward. "Aren't you feeling well, Mrs. Tree?"

Sam hadn't taken his eyes off Violet. She was gripping the back of the chair Sergeant Jones had brought forward for her. Color ebbed from her face.

"Steady," Sam said. He squeezed her shoulder. "It'll be over soon."

She tossed her head and smiled wanly at Banderson. "I — I'm nervous these days." She went around the chair and sat down and folded her hands in her lap. It was an effort for her to work up her placid pose.

"Now to business," Banderson said impatiently.

"Grover Langford isn't here," Sam said. "I can't imagine what's keeping him."

"See here," Banderson snapped. "I'm a busy — "

"We're all busy," Sam said mildly, "but I'm entitled to have my lawyer present. Yesterday's papers said that Earl Durand had murdered Felix Skinner and Martha Underhill. Are you convinced of that?"

"My office has issued no statement to that effect," Banderson told him stiffly.

"But you didn't deny it. You may be willing to let it ride that way. I'm not."

Grover Langford bustled in. "Hello, Sam," he said breezily, pulling off his overcoat. "How are you, Violet? Nice job you did on Shoeless Evans, Banderson. Well, well, Captain Gavigan. Sorry I was delayed. What's it all about, anyway?"

"Do I understand that even Mr. Tree's attorney doesn't know?" Banderson said dryly.

"Naturally Tree explained some of it to me," Grover lied blandly. Sam had merely asked him to be at the D.A.'s office at eleven. Neatly Grover placed his overcoat on a chair. "Fire away, Sammy boy. The legal brains of the state are behind you."

Sam opened his wallet and extracted a personal check and placed it on the desk. "I found Ira Pram's money. Do you know about it?"

"I have acquainted myself with all aspects of the case." Banderson picked up the check and stretched it between his fingers. "Eleven thousand, three hundred dollars. Well!"

Grover's eyebrows arched. Sergeant Jones clucked his tongue. At the windows Gavigan was still at last. "Where's the rest of it?" Gavigan said.

"That's all there was," Sam said. "Pram might have known that the police were closing in on him. Probably he kept eight or nine thousand dollars on his person in case he had to make a quick getaway. He wouldn't want to carry more than that around, and he thought he could always slip back to get the rest of it."

Banderson studied the check. "Why your personal check? And why is it postdated ten days from now?"

"That's another thing," Sam said. "You'll have to hang onto that check until I raise the money to cover the full amount. I have part of it in the original one-hundred-dollar bills, but I might as well turn it all over at one time."

Grover clucked his tongue and looked worried.

"And Skinner had one-hundred-dollar bills," Banderson mused. "Did they come from the same source?"

"I gave Skinner that money," Sam said.

"Sam!" Violet was on her feet, moving resolutely toward the desk.

Sam grabbed her arm. "You promised to let me handle this."

She looked at him and then unsteadily returned to her chair.

"Where did you find this money, Mr. Tree?"

"In a plaster figure in my home," Sam said. "The figure — a plaster cast of Pallas Athene, with a raven perched on her head — had been in Pram's house when he was married to Violet. Nobody suspected the money was in it until I found it by accident about a week ago."

"A week ago," Banderson echoed. "You knew, of course, that it was stolen money."

"I thought it probably was."

"Did you tell your wife?"

"Not at once."

Grover leaped in. "The fact is that Tree is making restitution in full. Suspecting it was Pram's money isn't knowing. He wanted to be sure. Besides, I fail to see where this matter comes under the jurisdiction of your office. My client resides in Queens County, and that was where he found the money."

Banderson smiled sourly. "I see now, Mr. Tree, why you were anxious to wait for your lawyer."

"That's right," Sam admitted readily. "I want him here to protect me if it becomes necessary, but I doubt if it will be. As for jurisdiction, I differ with my lawyer. Felix Skinner and Martha Underhill were murdered in this county."

Gavigan spoke from the windows. "Tree has something there. I told you yesterday that the way I figure it is that Skinner and Miss Underhill were murdered because of Pram's dough.

"What you imply, Captain, is nonsense," Grover said with legal indignation. "Would Tree have given Skinner money if he had planned to murder him? And Skinner's murder had been planned some days in advance — that's obvious."

"Nobody has accused Mr. Tree of murder or even implied it." The district attorney was being very patient now, very smooth, obviously anxious to give Sam plenty of rope. "I want Mr. Tree to speak for himself."

Sam pushed back his unruly hair. He was through with lying now, except where he would touch on the finding of the money. Violet was covered.

"Look," he said. "I could have waited another ten days for my loans to come through and then accumulated one-hundred-dollar bills issued in 1929 and handed over the entire sum in cash and pretended I'd just found it. But I don't want to take any more chances with my wife's life. So far Ira Pram has let her alone, but he might decide that she's as dangerous as the others were. I'm hurrying this up to play safe."

"Did you say Pram?" Grover muttered.

Gavigan laughed. "Aren't you getting tired of playing that record, Tree?"

"Wait for me to catch up." Banderson frowned at Sam and then at Gavigan.

"My understanding is that Pram was shot dead a long time ago."

"Tree's been nourishing a brainstorm," Gavigan explained. "He's been saying that Ira Pram is the killer. Now that he's turned up with Pram's dough, it's plain why he's dragging around that red herring."

"Pram escaped," Sam said. "It's not important how. Some days ago I began to suspect that Ira Pram was alive and had murdered Skinner. When Martha Underhill phoned me as she was dying and mentioned Pram, I was sure. It got so that I suspected every big fat man I saw of being the murderer, including the clerk in my store. That didn't mean that Pram was still fat. It's possible for a man that size to take off eighty pounds. He would no longer be fat, but he would still be a big man — a two-hundred-pounder, like Captain Gavigan here."

Banderson sat forward in his chair. "Are you saying that you know where Pram is?"

The three standing men also leaned toward Sam, as if to hear better. Behind him Violet's chair shifted. The stenographer's pencil was poised above the pad.

"That's why I'm here," Sam said. "It was as big as life, but I didn't see it. Not until Saturday night when Captain Gavigan murdered Earl Durand."

Banderson's head snapped back. "What's that you said? Captain Gavigan shot Durand in the line of duty."

"That's gratitude for you," Gavigan growled. "I save the guy's life and he calls it murder."

"Gavigan murdered Durand," Sam repeated stolidly. "He had to. Because Captain Gavigan is Ira Pram."

There it was. Sam felt no triumph, no satisfaction. He wanted to leave now, never again to see a policeman or a district attorney or a murderer, but there was more to be done.

At his side Grover's eyes were popping behind their glasses. Across the room Sergeant Jones stood with his jaw slack. The dapper stenographer's eyes danced. Sam looked around at Violet; her head was against the back of the chair, and her eyelids were half shut.

And at the windows Gavigan laughed

without mirth. "Is that another of your red herrings?"

Banderson sat stiffy in his chair. "Explain yourself, Mr. Tree."

"Let's go all the way back to Ira Pram's escape on Cape Cod," Sam said. "I don't have to prove he escaped; all I have to do is show that Gavigan is Pram. I don't know how soon Pram came to New York after his escape. It might have been at once, or perhaps a little later after he had shed eighty pounds or so through a severe diet. It was an easy disguise. One would have to have known him very well and to look at him closely to recognize him, but his chief disguise was the assumption that he was dead. If anybody who'd known Pram saw the resemblance, it would be put down as a resemblance and nothing more. I imagine Pram thought it was clever to join the New York police force. Where was a wanted criminal safer than on a police force, especially when he was assumed to be dead? Pram had never been arrested; his fingerprints weren't on record. And it was likely that nobody knew him in New York — not at that time, anyway."

Gavigan's mouth twisted. "And he gave up a fortune waiting for him in Provincetown?"

"You're the best judge of that," Sam flung at him. He faced the desk again. "Maybe Gavigan was willing to forget that money. He had eight or nine thousand dollars; he would be reasonably safe if he sat tight. But say he learned that the furniture was in storage. With at least one watchman in the building, he'd have to sneak in at night and locate that particular furniture and pull it apart, and he'd have to take that risk without knowing whether Violet had found the money or given Pallas and the raven away. Inquiries were dangerous. He couldn't show himself and he couldn't trust anybody.

"Maybe he decided to wait till the furniture was moved. Maybe several years later he actually did burglarize Mrs. Wilson's house, where the furniture was taken. He would have found all his furniture there, but not the figure. He would have reasoned that Violet had found the money or got rid of the figure. Why press the matter further?

His security was worth a lot more to him than eleven thousand dollars. He could let well enough alone."

"All that," Banderson said, "is sheer supposition."

"I'm getting down to what I'm sure of," Sam said. "Gavigan may or may not have known that Violet and Felix Skinner and Martha Underhill had moved to New York. It wouldn't have made any difference to him. New York is a terrifically big place; he was older; he was assumed dead. Who would suspect a respectable police officer of being a dead crook?

"Then, about a month ago, Felix Skinner was driven home by a drunk named James Artill, and it was Gavigan's bad luck that Artill ran over a boy in the district where Gavigan was a Homicide captain. As a material witness, Skinner was brought before Gavigan. Skinner, who'd known Pram well, had plenty of opportunity to observe Gavigan. What went on in Skinner's mind we'll never know, except that he convinced himself that Gavigan was Pram. Five days after that accident, Skinner lost exactly two thousand dollars in a gambling joint."

The office was deathly quiet. Banderson turned his head to Gavigan, and Gavigan said nothing. The two inverted triangles forming his body were motionless in front of a window. The inverted triangle which was his face seemed hacked out of stone.

He knows whatever he says now he cannot change the end, Sam thought. *He's always been vulnerable.*

"Skinner blackmailed Gavigan," Sam went on. "He was a gambler, always desperate for a stake in the hope that he could make a killing. He got two thousand dollars from Gavigan, lost it, held Gavigan up for two thousand more, lost that also. I don't know how much money a Homicide captain makes, but even if Gavigan had had the money, it was plain to him that a gambler like Skinner would never be satisfied. And Skinner was a drunkard, and drunkards can't be trusted not to blabber. There was only one way Gavigan could save himself from being exposed as an escaped crook. He took it. He murdered Skinner."

Gavigan grunted, but still he had no

words, and there was no laughter left in him.

"It was neat," Sam said. "Gavigan had murdered Skinner in his own district, which put him in charge of the investigation. What better setup could a murderer want? But there was one flaw. Immediately after the murder I told Gavigan that Skinner had been to see me the night before to ask for money. And Skinner had ten one-hundred-dollar bills in his wallet, all of a 1929 series, and the night before that Skinner had lost nine one-hundred-dollar bills in a gambling joint. There could be only one answer: that it was Gavigan's own money, and that I had found it in the figure, and that Skinner had gotten it from me. In short, Skinner had been blackmailing me also."

"Was he?" Banderson asked softly.

"Skinner believed that he had drained Gavigan dry, so he shifted his blackmailing to me."

"No!" Again Violet was coming forward from her chair. "He — "

"Violet!" Sam said. "Will you let me tell the truth?"

"The truth — "

"Sit down!"

Unsteadily Violet returned to her chair.

Sam said: "Grover, can I be arrested for withholding the information that I had paid a murdered man blackmail?"

"Make out your case against Gavigan and you won't have a thing to worry about."

"All right," Sam said, facing the desk. "Skinner told me that Pram was alive, but he didn't tell me who Pram was. My wife's daughter was about to marry into a snooty family, and I was afraid that a scandal would break it up, so I gave Skinner the money to keep quiet. When Skinner was murdered, I found myself in a spot. What better motive for murder has a man than to eliminate a blackmailer? It was likely that if the police knew I'd given Skinner money, they'd accuse me of killing him."

Sam paused to think over what he had said. It sounded all right because it was true, except that he had changed places with Violet.

Gavigan found his voice. "There we have it — the reason for the red herring. Tree is our killer."

Nobody seemed to hear him. All eyes were on Sam.

"Go on, Mr. Tree." Banderson's face was impassive now.

"When Skinner came to my store Tuesday evening, I couldn't get my hands on that much money at once. Not my own, I mean. But only the day before I had found Pram's money in the figure."

"Quite a coincidences," Banderson said sourly.

"Coincidences happen," Sam tossed the objection aside. "Anyway, that's how Skinner came to be in possession of nineteen hundred dollars of Pram's money." Sam uttered a muffled sigh. He was back to the truth. In all of the lying he had been forced to do within a week, he had lost none of his distaste for it. "And Gavigan was worried. He couldn't quite smother the case now. He had to find out how much Skinner had told me. He had to come to my store, even though it was dangerous because he might meet Violet there.

"That was what was wrong with the police investigation from the first. Maybe

387

I should have seen it before I did. Captain Gavigan was in charge of the case. Twice he came all the way to my store to see me, but he never went the four blocks from the store to my house to see Violet. She was a key witness; she'd been Skinner's wife for years. Besides, she was as much under suspicion of murder as anybody, yet Gavigan carefully stayed away from her, sending Sergeant Jones instead. And Gavigan stayed away from Martha Underhill for the same reason.

"After a day or two Gavigan was convinced that Skinner had not given him away. Then, on Friday, Sergeant Jones reported to him that Earl Durand had been in my house. Naturally that bothered Gavigan a lot. Why had Durand visited Violet? He couldn't ask Violet, so he hurried to my store. And there what he had been afraid of happened. Martha Underhill was in the store.

"The night before I had told her that Pram was alive, so she wasn't blinded by the assumption that he was dead. She recognized him. It was a terrific shock to her. At that time I thought she was so upset because she had reason to fear the police. Later the real reason helped form the pattern."

Gavigan's voice rapped crisply. "Jones, you were there. Did you hear Mrs. Underhill say I was Pram or in any way indicate that I was?"

Dazedly the sergeant shook his head.

"Why should she have?" Sam said to Banderson. "She probably assumed when she saw Gavigan that Violet had known all along that Pram was alive and that in some way she was involved in his new life. I doubt if Martha had more than a vague idea then that Gavigan might have murdered Skinner. She had to find out what it was all about before she gave him away. So when Gavigan drove her to the subway and suggested an appointment for later that evening, when he would explain everything, she agreed. She felt, though, that she would need experienced advice after she heard him out. That's why she phoned Grover Langford, but told him not to come until nine, when Gavigan would be gone. Gavigan was gone, all right, when Grover arrived, and Martha was dying."

"God!" Grover whispered.

Sam pushed all ten fingers through his hair. Banderson's face had become a featureless blob hanging above the desk.

"Killing wasn't solving anything for Gavigan," Sam said. "He was getting in deeper all the time, because now being in charge of the investigation had become dangerous. There was no way of keeping an alarm for Durand from being sent out. When Durand was caught, he would be brought before Gavigan and Durand would recognize him.

"Saturday morning Gavigan learned that I had taken a train to East Wiston. He was very jumpy now, and he'd always been worried about me. I knew too much. He went out there later that day to see what I was up to. In East Wiston he either saw Durand in the town without being seen himself, or he learned that a man answering Durand's description was staying at Mrs. Wilson's house. At the time Gavigan must have thought that that was a tremendous break for him. He'd lure Durand out of the house and shoot him down and say that Durand had tried to resist arrest. Durand would be blamed for the murders; the case would be closed; Gavigan could go back to being a respectable captain of detectives.

"Pram's phone call got Durand out of the house easily enough, but something went wrong. I was following Durand." Sam looked directly at Gavigan. "Aren't you sorry now that you didn't wait for the possibility that Durand would kill me before I could kill him? I suppose it all happened too fast for you to think it through. Maybe you didn't want to risk Durand killing me because you wanted me as a witness that you had shot Durand in the line of duty. You couldn't afford any sort of investigation by the local police. Ira Pram had been known on Cape Cod. Besides, you must have been afraid that Mrs. Wilson was watching us from the house."

Gavigan's eyes were steady as they locked with Sam's. The captain, at any rate, was no coward, except as every murderer is a coward. He said wearily, almost without interest: "How much longer do we have to listen to your crackpot ideas?"

"I'm nearly finished," Sam said. "Everything fell into place that night. I realized that it hadn't been necessary for Gavigan to kill Durand. Durand was only reaching for his gun. If Gavigan had made his presence known, Durand would have given up. At least, as a responsible police officer, Gavigan should have made some effort to take Durand alive.

"But that wasn't what told me either, until I traced back. It was urgent for Gavigan to send out an alarm to have Georgie picked up before he could go far. In addition, Gavigan should have called the local police at once and have been there when they arrived. Even I, who am not a police officer, know what is proper under the circumstances. There was a telephone in the house only a few feet away. Gavigan knew it, because I had told him that Durand had received a phone call there from Ira Pram. Yet Gavigan didn't use that phone or even go near the house.

"Mrs. Wilson came to the door and called out. At once Gavigan said good-by and started walking to the town, a mile away. It was awkward, but he couldn't help it, because Mrs. Wilson had once been his mother-in-law. She was one of the people who had known him well, and he couldn't have any of those people see him. It all cleared up then. Carefully Captain Gavigan had avoided Violet and Violet's mother. Two people who had known Pram well, and who had seen Gavigan, had been murdered. Pram's partner in crime, who would see him if he was picked up by the police, had also been killed. And there it was."

Breathing hard, Sam stepped back from the desk. He felt exhausted; his limbs quivered the way they used to after a mile run in college. Silence hung stifling in the office.

Slowly Banderson's head swiveled toward Gavigan. The big man had turned his back to the room and appeared to be looking out of the window. For a moment Sam thought he would jump. It would mean death, but Gavigan must have known from the moment Sam and Violet entered the office that he was doomed.

"Evidence," Banderson was saying. "Have you concrete evidence?"

Gavigan turned from the window then,

and his mouth was thin with a crooked smile. He was looking at Violet.

"Gavigan — or Pram — knows there's evidence," Sam said. "Violet was his wife and is the mother of his child." He went to the side of her chair and dropped a hand on her shoulder. "You had a severe shock when you came in here. Why?"

"I saw Ira," Violet whispered so low that she could scarcely be heard.

"You mean Captain Gavigan?"

She closed her eyes. "Yes."

Banderson slouched back in his chair and studied his fingernails: "Obviously the weakness of that identification is that she's your wife, Mr. Tree. She would want to save you." He touched the check. "After all, you found Pram's money."

"Ridiculous!" Grover exploded. He had remembered that he was a lawyer and Sam his client. "Would my client have come to you of his own free — "

"Never mind, Grover," Sam said. His voice was husky with too much talking and with the tiredness he had felt for days. He wanted to get it over with quickly. "Gavigan doesn't question Violet's identification. He knows how vulnerable he is. I think that investigation will show that twice within recent weeks he withdrew two thousand dollars from his bank. He couldn't have changed much in fifteen years, in spite of the fact that he's thinner, because Skinner and then Martha Underhill had little trouble recognizing him. He knows that other people who had known Ira Pram well will be brought here to identify him. He knows he's lost if his background is checked. That's why he murdered — "

Gavigan's gun fell into his hand. He moved in from the windows, his black eyes wary, his face taut.

One of the men, probably Grover, squeaked like a mouse. Banderson and the stenographer were on their feet, each frozen behind his desk. Sam felt his arm grabbed by Violet, though she was in the chair, her weight pulled down at his shoulder.

"Captain, I order you to put that gun down," Banderson said with futile authority.

Gavigan's eyes shifted to the door and then back. "All I want is to get out. I'm not out to hurt anybody, but I've killed before and, by God, I'll — "

He realized then that there were not enough people in front of him. He started to wheel, but by then Sergeant Jones was too close to his back. Jones had his gun out. Expertly he used it to tap Gavigan on the base of the skull.

Gavigan reeled drunkenly, clawing air as if to push aside growing darkness. Jones tapped him again. Gavigan crumpled and lay still.

"Nice work, Sergeant," Banderson said.

Jones grinned. "Never throw a murder charge at a man while he's carrying iron. A few minutes ago I saw what he would pull, so I got set behind him." The sergeant looked down at the still form, and awe crossed his plain features. "Who'd ever think I'd take a couple of socks at the Skipper and get away with it?"

★ ★ ★

Ten minutes later there were only four in the office. Sergeant Jones had helped carry the unconscious body out, and

Banderson had dismissed the stenographer. Violet leaned against Sam in the circle of his arm. Banderson sat behind his desk and studied Sam's check as if he had never seen it before.

Sam said: "If it's the amount of the check that's bothering you, I think Pram will admit that that was all he had left behind."

"It's not the amount," Banderson said. "You stated that you knew on Saturday night that Gavigan was Pram and the murderer. Why did you wait until today to come here?"

"I wanted to be sure I could raise the money."

Banderson shook his head and snapped the check between his hands.

"Don't tell me you propose to take action," Grover Langford protested. "You have no legal basis. Besides, my client dropped a murderer into your lap, for which you should be eternally grateful."

"I am." Banderson placed the check into a desk drawer. "I'm not only grateful. I'm impressed by gallantry. Of course, Mr. Tree, you weren't the one who found the money and spent some of it and gave some to Skinner. Your wife did. And she didn't find the money a week ago."

Sam felt Violet press against his side. He forced himself to meet the district attorney's gaze squarely.

"You're wrong," Sam said.

Banderson smiled and shook a cigarette out of a pack. "As far as I'm concerned, your story will remain the official one. We prosecutors are human, Mr. Tree. And often sentimental. I am also very much in love with my wife. A cigarette?"

"I don't smoke, thanks." Sam's arm tightened about Violet's waist. "Let's go home," he said.

THE WILDERNESS WALK
Sheila Bishop

Stifling unpleasant memories of a misbegotten romance in Cleave with Lord Francis Aubrey, Lavinia goes on holiday there with her sister. The two women are thrust into a romantic intrigue involving none other than Lord Francis.

THE RELUCTANT GUEST
Rosalind Brett

Ann Calvert went to spend a month on a South African farm with Theo Borland and his sister. They both proved to be different from her first idea of them, and there was Storr Peterson — the most disturbing man she had ever met.

ONE ENCHANTED SUMMER
Anne Tedlock Brooks

A tale of mystery and romance and a girl who found both during one enchanted summer.

CLOUD OVER MALVERTON
Nancy Buckingham

Dulcie soon realises that something is seriously wrong at Malverton, and when violence strikes she is horrified to find herself under suspicion of murder.

AFTER THOUGHTS
Max Bygraves

The Cockney entertainer tells stories of his East End childhood, of his RAF days, and his post-war showbusiness successes and friendships with fellow comedians.

MOONLIGHT AND MARCH ROSES
D. Y. Cameron

Lynn's search to trace a missing girl takes her to Spain, where she meets Clive Hendon. While untangling the situation, she untangles her emotions and decides on her own future.

NURSE ALICE IN LOVE
Theresa Charles

Accepting the post of nurse to little Fernie Sherrod, Alice Everton could not guess at the romance, suspense and danger which lay ahead at the Sherrod's isolated estate.

POIROT INVESTIGATES
Agatha Christie

Two things bind these eleven stories together — the brilliance and uncanny skill of the diminutive Belgian detective, and the stupidity of his Watson-like partner, Captain Hastings.

LET LOOSE THE TIGERS
Josephine Cox

Queenie promised to find the long-lost son of the frail, elderly murderess, Hannah Jason. But her enquiries threatened to unlock the cage where crucial secrets had long been held captive.

THE TWILIGHT MAN
Frank Gruber

Jim Rand lives alone in the California desert awaiting death. Into his hermit existence comes a teenage girl who blows both his past and his brief future wide open.

DOG IN THE DARK
Gerald Hammond

Jim Cunningham breeds and trains gun dogs, and his antagonism towards the devotees of show spaniels earns him many enemies. So when one of them is found murdered, the police are on his doorstep within hours.

THE RED KNIGHT
Geoffrey Moxon

When he finds himself a pawn on the chessboard of international espionage with his family in constant danger, Guy Trent becomes embroiled in moves and countermoves which may mean life or death for Western scientists.

TIGER TIGER
Frank Ryan

A young man involved in drugs is found murdered. This is the first event which will draw Detective Inspector Sandy Woodings into a whirlpool of murder and deceit.

CAROLINE MINUSCULE
Andrew Taylor

Caroline Minuscule, a medieval script, is the first clue to the whereabouts of a cache of diamonds. The search becomes a deadly kind of fairy story in which several murders have an other-worldly quality.

LONG CHAIN OF DEATH
Sarah Wolf

During the Second World War four American teenagers from the same town join the Army together. Forty-two years later, the son of one of the soldiers realises that someone is systematically wiping out the families of the four men.

THE LISTERDALE MYSTERY
Agatha Christie

Twelve short stories ranging from the light-hearted to the macabre, diverse mysteries ingeniously and plausibly contrived and convincingly unravelled.

TO BE LOVED
Lynne Collins

Andrew married the woman he had always loved despite the knowledge that Sarah married him for reasons of her own. So much heartache could have been avoided if only he had known how vital it was to be loved.

ACCUSED NURSE
Jane Converse

Paula found herself accused of a crime which could cost her her job, her nurse's reputation, and even the man she loved, unless the truth came to light.

CHATEAU OF FLOWERS
Margaret Rome

Alain, Comte de Treville needed a wife to look after him, and Fleur went into marriage on a business basis only, hoping that eventually he would come to trust and care for her.

CRISS-CROSS
Alan Scholefield

As her ex-husband had succeeded in kidnapping their young daughter once, Jane was determined to take her safely back to England. But all too soon Jane is caught up in a new web of intrigue.

DEAD BY MORNING
Dorothy Simpson

Leo Martindale's body was discovered outside the gates of his ancestral home. Is it, as Inspector Thanet begins to suspect, murder?

A GREAT DELIVERANCE
Elizabeth George

Into the web of old houses and secrets of Keldale Valley comes Scotland Yard Inspector Thomas Lynley and his assistant to solve a particularly savage murder.

'E' IS FOR EVIDENCE
Sue Grafton

Kinsey Millhone was bogged down on a warehouse fire claim. It came as something of a shock when she was accused of being on the take. She'd been set up. Now she had a new client — herself.

A FAMILY OUTING IN AFRICA
Charles Hampton and Janie Hampton

A tale of a young family's journey through Central Africa by bus, train, river boat, lorry, wooden bicycle and foot.

THE PLEASURES OF AGE
Robert Morley

The author, British stage and screen star, now eighty, is enjoying the pleasures of age. He has drawn on his experiences to write this witty, entertaining and informative book.

THE VINEGAR SEED
Maureen Peters

The first book in a trilogy which follows the exploits of two sisters who leave Ireland in 1861 to seek their fortune in England.

A VERY PAROCHIAL MURDER
John Wainwright

A mugging in the genteel seaside town turned to murder when the victim died. Then the body of a young tearaway is washed ashore and Detective Inspector Lyle is determined that a second killing will not go unpunished.

DEATH ON A
HOT SUMMER NIGHT
Anne Infante

Micky Douglas is either accident-prone or someone is trying to kill him. He finds himself caught in a desperate race to save his ex-wife and others from a ruthless gang.

HOLD DOWN A SHADOW
Geoffrey Jenkins

Maluti Rider, with the help of four of the world's most wanted men, is determined to destroy the Katse Dam and release a killer flood.

THAT NICE MISS SMITH
Nigel Morland

A reconstruction and reassessment of the trial in 1857 of Madeleine Smith, who was acquitted by a verdict of Not Proven of poisoning her lover, Emile L'Angelier.

SEASONS OF MY LIFE
Hannah Hauxwell
and Barry Cockcroft

The story of Hannah Hauxwell's struggle to survive on a desolate farm in the Yorkshire Dales with little money, no electricity and no running water.

TAKING OVER
Shirley Lowe and Angela Ince

A witty insight into what happens when women take over in the boardroom and their husbands take over chores, children and chickenpox.

AFTER MIDNIGHT STORIES,
The Fourth Book Of

A collection of sixteen of the best of today's ghost stories, all different in style and approach but all combining to give the reader that special midnight shiver.